The Flip

Doyle Weldon Knight

True Southern Gentleman Publishing
A Subsidiary of HOSS International, LLC

For information contact:

Email: dweldonknight@gmail.com

Website: http://www.hossintl.com.

THE FLIP

Book and Cover design by: Doyle W. Knight

ISBN: 978-1-7350923-0-0

First Edition: August 2020

The Pentacle Virus drove the human race to the brink of extinction. Humanity is determined to complete the job.

It's now 2020 A.D. or 0004 A.P. (After Pentacle), depending on how you relate to things since the world flipped. The existence that Dinky knew prior to the pandemic, died four years ago. The microscopic warrior devastated ninety percent of the global human and animal population. The remaining individuals have no laws, no government, no social services or communication. Survival of the Fittest is the current standard.

Travelling on foot to a town 35 miles away, Dinky must expand his scavenging area to find the needed medication for his wife Sarah.

Will he survive the perils of the trip or will he be just another victim of

The Flip

This novel is dedicated to Betty Sue.

My harshest critic, greatest fan and beautiful mother. She never got to read the final manuscript. She went to meet up with the loved one's who have gone before. I hope she and Dad found the perfect cloud to reside on. They sure are missed around here.

A special thanks to Rick, a colleague that told me in 2015 I should be writing stories and not reading them. I'm glad I took his advice.

Table of Contents

Table of Contents

Or if I send a pestilence into that land, and pour out my fury upon it in blood, to cut off from it man and beast:

Ezekiel 14:19 – The Holy Bible (King James Version)

The Flip

The LORD shall smite thee with a consumption, and with a fever, and with an inflammation, and with an extreme burning, and with the sword, and with blasting, and with mildew; and they shall pursue thee until thou perish.

Deuteronomy 28:22 – *The Holy Bible* (King James Version)

Chapter 1: Day 1, Spring, 04 A.P. (After Pentacle)

In the new topsy-turvy world, the one thing I loved, almost as much as Baby Girl and our Blue Heeler, was the fragrance of the southern outdoors at daybreak. On a spring morning, the aromatic smell of the flowers mixed with a hint of marsh bog create a false atmosphere of pre-Pentacle home. I knew it was one of those mornings as I took in a deep breath.

I was thankful that the smell of nature had returned to a natural earthy aroma. A gracious reminder that the pungent odor of death had subsided. The odor that seemed to penetrate your skin, invade your soul and suck you into it's sickening bouquet.

There was a sense of tenderness and serenity in the quiet southern morning. I garnered a glimpse of the majesty of springtime as I stood on the boat dock and gazed across my kingdom.

The leaves had started to form on the hardwood trees, and the grass had begun to thicken and turn green. Baby Girl's azaleas showed a glimmer of the beautiful lavender they would display within a week or two. The gladiolas were already bloomed and on full display and the Easter lilies had opened to show the snow-white linen of their petals.

It had been four winters since the Pentacle pandemic reached its crescendo, but judging by mother nature's sneak peek, it's springtime. I estimated somewhere around early April.

The lake was calm with barely a ripple on the water. It was too early for the birds, and the crickets were exhausted from their all-night excursion. A few frogs would not give up and made the only sounds within what seemed like the whole universe. The dawn light crept in, and the long shadows slipped back into the realm of darkness.

In the giant pecan tree, a red fox squirrel exited his nest, slow and deliberate. He took off down the tree's limb and sailed through the air, landing on a branch that shouldn't have been able to hold a dragonfly, much less the old fuzzy tail. He navigated it with perfect ease and settled to have his breakfast. Old Blue looked up at him, as if to say, "If I really wanted to, I could have you for supper."

Old fuzzy tail and I both know he was only fooling himself. My imagination displayed the cartoon version of Rocky laughing his ass off. I smiled.

"If you see Bullwinkle, tell him I said hello," I whispered to the rodent and tipped my hat in his direction.

I picked up a stone and threw it in the water to watch the ripples make circles and expand larger. I never lost the thrill of throwing a rock in the water. Something about it, in conjunction with the morning quiet, brought my soul to another place and time, one where death and carnage was only in my nightmares. The perils of the world in the four years since Pentacle warranted any peaceful period to be a formal blessing.

There were around seven and a half billion people on Mother Earth the year that the NV-17 virus wreaked its havoc. In an effort to contain NV-17, the quarantine and lockdown mandates crippled the global economy. The cure became almost as bad as the disease. By the end of the year, they reported a global death toll of around forty-two million which was about 1% of the population. Of the forty-two million, ten million was from means created by humanity from the fallout of society in the presence of NV-17 virus, but not the disease itself.

Early the next spring at a research facility preparing for vaccine human trials, NV-17 merged and mutated with M.E.R.S. and became airborne. It was dubbed the Pentacle Virus. Becoming infected brought death within thirty-six hours in almost all cases.

Weeks later, just before the newscasters went off the air, the estimated death toll of the Pentacle Virus was eighty-five percent of the global population. If that actually came to pass, my rudimentary calculations being generous, about one billion, one hundred-twenty million humans survived or were immune to the Pentacle Virus worldwide.

That put the continental United States living population at around fifty million, give or take.

Living off the beaten path, Baby Girl and I have been relatively fortunate so far.

She smiles and tells me she is fine but I know that it is not all Presyscodine in the pill bottle in the medicine cabinet. She didn't want me go out into the cold of winter and added pills that resembled her medication. She has kept her legs covered up, so I know the Lupus rash has returned.

I was born, Richard Engelmann on the eighteenth of November 1963. Ever since, I can remember everyone that knew me personally called me Dinky. I'm not sure if I know how it started. My Mamaw once told me that my dad came out to the waiting room and told my Papaw that I was pretty and pink to make him think I was a girl.

"With a Dinky, about this big!" he said, holding his hands a foot apart.

Later in life, I was relieved that I wasn't stuck with Rich or Dick. Dinky was original, and it belonged to me. The one and only time the name got me in trouble was in the third grade. Forrest Whitney called me Dinky-Do, imitating that big-nosed fellow on the television.

"Red Rover, Red Rover let Dinky-Do come over," he had shouted.

That day, he developed an acute case of swollen lip and bloody nose. I got whipped by the principal and again by my dad, but I never heard Dinky-Do again. Case Closed.

Baby Girl was born Sarah Ruth Spiney, on the eleventh of October 1963. On the twelfth day of June in 1982, her last name became Engelmann.

When we were dating, I was at her house one night. We were sitting on the couch watching the boob-tube. Her daddy, Mr. Harry, got out of his recliner and stretched as far as his five-foot nothing body would let him and worked all the kinks back in place.

"G-night, Baby Girl," he told her and nodded at me.

I watched her while she told her old man good night and that she loved him. A golden aura emitted from her which put the nail in the coffin. She has been Baby Girl ever since. I wanted from that day to my last day for that glow to apply to me as much as it did to her old man.

She didn't know that night that her last name would be Engelmann, but I did.

That glow is not as bright now as it was the first day, I saw it, but I can catch a glimpse of it now and then, and it warms my very soul.

The light expanded more, and the shadows retreated. A few birds had decided to awaken for the day. Some sang, and some took wing to check out the beautiful morning. A slight breeze formed causing a silver shimmer on the water.

A fish surfaced in the middle and splashed before he submerged.

I really should be out there with my fishing pole this morning. That was probably the biggest one ever that broke the water.

Maybe soon--- Today, I have to get my shit together.

I sat on the bench by the stone walk leading to the boat dock. Blue jumped up on the seat with me. I looked at him, knowing what he wanted, but acting like I didn't have a clue. He knew the game better than I did. After a minute or two of stalemate, he nuzzled my hand.

"All right, you old shit- eater!" I said.

I scratched him behind the ears until he stretched out his neck, cocking his head to tighten the skin, enjoying every bit of attention. In a couple of minutes, he figured that I had had enough and jumped down.

He looked at me with the I-got-you-again smile and then shook himself out. I've come to call that the hokey-pokey. When he got everything in place, he laid down and stared out at the lake.

Blue liked the early mornings, too.

The sun had broken over, and the silver had turned to blue on the water. It was time to chew the bones, as Jeremy Singer, my old straw boss at Alamos, often said.

"If you're going to suck up the gravy, son. You have to chew the bones, too," I told Blue, in my best Jeremy Singer imitation.

I looked up on the porch; Baby Girl was standing there in a pink cotton Terry-cloth robe and both hands wrapped around a mug with steam coming out of it. Her beautiful long hair, more silver than brunette these days, was pulled back behind her ears.

The greatest accessory to the ensemble was the black Wellington boots she wore.

It was a truer than true fashion statement that fit her to a tee and dipped to the center of my heart. As always, the sight of her filled me with love, peace, and joy. She saw me looking and waved at me to come back to the house.

My heart was already there.

"Come on, old shit-eater," I said. He gave me his typical go-to-hell look. If looks could kill, old Blue would have had me in the grave a long time ago.

I looked back at the lake again, taking in the scenery one more time. I wondered if Darrell was gazing upon a pretty sight somewhere and hoped that he and my grandbabies were still breathing. I took a deep breath, and started up the stone path.

I got to the porch and Baby Girl asked, "You want some breakfast?"

"No, ma'am," I said. "I'll get something later on today."

I cocked my head at her with the best sexy eyes I could muster. "You sure are looking sexy in your morning ensemble, Baby Girl," I crooned, batting my eye lashes.

"Don't make promises if you can't keep them. If you stir up the tiger, you're gonna get scratched." She giggled.

"Ooh! My Lady, I be scared," I said.

"Which direction you going?" she asked, getting serious.

"I think I'll go north this time," I said. "Make a trip into Anson."

"Anson?" she asked. "That is a long way on foot. Want me to come?"

"No, ma'am! I'll be gone about five days, a week tops," I said. "It'll be a pretty tough walk, and besides, I'll have the old shit-eater with me."

"You know one day he is going bite your ass. Come here, Blue." She stooped down and scratched him behind the ears.

Two times in one morning—he was in hog heaven.

She placed her hands on both sides of his face and looked straight in his eyes.

"Take care of the old fart for me," she said.

The look he gave her said, "Okay, if I must."

He gave me a different look. It said, "Come on old fart, we're burning daylight."

"Okay, okay! Let me get my gear!" I told him.

He trotted back to Baby Girl, begging for more attention.

The old lake house was never supposed to be permanent when my uncle gave it to us for a wedding present but we fell in love with the place as much as with each other. Baby Girl will never leave. Every day since the Pentacle pandemic finale, she has stared down the old driveway longing to see Darrel make his way home.

That crazy little thing called hope.

I walked in through the back-porch door to the kitchen. Although nothing was being cooked, it smelled like a kitchen should smell. The aroma of home; lingering pot-stirred fragrances with hint of "Baby Girl" clean. Sanitized to the tenth power!

Sometimes, just being in there made me hungry. I grabbed a day-old biscuit and started through the door to the living room. Some people would call this a den or a family room, but to me, it will always be the living room. I looked at the years of accumulation and had to smile. Every bit and bob in here told a story; I was fortunate enough to already know most of them.

My eyes focused on the calendar, the one we got for Christmas with a different picture of the Engelmann family on each month. It still displayed Darrel, Brenda, Little Darrel, and Sweet Baby Jane with a grassy-hill background full of wild flowers. That was the picture for May of 2016. Brenda didn't make through the first wave; my son and grandbabies could still be alive though.

That crazy little thing called hope.

The recently added appliances and piping reminded me of how spoiled we had become to the amenities of modern life prior to Pentacle. A gravity-fed cistern and hand pump had replaced pressurized water lines, a gas-powered stove for cooking. Lighting was mostly candles, with some battery powered and oil lanterns.

I grabbed "Old Beulah," my Remington pump shotgun and a few extra shells. Then I threw on my backpack with all the essentials contained: toilet paper (most essential), change of clothes, a blanket, a Louis L'Amour, a couple of water bottles and some munch rations. Some of the rations were for old Blue, but I would never tell him that. I had grabbed my walking stick by the time Blue and Baby Girl walked in.

"I got to get going, but I got time for a quickie!" I said.

Baby Girl threw her hand forward like she was brushing away a fly from the dinner table. "Save your strength for when you get back. I'll whip you up some shaky pudding."

She walked up and wrapped her arms around my waist and gave me a kiss. She gave me a, you-better-be-careful look, and then smiled. It was not the bright eyes and I-love-you-with-all-my-heart, ear-to-ear smile. It never was when I went out for more than a day trip.

"Be careful and stay out of sight. I love you," she whispered in my ear.

I stared into her eyes. "What's the drill while I'm away?"

"Don't stray far from the house. Stay armed at all times. Minimize noise. Make sure the batteries are good in the alarm sensors. If alarm sounds, make it to the basement panic room and wait it out. If discovered or surprised, shoot to kill," she said.

I couldn't help myself and gave her a bear hug squeeze that about took her feet from the floor. "Good girl. Do you want me to leave Blue with you?

"No, you need him more than I do. I'll be fine," she said. "Do be careful and no He-man bullshit, okay?"

"I Love you, Baby Girl," I whispered and caught a hint of glow around her and smiled inside.

"Come on, you flea bitten shit-eater," I yelled in my best Yosemite Sam voice. I don't think it impressed Blue one bit, but he got up, did the hokey-pokey; shake-it-all-about thing, and trotted towards the door.

On impulse, I did the old Michael Jackson spin and backed toward the door in the moon walk for good measure.

Blue ignored me, but I got a giggle out of Baby Girl. That made the deed worthwhile. My ankles will probably recite the "Paul Harvey -- Rest of the Story" by the end of the day.

Blue went on ahead, like he sometimes does, and I made it down the steps into the front yard. The ties of society no longer necessitated lawn grooming, but old habits die hard and the fact that the grass needed mowing crossed my mind as I closed the gate and started down the driveway toward the highway.

I walked this walk many, many times and never got tired of looking at the hardwoods, especially the old live oak trees. They stand to the testament that all things beautiful take their time arriving. I have seen all manner of wild game in this stand of forest and taken several of them home to keep the aroma of Baby Girl's kitchen in good standing.

Pentacle took its toll and there were not as many animals left in the new version of our world. Mother Nature, hopefully, would allow them to make a comeback. It would have been nice if the virus would have wiped out mosquitos, ticks and roaches, but it seemed to target mammals and birds. I don't think the reptiles and insects were affected.

Blue performed his normal ritual. Anything that entertained the thought of leaving a scent on his turf got a smidgen of piss applied to it to let them know who big kahuna was around these parts.

I don't think he is fooling any of them, either.

He finally settled on a place to do his morning deposit and looked to make sure that I was not watching. That three-circle thing is a dead giveaway to turn your head and look somewhere else. If he caught you watching, he would hold it in till he busted.

I gave him his privacy and moved on down the road, picking up the pace, and tried to settle into the old walking rhythm. He caught up, giving me the stink eye as he passed, and went on up ahead to investigate some more smells.

I got into my stride and sang a cadence-style jingle in my head.

The walkin' man walks with a swagger and a step.
Getting in the rhythm and making them count.
Do we have a really long way to go, You Bet!
Me and Old Blue's gonna make it no doubt.

As I covered the ground that was all too familiar to me, my mind drifted to yesteryears, a time when Baby Girl and I were young, and Blue's ancestors were domesticated cattle dogs.

I particularly loved the 1980's. I was full of piss and vinegar, and Baby Girl was the Belle of the Ball.

Chapter 2: The Paul Jones Tradition

"Baby Girl, you sure look purty in that dress," I said with a lopsided smile.

"We ain't got time for that. We are late already," she said, smiling all the same.

"I swear, girl, that is the prettiest hickory nut ass I have ever seen," I said, looking appreciative at her attire.

"Hush, you want them to hear you?" She was talking about Darrell, who she probably imagined was at the door with his ear up against a high ball glass pressed to the wood.

Darrell wasn't even two yet. I was more concerned with her mama, Mrs. Emily, and her knowledge of a high ball glass as an eavesdropping espionage device.

"I doubt he knows what a hickory-nut ass is. Well, maybe he does," I said. "He definitely seems to be a chip off the old block, if you know what I mean." I worked my eyebrows up and down as fast as I could.

"All too well," she said, laughing. "All too well."

She ran over and gave me an, if-you're-good-this-is-what-you-can-expect-later kiss. She had my blood boiling, and we hadn't even left the house yet.

Maybe I could talk her into parking the old Ford on a back road somewhere like we used to.

She checked herself in the mirror; I never understood why. She shined like a new penny everywhere she went.

"Ready or not, here we come," she said.

We headed out. She needn't have worried about any eavesdropping; Darrell and Mrs. Emily were having too good a time in the living room to be worried about us.

"Mom, the number to the hall is on the fridge under a magnet. You'll have to let it ring a bunch till somebody answers it if you need us," Baby Girl said.

Her mom looked at her like she had fallen off a turnip truck. "This is 1986. I'm fifty-four years old, and this for sure ain't my first rodeo. Ya'll get on out of here."

We all laughed and my imagination displayed the image of Mrs. Emily riding a bull. A hell-u-va eight seconds that would be, and my bet would not be on the bull. Mrs. Emily could be a formidable adversary, when inclined to.

On the way over to the dance hall, we talked and laughed. She was on the seat right beside me in the middle of the old Ford truck. I tried to get a little frisky and got my hand slapped for my efforts. She made me a promise for later with just a look in her eye.

I parked the Ford by Jason Connelly's Chevy. His truck was newer than my old Ford, a 1976 model, but he had already ragged it out. Even when we were kids, he would have his toys torn up before the new wore off of them.

For whatever faults he had, he was my best friend in the entire world, more like a brother than a friend, really.

I always thought we would grow old together after retirement, but life has a funny way of throwing a curve ball. Damn sure didn't expect apocalyptic survival techniques to be in the line-up.

His wife, Melanie, and Baby Girl were on the same cheerleading squad when Jason and I had aspirations of the NFL. Their cheering turned out to be a lot better than our athletic abilities because we didn't make the high school playoffs in the three years we played.

After a couple of nights on the town with Baby Girl and Melanie, we decided there were a lot of better things in life than the NFL.

I knew right away what the future held for Baby Girl; I just had to convince her of it.

I opened the door and held out my hand for Baby Girl to come out the driver's side. Her skirt rode up a little when she scooted across the seat, and I looked at her batting my eyelashes real fast and grinning the I'm-a-gonna-git-you grin.

"Behave, you heathen," she said and rolled her eyes, but the glow told the truth.

When she composed herself and got out, I stood at attention and extended the crook of my right arm. Shaking her head and giggling, she locked onto my arm, and we started into the dance hall.

The dance hall was actually the V.F.W. Hall, but they brought in a band on Saturday night and charged a small cover charge that was called a donation.

The fixings- Coca-Cola, ice, and Dixie Cups- were free. They had a pretty severe mark-up on the whiskey, which was only sold in half pints from behind the partition, of course, and keg beer only served in Dixie Cup draft.

They did all right as far as donations went. They hired a local sheriff deputy to walk around and keep the peace, and they paid the band. Their intake allowed the hall's charitable inclinations to be admirable in the eyes of society.

The majority of the bands only played three chords, but they all made them three sound pretty good. They played mostly country and western until the Geritol crowd played out. That was about 9:30 because, after the 8:45 band break, we all lined up for the Paul Jones.

The Paul Jones was a time-honored tradition that stemmed way back. No one remembered when or why it came about, but everyone maintained it was tradition and had to be performed.

The women formed a circle on the inside. The men lined up in a circle around them on the dance floor. The band cranked up a fast ditty, and the girls sashayed to the left and the boy's heel-toed to the right.

Very much like musical chairs, when the music stopped you turned and faced whoever was in front of you. That was your dance partner.

They played about two minutes of belly-rubbing music, and you were at the mercy of fate for those two minutes.

The music stopped, and the fast ditty started the ritual all over again. That went on till around 9:30. After that, the Geritol crowd faded away. If they stayed any longer, they might miss Sunday School the next morning and be the topic of the next week's gossip.

In the second song of the Paul Jones, I got captured by Mrs. Pearly, the widow Newman.

Bless her heart, I loved her to death, but she tipped the scales at about three hundred.

She grabbed me up to a George Jones medley, and I don't think my boots touched the floor until the ditty started again.

As I was being flung around the hardwood floor, I recalled how many times she tore my butt up when she was my Sunday School teacher and apparently had a grin from ear to ear the whole dance.

Baby Girl ended up with Mr. Hiram, the reigning Monarch of the Geritol crowd, and you'd have thought he had hit the jackpot. She looked over at me and was visibly shaking from trying not to laugh and spoil Hiram's dance; he was trying so hard to be graceful.

Jason had given up. He was with April Green, and they had quit their dance to watch me and Mrs. Pearly. Both of them were bowled over laughing and I was the brunt of the joke.

I didn't catch where Melanie was, but when the Paul Jones was over, they all were about to pee their pants as they debated my excellent dance skills in the presence of a master. Within a minute, I was about to pee my pants, too.

The explanation of what it looked like was funnier than the experience.

Around 10:30, things livened up and a little Rock & Roll was thrown into the mix. That was my time to get Baby Girl on the floor and work my magical charms.

Of course, I had no formal training; everything I knew about the art of dance was self-taught. I didn't foresee my style of jitterbug ever being acceptable on *American Bandstand*, but Baby Girl followed me like it was second nature to her.

Seemed like she knew what I was going to do before I did.

I few good slow belly-rubbing songs along with a little butt-shaking, and I was back to thinking about the dark end of a back road.

Jason and Melanie got a little closer on the dance floor. They wouldn't be hanging around much longer, either.

"You wanna blow this joint, sweet cake?" I whispered to Baby Girl in my best Bogart voice. All I got in return was that come-and-get-me smile.

I couldn't get out of there fast enough.

We made it back to the table, talked with Jason and Melanie a couple more minutes, and made our escape. We all walked out together to the parking lot.

As we said our goodbyes at the truck, Jeff Gentry and his wife, Jenny, came staggering and stumbling out of the dance hall. I looked over at Baby Girl.

She gave me, The-Look, and sighed. I knew the woods thing was out of the question and started toward Jeff, who was trying desperately to remember where his old Buick was.

"Hey, Jeff," I said, "why don't you let me bring you home and we'll come back in the morning and get your car? It is on the way to my house anyway."

"Thanks-sh, Dinky," he slurred. "Probly won't sh-start widout a jumpin' nohow."

"Ya'll, jump in," I said.

This made some sho'nuff brownie points with Baby Girl. Oh well, maybe we can go parking another time, but that bedroom door will close tonight and I'm gonna have a big bate of shaky pudding!

We got home, and Baby Girl checked in on Darrell. Mrs. Emily eased on out to get in her car and head home. Baby Girl tried to get her to stay, but she wouldn't have any of it.

I was glad that she was stubborn that way.

After her mama left, Baby Girl made good on all her promises. After the cuddling and cooing, she whispered soft to me.

"I love you, and I am proud of you. That was a good thing you did tonight, bringing Jeff and Jenny home. You are a decent man; don't let anyone ever tell you different."

I fell asleep that night like every other night, the most fortunate man in the world.

Chapter 3: On the Road

"Blue! C'mere boy!" I said.

Trekking and reminiscing made me lose track of him. I looked up as he trotted back toward me from around the curve.

"That's okay. I just wanted to know where you were,"

It was as if he understood the English language. He stopped, did the hokey-pokey, and sat on his butt until I caught up with him. When I got close, he came and walked beside me, keeping pace. His tongue was lolled out to one side, so I stopped and got out the water bottle. I took a swig and poured some in my cupped hand for him.

"It is warming up a little bit today, ain't it, old boy?" He looked at me and seemed to be grateful that I didn't call him shit-eater. We cranked up the walk again.

The walkin' man skips with jingle and a hop
He's got the whole world on a string
Walkin' man hurries and he just can't stop
Cause Blue will do the hokey-pokey thing.

About two o'clock in the afternoon, we came to a rusty signpost that read Anson to the right and Langston to the left. I took a right and headed toward Anson. If luck held out, I would be there in a couple of days. I had not been to Anson since I took Baby Girl to the Lupus Doctor in the fall of 2015; I tried to keep things as close to home as possible after Pentacle. I hated being away from Baby Girl at night, even though she knows where and how to hide if strangers ventured that far and found our house.

Anson was a bigger town, though, and I needed to locate Baby Girl's medication.

Maybe I'll be able to find it, just maybe!

Another four hundred yards down, the rusty road sign read, "Anson, 28 miles."

The sky was clear with only a few puffy clouds overhead; the air was crisp. I didn't need a jacket but I probably would have been a little uncomfortable in short sleeves. The wind had almost stopped, but every once in a while, a gentle puff would pass by.

The day was almost perfect.

Half a mile past the road sign I came upon the railroad tracks. They crossed the road going north to south. The once-shiny rails were now dull brown rust. Thistles, bull nettles, and Johnson grass were stretched out from underneath the rocks. The underbrush had taken over the embankments.

Seemed like reminders of the old ways were everywhere in the world.

"What do you think, Blue? Want to rest a minute?" I said. "Look at that old oak by the road. It's gotta be some sho'nuff shade under that one."

I looked at my watch, Old-T, and it said 3:45. We had been hoofing it for about eight hours. I was a little tired but hadn't gotten winded yet.

That is the beauty of walking; it keeps your stamina up, which is always good come shaky pudding time.

I cleaned out a spot under the oak, settled down to get the weight off the old bones, and pulled out the water bottle. I took a swig and cupped my hand again. Blue lapped up every bit, did the hokey-pokey, and lay down right beside me. I couldn't help but give the old ears a little scratch; he didn't object one bit.

I pulled my old ball cap down over my face and rested my head against the old oak. I felt her heartbeat in the quiet and still of the early afternoon. There was not a sound of anything fabricated by home sapien, just the quiet calm that only Mother Nature can provide.

My body wanted to slip off to the place where I wasn't asleep but not quite awake either. I shouldn't have let it, but it seemed like the right thing to do at the time. When I came out of that special place, it was 4:30.

Chapter 4: Baby Girl's Journal

As I stood on the front porch and looked down the long driveway, most of me wanted to see Dinky and Blue return with the decision to abandon the trip. I knew that would not happen.

It was amazing the difference it had made when the world had cell phones. We got used to being able to call or text at any time and now are back to hoping and wondering.

"I guess we have come full circle Lord," I said, and hoped the Lord could still hear me. "Please keep him and Blue safe."

I put cortisone cream on my leg rashes, two splotches felt warm and possibly feverish.

I pulled my journal down from its hiding place on the closet shelf and started to write.

Dear Diary – Early in the Forth Spring, After Pentacle (Gladiolas Blooming)

Dinky and Blue left out this morning to go to Anson which is about thirty-five miles away. I wish he would have taken the old Ford truck but Dinky stopped using vehicles for travelling due to the noise they make. The highway men use motorcycles to overtake individual travelers.

My stomach tied up in a knot as soon as he went out the door and will stay that way until I hear his voice again. This upcoming week will be a long one. My imagination displays him on the side of the road with a broken leg, choked to death eating those damned Vienna Sausages, taken hostage by raiders, dead of a heart attack, or killed in a shootout over something probably stupid.

He is a tough old coot; I'll give him that. He will try anything if it is for me and he knows I am about out of Presyscodine. Dinky will find the medicine or die trying, I am sure of that. I am going to start taking the correct dosage again with what little I have left.

I should go out and work the garden but the Lupus has kept me drained of all my energy. I will have to force myself to get moving.

I am glad that Blue is with Dinky. I get tickled at the way they act when they think I am not watching. Dinky loves that dog as if he were his own son. They sometimes remind me of Dinky and Darrel, when Darrel was young and so wanted to impress his daddy.

Dinky was always a hardworking and hard playing man. I guess he can't do anything the easy way. It always has to be all out or nothing. I have stated before that he is a generous man, even though he didn't want anyone to know it.

I guess we had not been married but four or five years when the Benson boy, his pretty little wife and infant boy became homeless when their house trailer burned to the ground. Bartholomew was his name, but everyone called him Bart.

Nobody would help him, not even his own parents. Joshua Benson was a tight wad old bastard and never did anything to help any of his family unless there was a profit in it for him.

Dinky and I could barely keep a roof over our own head. Darrel was still a toddler, barely out of diapers and we were living paycheck to paycheck.

It didn't matter, Dinky swung a deal with Mr. Ledbetter on the little rent house on the corner of Edgeworth and Hemmingway street.

Bart worked with Dinky at Alamos and Dinky promised old man Ledbetter that we would vouch for Bart and if Bart couldn't pay the rent we would.

I don't know how or why I got drug into it; it was a done deal before I even knew about it. It was always funny to me who and what Dinky would come to love and want to take care of. Some things that you would think he would just go crazy over, he didn't care a thing about. And other times some things that didn't make a hill of beans, he acted like it was better than gold.

Anyway, Dinky put his faith in Bart and he didn't let him down. He paid his rent when it was due. After a month, he was able to have the electricity turned on. About six months later, he bought Dinky's old truck, the one he called Smokey and Dinky didn't have to pick him up and drop him off every day. It showed the love he had for the young man because I never thought Dinky would ever part with that old truck.

Dinky became more like a father to him than his own father was and they would spend their off time together fishing, hunting, cutting wood, or building on something.

Dinky loved that young man like he was his own brother.

Bart was really smart and caught on to everything very fast. Within a year and a half of the trailer fire, Bart was asked to take a promotion. I think the day that Bart got the promotion to line foreman, Dinky's head was swollen bigger than Bart's was. The only sad part was that Bart would have to move to Little Rock, Arkansas.

It was a tearful good bye and I'll never forget what Bart whispered in my ear the last time he hugged my neck.

"Take care of him. When I grow up, I want to be just like him." He pulled away with a tear in his eye. I knew he meant it.

It was his way of thanking me for what we had done and to this day I know in my heart that if the roles were reversed, that is exactly what Dinky would have said. We got cards at Christmas and every once in a while, Bart would call and promise when things slowed down, they were going to come home for a visit.

To this day, I know Dinky still thinks about him.

The day we got the news, Dinky eased himself from the lazy-boy and walked down to the lake. He stayed down there for at least two hours; it had gotten dark by the time he came back. Darrel had wanted to go down where he was, but I wouldn't let him. I think he was about five, maybe six at the time.

When Dinky got back to the house, he picked Darrel up and hugged him so tight I thought he was going to crush his ribs. I could tell he had been crying.

The only thing he said was. "Baby Girl, we need to see if we can find out the funeral arrangements."

He got back in the lazy-boy and Darrel crawled up in his lap, laying his head on Dinky's chest. They sat there until both of them went to sleep with Dinky slowly rubbing Darrel's back.

I got the funeral arrangements. They brought Bart home and buried him in Pine Grove Cemetery. Dinky didn't shed a tear and was very tight lipped through the whole ceremony. I clipped out the copy of the newspaper article about the Industrial Fire at the Alamos Little Rock facility.

I don't think Dinky ever asked what really happened; I don't think he really wanted to know. The article said that Bart was a hero and that he saved the lives of at least twenty men when he lost his. That was good enough for Dinky.

We never once talked about it and probably never will. All I know is that from then on, Dinky and Darrel were inseparable when Dinky was not working.

I flipped through the pages, about the fifth or sixth page in the journal and started reading. Memories flooded in.

Dear Diary, Date Unknown - Early Spring of the first year A.P. (After Pentacle)

Now that Dinky ain't here to be in my hair for a couple of days, it gives me some alone time to write to you. I never write when I think Dinky might see me. Not that he would say anything, but he would want to read you because you are filled with my personal thoughts. Your job is to someday let society know what has happened here.

The smell is a little better these last weeks, not much though. I guess it has been about eight or nine months since the final stage of Pentacle Virus started. We do not have to go down into the basement and breathe the bottled air as much as we used to. I swear at times I would have gone completely out of my mind if Dinky would not have made the breathing air space for us. It was a little bit stale, but for a short while, you were able to be away from the smell of death.

The temperature is getting a little warmer and I am glad that Dinky and Gordon are getting to leave out more. Both of them are about as stubborn as plow mules, it was a wonder they didn't get frost bite during the winter. I think they did more playing than they did working.

Gordon has told us that he was leaving and going to try to find his family. I know in my heart that it is more about feeling like he is "wearing out his welcome" than the possibility of finding his daughter. I never say a word about it though. We have told him many times that he is welcome to stay.

His temperament is a lot like Dinky's and Dinky would not have stayed this long. We would have been out walking in a blizzard before we let his big old pride feel like he was imposing. I must be crazy for loving him the way I do.

I messed up the other day and said something about Jason and Melanie. I hope that I don't forget and do that again. Dinky instantly became down hearted and it took a couple of days before he acted like himself again. I have to remind myself of what he did that day at their house.

I have to admit that day Dinky was probably in the worst shape I had seen him in since Bart got killed in the explosion. He never let on that he was down but I can read him like a book and he can't hide it from me.

I can tell he has become accustomed to having Gordon here and it will be a great loss when he is gone. My saving grace is my "Blue". He can argue all he wants to, but Blue is my baby, not his dog.

I never thought I could become attached to an animal as much as I love that dog. I often wondered if Blue reminds Dinky of that particular day. Dinky will not admit it, but he loves that puppy as much as I do. I've seen him scratching him behind the ears when he thinks I am not looking.

Looking forward to getting a garden started. Some fresh vegetables will help feed the soul and some blooming flowers sure can't hurt the smell.

That's all for now.

Flipping through the pages, I landed on another one.

Dear Diary, Sometime in Late Summer of the first year A.P.

Something is wrong with Dinky. He is down and melancholy. He is trying so hard not to act like it. Last night he was having a nightmare and tossing in the bed. He hasn't done that since we were first married.

I know something happened on his last trip into Barkston. He will hardly go anywhere anymore unless he has that old shotgun with him. I found him sitting down by the lake the other day and thought he was sleeping. When I got to him, I could tell had he been upset and troubled. He immediately perked up and started smiling and acting like nothing was wrong. I wish he would let me help him, but I know he won't.

I flipped a few more pages.

Dear Diary, Fall in the Second Year A.P.

The trees are beautiful this time of year. They are changing colors and the leaves are starting to fall. The smell is about gone and every once in a while, you get a fait whiff of what it was like. I waited for Dinky and Blue to get home today and I am worried for them. I hate it when they stay out overnight. I know they can take care of themselves but I still worry.

Dinky seems more like himself these days, but he is harder than he used to be. Not as resilient as he used to be. I guess you have to adapt to the way things are now. I know he is keeping things from me about how bad it is. He will not lie to me and if I was to press him, he would tell me. I am not sure that I want to know. I hope they make it back from Langston tomorrow. They might drag in late tonight.

I closed the book as my mind wandered back to that time period as I stored the journal back to the hiding place.

Gordon had been gone since spring and we had not heard from him. There was not as much coming over the CB channels anymore. The times we heard a combustible engine out on the highway happened less and less.

Dinky had started pretty much walking to gather the supplies or pulling his wagon. He only took the Ford if I was going or he needed to carry a big load. He said it was better on foot and he could get out of sight if he heard a vehicle. He had entered most of the houses in Barkston, our supply inventory was built up pretty good.

He had devised a filtering system and we could get water from the lake if we had to. He rigged it to pump up into a cistern beside the house and converted a gas water heater and gas oven to butane that we could hook up to bottles. At this point we must have had fifty of those five-gallon bottles and a few ten-gallon ones that he picked up from all over. He would take them down to the old farmers coop and fill them from the big tank behind the seed building.

There were lots of things that Dinky did to try to make my life as easy as possible. He rigged a hand pump up in the kitchen where I could pump water from the cistern. A gravity fed reservoir from the cistern was mounted above the toilet so we could fill the toilet tank to make a flush.

The simple things in everyday life that we used to take for granted. I loved him for it and it made him happy to be my protector and provider.

I never dared to ask him, but I know that one particular outing, something bad had happened. It was something that ate away at his very soul. I could only speculate that he had to have either harmed or killed someone. Nothing else would have had an effect on him. As months went by, he came to grips with whatever had him upset and settled back to the Dinky I knew and loved. I've often wished he would let me help with these things.

I looked out the window and down the driveway again, just for good measure.

Chapter 5: William and Smitty

Old Blue looked up at me as if to say, "Did it again, didn't you?"

"Shut up, old shit-eater. You could've kept me awake," I said. He got up nonchalantly and did the hokey-pokey, trotted ahead a few feet, and turned back to watch me wrestle my way back onto my feet. He gave me the, c'mon-you-old-fart, look and turned toward the road.

It looked like some dark clouds were in the distance to the southwest. The shadows were lengthening, and the temperature dropped a little. We started out again.

The walkin' man struts with a stride and a giggle
The walkin' man listens to the birds
The walkin' man skips with a hop and a wiggle
Whistling the pretty sounds that he heard.

We rounded a curve in the road; there were cattle in the road ditch. The fence was down in several places. They didn't mind greener grass, but they didn't want to stray too far from home. I checked this spot in my memory bank for the trip home. A fresh rib-eye steak would brighten Baby Girl's world, and I could use some more rawhide.

The hair on Blue's back started to stand up; he was transforming into what I called the "Pink Panther Mode." Every time he focused in that manner; *The Pink Panther* theme started playing in my head.

He crouched and readied himself for the chase, every hair on his back raised.

"Not this time, Blue," I said. "We'll get them on the way back."

He instantly relaxed and started trotting beside me again, but he never took his eyes away till we passed.

He was a little stirred up by the cows, so when a rabbit crossed in front of us about thirty yards away, I said, "Sic 'em, Blue!"

That was about like throwing a stick of dynamite in the shitter: all manner of hell breaks loose. A little hare for supper wasn't a bad idea, either.

Blue left for a few minutes and then trotted back up to me with it hanging in his mouth. To his credit, for once, it was whole. I reckon Baby Girl's speech worked after all. He stopped and dropped it at my feet, and I gave him a quick scratch. He stretched out his skin and gave me his smiley face. I stuffed the rabbit in the side pouch of my backpack while Blue did the hokey-pokey.

An hour later, the light took on the translucence of late evening. The night crawlers had risen and made ready for another all-nighter, the warmup version of the buzzing and ringing that played every night was escalating.

Jiminy Cricket was standing on his podium in a tuxedo and waved his baton in preparation for the orchestration.

It occurred to me that a roof would be nice. Two hundred or so yards ahead I could see the roof line of a deserted farmhouse.

Of course, it's deserted; they all are.

It looked like the driveway wasn't very long either. I noticed a chimney, another plus. By the time we got to the porch, the crickets were starting to sing their night song in complete harmony.

Old Jiminy was waving the shit out of that baton.

No frogs were harmonizing because there wasn't enough water around, though there was one single solo tenor off in the distance; a whip-or-will sang his ballad.

I performed a sight survey as we approached and spotted a wood pile in front of the house. I stopped and got a few good sticks, focused on oak or pecan for the rabbit's benefit, and started toward the porch.

"Perimeter check, Blue!" I whispered.

Blue immediately reverted to what I called "Alert Mode." It was similar to the Pink Panther, but not quite the same. In the Pink Feline Mode, the prey was already identified. In Alert Mode, his ears would lay back against his head, and he started an immediate visual, audio, and olfactory search for anything out of the ordinary. He smelled and sniffed at the door and made a complete circle around the house.

When he came back to the porch, he was Blue again, no sense of alarm or curiosity. The house was empty. I went to the door and tried the door handle.

It opened with ease; Blue and I went inside.

It was a nice ranch-style dwelling, and the porch opened into the living room. I did another sight survey and determined nothing appeared ransacked or misplaced. It was kind of dusty, but I had seen a lot worse in my travels.

One plus; there were no shriveled-up corpses or lingering smell of death and decay.

There was nothing in the fireplace but old ashes. I looked up through the chimney to see if birds had made a nest there. There was a damper in it, so I figured that it was usable.

I went back out to the porch, got the wood I had left, and brought it inside.

"Let me get a fire going, and we will barbecue, Mr. Rabbit," I told Blue. "How would you like that?"

It didn't seem to impress him as much as it did me.

Some old newspapers piled up in the corner and a few sticks of kindling waited in the kindling box. I took a couple of matches from the dry box in my backpack and, within a few minutes, had a decent fire started. The light was fading fast; I did a quick search for candles. I found four candles and two oil lamps in the kitchen. I got them lit and placed them around the living room.

I took the oil lamp outside and removed Mr. Rabbit's pelt and insides. I got him prepared to meet Mr. Fire. I took the fire poker and some bailing wire from my backpack and made a skewer out of it. I pulled the log tray over close to the fire and set Mr. Rabbit on broil over the edge of the fire.

It wasn't long before the olfactory device signaled delicious, and Blue licked his lips.

"Not yet, old boy," I said.

I took the oil lamp into the kitchen and rummaged around. I found some spices in the cabinet over the stove. I shook a box of salt, a box of pepper, and a container of Soul Seasoning. They seemed to be okay. There was also a bottle of extra virgin olive oil. Jackpot!

I mixed up a little home seasoning and took down Mr. Rabbit long enough to wipe him down, inside and out, with my concoction.

Back to broil mode he went.

Blue had settled in, resting on his belly with his face on his front paws. I looked in the corner at the newspapers and tried to recall how long it had been since I had read one.

I took the one underneath the top bundle. It looked like it was a complete paper, although faded to a yellowish color. I dug into my backpack and extracted my cheaters. I slipped them on and looked over the top of them at Blue who appeared to be smiling a little too big.

"Shut up about it, shit-eater," I said and went back to the newspaper.

The headline report was about the second phase of the vaccine. Second Phase was Animal Trials, which rushed right into the Third Phase, Human Trials. The date was April 7, 2016. That was four years ago, give or take. By the time the vaccine was produced, it was too late.

No way to tell anymore about the exact days and months. It has been at least four winters. I returned the paper to the burn pile.

I lived thorough it once; don't need a reminder of the events. If the bureaucrats had agreed on anything, anything at all, Jason and I would probably be out fishing today.

I took Mr. L'Amour from my backpack and fell into the romantic setting of the Wild West. One of the Sacket boys was undoubtedly in deep doo-doo again.

After about ten pages, I checked on Mr. Rabbit. His aroma had definitely improved the place. I rotated the poker and let him get a little bit on the back side going. Blue was being patient, but I reckoned he was as hungry as I was.

"Not long now, old boy," I said and went back to the Wild West.

Suddenly, Blue went into Alert Mode. He didn't get up, but he tensed and turned his head toward the back of the house, ears laid back.

I eased the book down and picked up old Beulah. It never hurt to be prepared. Blue cocked his head again, and that is when I heard it.

A board creaked.

The noise emanated from the back-porch steps. I eased out of the chair, and Blue went into Pink Panther. He crouched at the door with every muscle set on spring.

I heard the back door open. Whoever approached was being especially quiet.

I took the safety off of Old Beulah.

My heart hammered in my chest, and I considered shooting through the door. I tried the only play I could think of.

"I am locked and loaded. Are you a friend?" I said loudly.

Everything in the entire universe got deathly quiet. A voice that I thought was long in the grave came through the door. "Dinky, is that you?"

I was sure it was him, but I yelled out anyway. "This is Dinky, who am I addressing?"

"Dinky, it's Byron, Byron Adams," he said.

"Where do I know you from?" I asked.

"We worked together at Alamos for three years," he said in a distressed voice. "You know me."

I still didn't let my guard down, and Blue was still in Pink Feline.

Byron was the welder at Alamos and did some blacksmith work on the side. This earned him the nick name of Smitty. Byron was a glass-half-empty kind of man that most people didn't take a shine to, me included.

I lowered my voice to show I was not joking in the least bit. "Are you alone, Smitty?" I asked. He took too long to answer, so I knew he wasn't. "Smitty, you don't sneak up on a man unless you mean him harm. I don't have anything here, but I'll protect what is mine." I yelled through the door. "I'll ask again, are you my friend?"

"Hell, no!" he yelled, as he kicked the door open.

Old Beulah roared.

Byron achieved nothing but double-ought-buckshot in his chest.

It looked like someone had tied a rope around Byron and jerked really hard on it. Both of his feet left the ground, he landed hard on his ass and then rolled to his side.

The man with him that was carrying a rifle, hesitated. He looked at Smitty like he was in a dream; like none of this was real. Blue was on him within a millisecond and targeted the throat. The man dropped the rifle and went down, keeping one arm around his neck and beating Blue on the side with the other. Blue was unable to establish a throat hold and I was grateful that the man didn't have a knife or a club in his hand.

I took a glance through the door frame. I didn't reckon anybody else was out there. If they were, Blue would probably have been sent to doggy heaven.

"Dammit, Smitty, I told you I was loaded," I shouted, shifting another shell into Old Beulah and pointed her at the other man on the floor. It was obvious that Smitty was no threat. Within a minute or two he would converse with St. Peter as to whether or not he could enter. It's doubtful he made it through the gate.

"Blue, perimeter check!" I yelled, as I kicked the rifle out of reach of the wide-eyed pilgrim on the floor.

Blue stopped biting the man on the floor and jumped back fast enough not to get another punch in the ribs. He backed away and stopped near the back door. His body stiffened as he immediately switched to Alert Mode and he slipped outside without a sound.

I lowered Old Beulah to point at the man on the floor. "Who are you?" I said.

He was scared, but he also looked like he might be a couple of bricks short of a full load. "W—W-William," he stuttered.

"Well, William, what did you and Smitty think you were going to do here tonight?" I asked. "I ain't got nothing worth stealing, and I value what little bit of life I have left."

He looked embarrassed and kept looking away.

A light bulb went off in my head as I came to the realization that I was very fortunate on this eventful evening. Blue's keen senses had saved me from being sodomized and perhaps murdered. I got pissed.

"Look what kind of mess we have made here," I said, my anger rising higher. "Why didn't you and Smitty just diddle each other?"

The more it was sinking in on me, the angrier I got. Blue came through the back door, still on alert status, but there was no sense of external danger.

I kept Old Beulah trained on William and backed over to the door and closed it.

William had not said anything. He looked up, "Who's Smitty?"

I pointed to the corpse in the floor. "He was. We used to work together in the past life. How long have you two been robbing and raping pilgrims on the road?" I asked, my blood pressure was through the roof.

He looked down and would not meet my eyes.

"How long, God-damn it!" I screamed.

"T--t-t-two years," he said. "N-n-n-ot many women folk left."

He shook his head slowly, obviously in shock.

"Byron said if we got caught, you wouldn't put up a fuss. He said you were a good man," he mumbled, almost to himself.

I looked straight at him, "He knew me as such, but that was then, and this is now. Get up and come in the living room."

He slowly got up sliding his back against the wall for support and never took his eyes off of Old Beulah. I read his body language.

"If I was going to shoot you, you would be dead by now. Get on up!" I barked.

He was almost up but slipped in Smitty's pooled blood and fell back to the floor. He landed hard and lay there moaning.

I had the immediate urge to kick him in the ribs until he couldn't move. I started positioning myself, but Blue got in between us, planted all four paws.

"Okay, Blue, okay!" I said and took a deep breath to calm the adrenaline rollercoaster.

"I'm okay, boy!" Blue backed up but kept his eyes on me and William.

"Get up, William," I said. "Let's go in the living room."

Here we go again, same as last time. This time he was aware of the slippery coating on the floor and was able to keep his footing. All three of us went into the living room, and I closed the door.

"Blue, watch him," I said. Blue went to full alert again and locked eyes with William.

William probably preferred Beulah over Blue.

I dragged the end table by the couch over to the door so it would stay closed. Smitty had busted the latch when he kicked it.

"Get on the couch," I told William.

He sat on the couch, and I told him to put his hands together.

"Blue, catch," I said. Blue jumped up on the couch and before William knew what happened, Blue was locked onto his throat, not enough to break the skin, but enough to let him know that any shenanigans would end up a very bad time for William.

I got the bailing wire out of the backpack again, only this time I wasn't using it to cook up old Mr. Rabbit. William was glossy-eyed and started to tear up, but he crossed his wrists and held them out for me to tie them together.

I thought about it, still a little pissed, and decided that William had no need for comfort this evening. Blue seemed to read my mind and moved over towards the side of the couch which caused William to turn his head with him. He planted his hind legs on the couch armrest and uttered a low growl through the teeth holding Williams throat.

I took his right hand and triple wrapped the bailing wire to his left knee, making the tightening twist underneath and leaving the ends sticking up towards the underside of his knee. I did the same thing with the left hand on his right knee.

I took the fireplace wrought-iron shovel and placed it down his back with the shovel on the back of his head.

"Release him, Blue." Blue turned loose; I straightened his head to the shovel and double wrapped a wire around his throat to the shovel handle.

I laid William on the couch on the flat of his back and stuffed pillows under his legs to keep his knees supported. I wanted him comfortable enough to speak but not comfortable enough to sleep. He needed to contemplate on his sins tonight, and I hoped he'd make peace with whoever he considers his God.

I was not entirely convinced that William and Smitty weren't destined for a reunion, real soon.

I checked on Mr. Rabbit. He was one hundred percent ready to make his contribution to the evening. Blue and I feasted on wild hare while William let out an occasional moan.

When Mr. Rabbit was all gone, Blue lay down within springing distance of the couch. I settled into the recliner and let the footrest out. Old Beulah stood right beside me on the wall within easy reach. Blue and I locked eyes, and he understood that he was taking first watch.

I pulled my ball cap down and closed my eyes.

Mr. Rabbit had satisfied my hunger for food, but my mind would not let me sleep. Even the despicable soul that he is, William could make conversation. I picked my hat back up, set it right on my forehead, and noticed that William watched my every move. He had settled a bit and come to the complete awareness that Byron was really dead, and he was in a tremendously bad situation.

"You're gonna kill me, aintcha?" he asked. I was glad the stuttering had stopped.

I stared straight and hard into his eyes.

"William, that depends entirely upon you," I said.

"Whatchu mean?" He looked at me like I imagined his victims had looked at him.

"Nothing like that!" I said, letting him know that he would not be molested in any way, form, or fashion.

"I want you to talk to me," I said. "I want you to quit stuttering and talk to me. If you can do that, I will see about making that tie on you more comfortable."

He did not speak but nodded his head as best he could with the shovel binding him.

"Good," I said. "You and Smitty seen me on the road today, didn't you?"

He nodded.

"You had to have seen that I was carrying Old Beulah with me and that Blue was tagging along. What in God's name were you two thinking, coming in here at me like that?" I shook my head in disbelief.

He tried not to look embarrassed.

"B-Byron thought we could j-jump you and take your gun. He wanted another shotgun and figured you would have extra shells. We are out of shotgun ammo. Everyplace we have found has already been picked over or the shells we found weren't no good. N-neither of us is any good with a rifle, we tried. The raping is -- was his idea, he said that hitting the b-booty was just going to be an extra."

Did Smitty really think I could be taken that easily? How little has the price of a man's life become? Even in the Old West, the general populations were decent, honest living folks. How did we become so spoiled that we forgot our own moral instincts?

"How many times did you and Byron pull this off?" I asked him.

"M-Maybe a dozen times all total," he said. His voice was getting calmer and his stuttering much improved. "It's nothing to be ashamed of really. Bryon says it is a new world since the Flip, and we make the rules." William closed his eyes and started tearing up.

"If both of you really thought the new world gave you the right to make your own rules, why are you tearing up like that?"

William shrugged and stayed silent.

I pushed down on his knee to make the pointed end of the tie-wire impact the soft skin underneath.

"Okay, okay. The little girl over towards Barkston. He didn't have to kill her."

I could feel my anger starting to creep up again, but I held it out of my voice.

"How old do you reckon she was?" I asked.

His eyes got wide, and he started explaining really quickly.

"It wasn't nothin' like that. She was at least sixteen and full growed. She just wouldn't shut up and quit crying. Truth be known, she should have never been out on the road by herself. She said she was running an errand for her grandma when we first caught up to her."

Tears started to flow from his eyes.

"She just would not shut up crying. I begged her to, but she wouldn't," he said.

"I knew he was going to do it. I saw the look in his eyes," he said, actually bawling. He wanted to make the confession. His chest was racking, and he was sniffling.

"He didn't have to kill her. There were so few left and she was pretty. Why did he have to kill her?"

I let him wallow in his thoughts for a minute.

"Was she the only one that ya'll killed?" I asked.

He locked his eyes on mine. "I have never killed anyone in my life. The times I was with Byron, I saw him kill that girl and one other person." He sniffled again. "It was a younger man that would not have it no way, form, or fashion. He fought tooth and nail against us both. Byron landed the barrel of the shotgun on top of his head and knocked him out cold. Then he took him while he was out. It didn't settle right with me, so I didn't get any."

He reflected on the memory a few seconds.

"Byron said I was crazy because it doesn't happen very often and we take our pleasures when we can. When the man came around, Byron shot him in the face with the shotgun. He dragged him off of the road into the woods and didn't even pull his pants back up. When he got back to the road, he said he reckoned he didn't have much fight left now. I kept my m-mouth shut because the look in Byron's eyes scared me a little."

I gave him another minute or two to reflect.

"How did you and Byron get together? How long have you been on the road?" I asked.

He looked at me, sizing me up again. His voice got a little stronger.

"Not long after the Flip, that's what Byron called it. I was sitting in the old honky-tonk I used to stop at after work. Nobody was around anymore, and I found myself more and more going out to the Wagon Wheel, out on 68, near Blackstone. It was still easy enough to siphon gas then and the road was not totally blocked. Besides, the smell was almost tolerable out there, but it was sickening closer into town."

The smell I remember well. I never thought to call it the Flip, though.

He was deep in thought and reflection, and I didn't say a word. His eyes were distant as he said, "Byron came in the Wheel, walked up to the bar, and hollered for the barkeep to give him a whiskey. I told him there weren't no more barkeeps left in this world, and we struck up a conversation. We'd been together since then."

He took a breath and sighed.

"In the early days, it was good. We helped people and they helped us. The people got fewer and fewer over the next year. I didn't know how quiet time could be until then. I reckon by that time we couldn't stand being alone."

He sniffed a hitch, but the real tears had left him.

"I never thought it could turn out this way," he said, almost a whisper.

I reflected for a moment.

"I reckon that the word Flip states it all; we are all definitely upside down these days," I said.

Chapter 6: The Pentacle Days

The death toll from Pentacle rose so fast that all the public services shut down almost at once. Within the span a few weeks, 55 percent of the already weakened human population was dead or dying at an exponential rate.

The NV-17 virus spread out across the globe when it was in its original stage and had done damage on a fairly large scale. For a period of about a year, the death toll from the NV-17 Strain had escalated to forty-two million, six hundred and fifty thousand people worldwide, almost half of that in the United States. The ones infected that were most likely to become fatality was the elderly and individuals with underlying diseases.

Children and healthy young to middle aged adults recovered better with many survivors being cleared of the virus. The medical community developed treatments that minimized the symptoms and lessened the death rate but this was primarily trial and error with lots of errors during the early onset of the NV-17.

The race for a vaccine escalated. The legalities and the approvals kept a vaccine out of the general population far too long.

The NV-17 virus mutated again.

The NV-17 Strain merged with the Middle East Respiratory Syndrome (MERS) and became airborne. It was called the Pentacle Virus because the first known case came from a lab attendant at the Pentacle Pharmaceutical Research Facility.

The Pentacle Virus had the ability to infect almost every living warm-blooded animal. It spread across the planet in the early summer of 2016. I am not sure how long the disease spread and wreaked havoc but communication lines went down by mid-summer, the world wide web would no longer connect around the same time. The news networks and radio stations were off the air shortly thereafter with their final broadcasts being confirmation of the death of POTUS and the complete breakdown of the federal government. All social services, including the armed forces were shut down.

The world was thrown into the dark ages and the poor souls who contracted the new Pentacle strain had little to no hope of survival. The vast majority who caught it, died within a twelve to thirty-six-hour period; regardless of health, age, gender, or race. Those that survived the thirty-six-hour period, in general, were stricken with continuous pneumonia type symptoms that eventually caused the individual's death. Most within two weeks.

In the early days of Pentacle awareness, conspiracy theorist blamed the government, accusing them of building biological weapons. If they did, they forgot to develop the antidote first.

The Muslims blamed the infidels, the Vatican declared it was "wrath of god", and atheist supremist blamed all society for global warming.

Personally, I think the Good Lord and Mother Nature had had enough of the parasitic homo sapien ruining the planet.

After the fifth or sixth week of Pentacle, the television shut down to just the signal in the middle that looked like a radiation emblem and that annoying ring. The predicament of the rest of the world was lost, and the remaining citizens of the United States were in panic mode.

They either held up behind their quarantined locked doors or took to the road in an attempt to outrun the disease. Neither option was a workable solution. Pentacle escalated to the point of no return, and soon the only humans left alive on the planet were the few that was immune to the virus.

No more local or cable news. No more WCPT - Where the Country Legends Live. The cell phones died. It was rumored that the land line telephones worked for a few more weeks. Baby Girl and I tried to use the land line; we got a dial tone but we never could connect to anyone. I guessed the gurus that kept everything going keeled over or headed for higher ground.

Within six to eight weeks, the world as Baby Girl and I knew it, had flipped. No more commerce, no more social services, no more police, no more armed forces, no more president, no more government.

After the electric lines went down, and the communications went silent was the hardest time for Baby Girl and me; waiting to get sick and knowing that it was coming.

We did everything the CNN newscaster had advised when the news first hit the press. We stayed indoors, didn't allow contact with other humans, and wrote our names and social security numbers on our chest with a marks-a-lot.

Baby Girl and I waited for the end.

Time slowly passed by, probably three weeks after the broadcasts stopped. We were still alive and still okay. No sign of the sniffles, fever, rashes, or the boils.

By that time, a constant and unpleasant odor drifted through and around the house. It was getting stronger by the day. On occasion, when the wind was right, I would get a whiff of smoke mixed in the smell. Somewhere, either by natural or man-made causes something had burned or was still burning. There was nothing to stop it from spreading and I didn't know how close it was to Baby Girl and me.

The worst had happened. After two months, we were still alive and almost out of canned food. What choice did I have but to go see?

I drove into Barkston and was amazed at what I saw. The God-awful stomach-wrenching odor of the corpses was far worse than the terrifying sight of the carnage.

Cars were parked in all different places and angles. Some with doors closed and some with doors open. Most of them had human remains in them, some bloated and some shriveled. Some were broken open and oozing fluids. Mother Nature's cleanup crew reveled in the easy access of the putrid decay. The buzzards, coons and rats were having a field day, but the insects were, by far, the worst.

It came to a point where the traffic jam would not let my truck pass.

I got out of the truck and walked toward town. I tied my old bandana around my mouth to help with the smell, but mostly it was for the flies. Flies and maggots seemed to be on everything in sight; they were everywhere.

A generator hummed in the distance. That meant someone was still alive, and they could inform me of what was going on. I walked through the maze of vehicles that got more confined as I entered onto Bolton Avenue. I wished that I had never come and was so thankful that I had had sense enough not to bring Baby Girl.

I headed for the one place in Barkston that held a special meaning for me: 1321 Sycamore Lane. I hoped and prayed that I would not find what I suspected I would.

The streets in this particular neighborhood was not crowded with traffic jam. It looked like a normal late morning in early summer; the lawns needed mowing, and the cars were in the driveways. The difference was the sound, or the lack of it, and the smell that was so awful that it seemed to have mass and weight to it.

I got to 1321 Sycamore and walked up the driveway as I had done so many times in my life. I expected Jason to jerk the door open and give me that shit-eatin grin of his. That didn't happen. I told myself that maybe they got out, but I knew better. He and Melanie would have come to our house if they would have left, and besides, his new Ford was still in the driveway.

I walked up the steps and knocked on the door. Nothing but sounds of the flies and the insects came back to me.

I knocked again, louder.

"Please, Lord," I begged.

No sound came from the other side.

Every bone in my body told me to turn away and go home, but I was obligated by love and friendship to know the truth.

I tried the lock on the door, and it held fast. I looked around to see if anybody was looking: old habit, I guess. I lifted the stone flowerpot under the porch light and got the spare key.

I unlocked the door and stepped inside a house that I loved as much as my own. Things were messier than I had ever known Melanie to be. One thing was very certain, the smell inside the house was extremely strong. My heart sank and my eyes flooded with tears.

I knew where I would find them.

I steeled myself and walked to the master bedroom. Memories of Jason flooded my thoughts: how he was strong and proud, the way he smiled and laughed, how he had my back no matter what, and how much he loved Melanie.

I opened the bedroom door, and the odor nearly knocked me to my knees. I leaned against the door frame and dry heaved a couple of times but managed to keep everything down. Once I thought I could go on, I looked into the room. The curtains were drawn, but there was enough light in the room for me to see their final moments.

Jason had his back against the big oak headboard and was sitting up. Melanie was curled in a ball against him with her head on his chest and her arm draped over him. He had his arm around her shoulder in a hug.

It would have been a sweet scene of surrender had not the forces and creatures of nature intervened. It appeared they had already bloated and then released. There were fluids on the sheets mixed with larvae and that was more than I could stand.

I backed out of the room and eased the door closed.

I walked to the kitchen and before I thought about what I was doing, I opened the refrigerator door. That was a big mistake. The odor of rotten food instantly mixed with the intolerable fragrance of carrion.

I lost what little bit of breakfast I had left.

I sat on a kitchen table chair that I had sat in many times before and cried like a newborn babe.

I went to the sink and was surprised that the water was still running. That was what the generator was doing, I realized. I washed my face and rinsed my mouth out, got a glass from the cabinet, and took a long drink. Even the water seemed to have that smell and taste to it.

I went to the back door and looked out over Jason's backyard. He always had kept a beautiful backyard. The best feature was the big live oak in the right corner.

I stepped off the back porch and headed for the tool shed on the side of the house. I found a spade and a shovel and took them out to the live oak and started my labor. It was not six feet deep, but it was deep enough to prevent any animals from disturbing them.

It was midafternoon by then, and I was wringing wet with sweat. I guess that at some point I got acclimated to the smell. It did not seem to have the effect on me that it had earlier, and the flies had dwindled some due to the heat of the day. I did a final survey and nodded; I headed back toward the house.

The next part of this chore was not as easy as I thought it would be. They were stone cold rigid in the positions they were in when the end came. I started with Melanie.

I got her pulled over to one side of the bed. I lifted Jason and pulled the soiled sheets from under him and off the bed. I balled them up with everything that was in them and threw them in the corner.

I went to the kitchen and wet a big sponge. I cleaned the once beautiful face that had turned into a nightmarish scene of putrid decay. She was still in the curled position when I wrapped her up in a clean sheet like a cocoon.

Jason was not as soiled as Melanie. I wiped the remnant of the face that belonged to the brother that I never had. As my tears streaked, I threw the sponge in the corner with the soiled bedding and wrapped him in up with a clean sheet in the same fashion.

I don't know if it was the adrenaline or the fact he'd already decomposed, but he did not seem to be as heavy as I thought he would be. I carried him down the hall and out in the yard to the old live oak.

A gentle breeze blew, and I got a shiver down my spine from the sweat soaked shirt receiving the blessing. The easy part was getting him out to the oak; the hard part was getting him in the grave. I managed to position him as best I could.

I went back to get Melanie. I wrapped her in the other clean sheet and picked her up. Again, she felt light to me as well.

I positioned Melanie as close to the position that she was in when they said their final farewells. She was lying beside Jason with an arm over his chest and his arm around her shoulder.

The first scoop of dirt was by far the worst.

When I finished filling in the grave, I was more than tired. I was both mentally and physically exhausted. I went inside and filled another glass of water and drank it down, not caring what it tasted like at that point.

I collected my thoughts and went back into the bedroom. I picked up Melanie's Bible off the nightstand. I walked out to the old live oak, sat on the ground, and opened the book. I read from the Book of Psalms: Melanie had a lot of it highlighted in yellow.

I bowed my head.

I knew he was busier than he had ever been right about then, but I hoped he would hear the prayer of a stiff-necked old Christian.

"Lord, if you would here a sinner's plea, I ask only for your audience. Please make a special place for these two. You won't find a sweeter woman or a more loyal man in this universe. Keep them in your care if it is your will to do so. Amen"

I cried again.

I was about to get up when I heard a whimpering noise under the tool shed. The smell under there was strong as well. I got down on all fours and looked underneath.

Jason's old Blue Heeler bitch, Penny, was under there. She was bloated to the point I thought she would bust. Three puppies laid beside her in the same condition.

One puppy was still alive and trying to root an enormously swollen tit.

I took a breath and held it, crawled a little farther under the shed and picked the little fellow up. He could not have been more than four to six weeks old.

He was weak and his eyes were barely open.

I cradled him in my hands, took him in the house and put some water in my hand for him to lick up. I found some cans of potted meat in the pantry and opened one. He went at it like nobody's business.

My old heart melted, and I guess that was the first time I smiled since I had showed up at 1231 Sycamore Lane. As I walked back to my truck, I heard the generator go down. There was nothing but total quiet.

I got goose bumps all over my body.

When I got home, I told Baby Girl what I had found and what I had done. She hugged me as tight as she could and let me cry while she held me. We made love that night that was slow and gentle and then little Blue settled in between us for the night. He snuggled up beside Baby Girl; I saw her glow get a little brighter.

I fell asleep that night like every other night, the most fortunate man in the world.

Chapter 7: William Takes a Drink

"That was a bad time for all of us, but it doesn't mean you can live without morals and laws," I said, staring at William. He cowered a little at the accusation, a sign that he at least once had morals. "Where did this girl you remember so well meet her end? If she was on an errand for her grandma, it means someone she loved was still in this world and needs to know what happened to her."

He lowered his eyes and would not look at me.

"That was at least two summers back. I don't think whoever sent her is still around. Most everyone has moved into communities these days."

He was right about that. I asked Baby Girl one time if she wanted to try to get set up in a commune with other folks. We could leave a message for Darrel if he ever showed up to let him know where we were. She said that she wanted to live and die right there in our house. Good enough by me. We never brought it up again.

"It was on 485 near Barkston. You know where that big farm with the wrought iron gate that has the horse head on it is?"

I nodded but didn't stop him from talking.

"She is in the woods about fifty yards in on the south end corner of the fence line where it meets 485."

I made a mental note of it and saw the exact location in my mind. That was Doc Hanson's farm and veterinary clinic. He worked on large animals so I never had cause for his services, but I had met and liked the man.

"Have you been through Anson?" I asked.

He nodded as much as the wire would let him, "We just came through there about a week back. We stayed for a week, maybe ten days before we left. We heard gunshots on the south side of town and got the hell out of there. Anson ain't in as bad a shape as some others I've seen. The worst place I seen was in and around Tungstull. The smell was better in Anson, but there are still a lot of remains left drying up."

I saw a spark of recognition glistened in his eyes.

"There were more animals in Anson, more than anywhere else we've been. Byron killed a small doe in town, and we laughed cause of all the times we went out in the woods to hunt deer but never got one and here we go and kill one in town. He actually hit it with the rifle. We ate good for a few days on that one."

I was glad to hear that some animal population was starting to pick up, but that was not what I was after.

"Did you see any people?" I asked.

"If anybody was close around, they made no sound and didn't show themselves."

I figured as much.

"Has it been ransacked, you know, the stores, gas stations, the pharmacies?"

"Didn't look to be too bad; if they went in, they didn't tear everything up."

That was a good sign.

I stood up and Blue tightened, but he didn't stand. He looked like a coiled spring.

"William, it looks like you are about to lose your hands, so I'm going to let the ties loose. If you even think you want to make a move you will find your throat ripped out, understand?"

He nodded. There was no fight left in William anyway. Truth be known, there was never much fight in him to begin with.

"Blue, watch him," I said, just for good measure. The spring uncoiled and was inches from William's face so fast that the man flinched and let out a little squeak.

I didn't bring Old Beulah over. Blue was more than enough for this operation.

I took the wires off his neck and then removed the wires on both wrists. I sat back down in the recliner, but I did not set back. I eased Beulah up and laid her across my lap with my finger in the trigger guard.

He sat up straight on the couch, real slow because there was an ever so slight rumble in Blue's throat. I was certain he would be feeling the bee-stinging sensation as blood returned to his extremities, but he kept still and never took his eyes off of Blue.

I gave him a couple of minutes to adjust and tossed him my water bottle.

"Here, take a swig."

He caught it in his lap, not wanting to make any sudden moves.

"Thanks," he said.

He took a drink, not a big one, but one good enough to coat his throat. He looked me straight in the eyes, a look that was almost like resignation came into his eyes.

"Now you are gonna kill me, ain't you?" he asked.

I pondered in my resoluteness what my words would be, and the suspense was eating him alive.

"I am not going to kill you. I probably should for what you did, but I'm not. I told you earlier that it was up to you whether you lived or not. Two things I need to know. Where did you stash the shotgun and which direction were you heading?"

"The shotgun is out back of the house; it's a 20-gauge, but we don't have any shots left. All we have left is the three bullets in the 30/30 rifle. We were up on a hill in a farmhouse when you passed by. We had stayed there last night. That's when Byron started making his plans. Before he started tracking you, we were headed to Langston. We were told there was a colony there."

I glared at him. "I gave you my word to let you live, but this is how this is going to play out." I stood up and William squirmed a little on the couch. The rumble in old Blue's throat turned into a low growl.

William got real still again.

I walked over to the upright cabinet in the center wall and opened it. I found what I had expected to find and grabbed two bottles. One was about half full and the other had not been opened yet.

This was a waste but necessary. I took the one that had not been opened and screwed the top off. I took a sip and it tasted so good that I took a complete swallow. I instantly felt the warmed feeling in my gut.

I shook my head back and forth and let out a big sigh.

"Awwh! That is a good one. Kentucky's finest, you can't beat it," I said as I sat back down on the edge of the recliner and looked straight into Williams's eyes.

"William, you are going to drink this whole bottle of whiskey, right now, within the next ten minutes. If that is not enough for you to pass out, you are going to drink this other half bottle of Vodka. Do you understand what is going to happen here?" I asked.

"I understand."

I locked eyes with him. "Know this. When you wake up from your little nap, you will bury your friend out back. You will start down the road to the south and when you come to the Langston crossroads, you will head west in that direction, toward Langston. You will head in that direction until you reach the community. You will be at the mercy of the Good Lord, and the people of that community as to whether you get to stay."

I raised my voice a little, staring as intensely as I could into his eyes.

"There are too few people left in this world as it is. You deserve killing, but I gave you my word, and my word is all I have left."

I lowered my voice to be sure he got the point. "If I ever lay eyes on you again, I will kill you without hesitation. Do you understand?"

His eyes filled up with tears that bordered somewhere between gratitude and awe. "Yes, sir."

"Okay, then, drink up."

I handed him the bottle, and he commenced to guzzling the fifth down. He choked and coughed a little, but he was able to get it all down. After a third of the bottle was gone, I told William to bow his head and close his eyes. There was a second of panic in his eyes and afterward resignation. He did as he was told. I removed my hat and lowered my head, but I didn't take my eyes off of William.

I prayed.

"Heavenly Father, we come to you as lonely sinners in the world that you have laid out for us. We don't know your overall plan and can only accept the thanksgivings of each new day we have on this earth. Please reach out to William's heart and show him the way and the light as he ventures forth in his endeavors. Please watch over me and Blue as we go forth with ours. We ask only that your will be done... Amen."

William was crying when he said, "Amen." He took a really hard pull on the bottle, as if it were the lifeline to his future. In a way, it was. It took a few more pulls, but he got the rest of the fifth down.

After about five minutes, I noticed him swaying on the couch and within fifteen minutes, he was out cold. He never said a word. Blue watched the show, and about the time William started swaying, he lost interest. He moved off, did the hokey-pokey, and lay down where he could be comfortable but watch William.

I picked up the 30/30 rifle and removed the cartridges. William had not lied, there were three cartridges in the magazine and none in the barrel. They had not planned on me being any threat to them. I put the bullets in my pocket.

I took the oil lamp out back. The shotgun was where he said it was. I picked it up and carried it with me. I found a hiding place in the garage and stashed the shotgun. It was a pretty weapon but 20-gauge rounds were hard to find even before the Flip. I found a shovel and brought it into the house.

I stepped around Smitty and tried not to get any blood on my boots, set the shovel and the 30/30 rifle against the wall, and closed the door.

Blue was relaxed, but he kept watching William who was moaning and blowing his breath out hard.

It wouldn't be long before William would be looking for Ralph. I really didn't want to be witness to projectile vomiting.

By my old, not-so-trusty Timex, Old-T, which could be right or could be wrong, it was 10:30. I put on my backpack, picked up Beulah, grabbed the walking stick and eased toward the door. Blue made one last look at William, satisfied that he was out and not playing possum, before trotting toward the door.

We made our exit into the night. As I headed out the door, I heard William slur. "Thank you, mister. Thank you." His head lolled over, and he was out again.

I placed one 30-30 cartridge on the little table by the door on my way out. Even a sadistic being like William needs an opportunity to decide what life that cartridge might take. He is not the type of individual to cope with being alone and might want to talk to Smitty.

I hoped he'd use it wisely.

The night was cooler, and I wanted to put my jacket on, but I needed to get away from the farm-house and what happened there. Smitty was not the first man I have had to put down, but the manner in which it went down was so senseless.

Blue was on point and never got ahead of where I could see him. He could not help himself and had to leave a few drops here and there on the path out to the road. Once we got to the highway and started back towards Anson, I stopped and pulled my old Carhart jacket out of my backpack and put it on. It was headed towards midnight, and I was too keyed up for sleep anyway.

The walkin' man trudges with a sorrow in his heart
He sent old Smitty to his maker
Everyone in the world needs to do his part
Start giving and never be a taker.

This time Beulah was in my hands, and the walking stick was slung across my back. The moonlight was sufficient to walk by, but the shadows of the big trees seemed to be darker than normal. My wild imagination, with assistance from some of the books I have read over the years, took over, and I imagined a booger behind every tree.

I was glad Blue was with me, but I would never admit it in public. He didn't seem to be bothered at all. As a matter of fact, it looked like he was enjoying himself. We got into the stride and for the most part didn't have any obstacles to deal with. There were a few abandoned cars here and there, but it looked like they mainly were able to get off the road before they succumbed.

About two hours into the walk, we came upon an old Winnebago. The adrenaline roller-coaster ride had come to an end, and the carny called for everybody off.

When we got to the motorhome, Blue made a perimeter check, he sniffed and evaluated everything around the vehicle. He came back to me and seemed satisfied with the surroundings.

I leveled old Beulah and stepped up on the sidestep. I jerked the door open and stepped back, picking up Beulah to my shoulder. Nothing happened, and there was only darkness.

"Check it, Blue," I said.

Blue went inside, and I lost sight of him. He did not growl or bark, but I heard him moving through the cabin. He came back and looked satisfied that nothing living was in the motorhome.

I stepped through but left the door open to allow what little moonlight there was to come in. It smelled of a stale odor with basic old carrion but not to the point where it was uninhabitable. Some pilgrims had used it before for a short-term sanctuary. The only dried up body I saw was in the front passenger seat. Not much more than rags and skeleton at this point. From the rags, I surmised it was a woman.

I noticed the table area had been let down to make a bed.

There might have been bodies in the rear bedroom; I didn't need to find out.

I opened the curtains above the table-bed and closed the outside door to the cabin. I locked it for good measure. There was just enough light to allow me to get settled.

I hoped there were not any critters in the mattress, but I had slept in worse before. I stretched out and put my feet toward the wall. I didn't really see him, but I heard and felt Blue do the hokey-pokey. He jumped up and curled up in a ball beside me on the edge of the mattress. I reached down until I could feel him and gave him a quick scratch behind the ears, "Good night, old boy."

I heard him let out a big sigh, and then he was silent.

I can remember when the thought of sleeping near a mummified body would have terrified me.

"Good Night, Mrs. Balderdash," I said aloud, but she did not reply back.

I dozed off that night like every other night, the most fortunate man in the world.

Chapter 8: Day 2, The Walking Man Walks

When I woke up, there was a grey light drifting through the window. Old-T, my antiquated Timex, said it was 6:10.

Hell, I guess that's close enough.

Blue lifted his head and looked at me to see if I was getting up or going to hit the snooze button.

My leg and calf muscles had tightened and didn't want to get moving but the urgency of the bladder overruled the muscles.

"Let me up, Blue," I said.

He jumped down, did the hokey-pokey and sat on his haunches.

I half rolled, half pushed my way to a sitting position and tested both feet on the floor. I felt like I could stand up and did so with more grace than I thought I was capable of.

Next dilemma: should I try the toilet or hang it outside? I opted for outside and went to the door. I put my hand on the door and told Blue, "Perimeter check, Blue," and opened the door.

He went into Instant Alert Mode and leaped out the door. When he rounded the corner, I reached for old Beulah, just in case. Blue came around the other side and had relaxed the alert for the time being.

He stopped at the back tire and hiked his leg. I guess he had been holding it in too. I looked up and down the road as far as I could and aimed it off to the side and let fly, sighing the old relief sigh as I vacated. I retrieved the old plumbing and situated it back in place for the next part of the journey, taking a better look around in the camper. There might be something that could be useful, if it isn't too heavy.

I pulled open the drawers and looked in the cabinets. I did not find anything of great use except there was road map of the state. I know the state pretty well and could probably find all the major stuff about these parts. However, as time goes by, chances were, I would have to expand my scavenging area. I attempted a look in the toilet and found that it was still relatively clean and thought about leaving a surprise for the next happy camper but didn't. I did take the roll of paper though. I still listed it as "the world's most essential commodity."

I put the paper and the map in my backpack, slung Beulah over my back, picked up my walking stick, and headed out. I closed the door behind me gently and patted the door.

"Thanks for the hospitality, Mrs. Balderdash," I whispered and headed for the road.

Old Blue had gone ahead a little and was checking all the sights and smells he could take in. I put one in front of the other.

The walkin' man steps with the knowing in his heart

My Baby Girl surely is a good'un

The walkin' man yearns for the glow of love to start

And wishes for a round of shaky pudding.

By mid-morning we were getting closer to what used to be called the Good Falls Community. The houses got closer together and the abandoned cars were more frequent. It amazed me how some of the people had completely decayed almost to the skeleton stage and some looked shriveled up but still basically intact. I wasn't near enough amazed, though, to get any closer!

Someday someone would have the responsibility of removing all the poor souls that have now become part of the scenery. There will never be a way to identify them all and completely put them to rest.

I remembered that Good Falls had a country store at the crossroads and a gas station across the street, a couple of churches, and a post office. Dad and I stopped at the store and got Coca-colas when we drove to Anson. Mainly, it was so I could pee.

Dad said that he never knew anybody worse at holding their water than I was, but he always stopped and let me relieve myself.

Blue and I rounded the curve, and I could see the store building, but the cars were scattered around the area. The highway is blocked and not passable with a vehicle.

Blue stayed close by and was a little more intense around the car bottlenecks. Too many places to be ambushed by a man or a beast. As we approached the store, I saw decayed remains in almost every vehicle. I could see partial remains that were unfortunate enough to be outside when the final breaths came. It was obvious that either buzzards or creatures had dislodged most of what was left.

I slowed down before we got there and swapped out the walking stick for Beulah, and we proceeded forward at a slower pace. We looked everything over before moving to the next car. During the final hours, the pilgrims must have thought the old store to be a safe haven because there were vehicles of all shapes and sizes parked in the most unorganized manner.

The time that had passed had not been good to them either. Some were on flats now and all were coated with dust and grime and streaks from the last rain storm. In two places we had to back up and go around a vehicle jam. The space that was the original store parking lot, was completely jammed. These pilgrims could not have opened their doors in the end, even if they had the strength to.

We finally got to the store which had a double swinging glass door. Next to these were big plate glass windows that showed the inside of the store. Beyond that, it was nothing but a cinder block building. I looked at all the advertisements: the tobacco, the beer, cold drinks, energy boost drinks, a hand written flyer for Betty Stevenson who was trying to be "Penny Queen."

Once upon a time in the Kingdom of Innocence! I hope you got to wear the crown Betty.

I wiped an opening in the dust and peered into the store. I did not see any movement and it appeared that the shelves still had some items on them.

Blue was on semi-alert and didn't seem to be distressed about anything, so I lowered Beulah to the one-handed-plug-and-play mode and opened the door. Any surprises get a load of buckshot almost immediately.

The details inside the store were the same as I had seen in my travels. There were at least forty people that came into the store at the end and never came out.

The shelves were still lined with some canned goods, and I might need to return for some of them someday. I have cleaned out most of Barkston and stockpiled a pretty good inventory.

I remembered some tools and implements being here before. That's what I am interested in. I made my way to the back of the store. It was darker back here but adequate enough to move about. A big wood rat took off from behind one of the shelves, and Blue was in hot pursuit. The rat knew where he was going, and Blue didn't. Old Fur-ball disappeared into the store, and Blue looked around with a dumb look on his face when I got to him.

"Old bastard is sneaky, ain't he?"

He lost interest and took up beside me again. I could hear scratching and movement in the store and knew that Mr. Furball didn't live alone. This was a family business. I would not even attempt to try any cereal boxes or anything in here that was in paper or plastic. From the looks of things, the rodents have had a lot better time with the left overs than any people.

I found the section I was looking for and rummaged around. This was an old country community and surely there were some good ole boys that liked to play with guns. They have to have their bullets. I found the back counter, and there was a rack full of those short and fat LED flashlights.

What the hell—might as well try one? It came on, and I took it behind the counter to look for ammo. All the good stuff had been picked clean, only exotic caliber bullets remained. If it comes down to it, I might have to start disassembling these for powder. Shining the light on the shelves I hit the jackpot. There were three of the one-pound tins of gun powder.

I knew somebody around here had to be a re-loader. I also found a box of primers. Lucky Day! I took these and put them in my backpack. Too bad there wasn't any shot with it.

I shined the light around some more and went to look at the implements. There was a manual push plow that might come in handy and a couple of gardening hoes were still on the rack.

I checked out the seed rack and discovered that the rats had had enough to deal with and for the most part had left the seeds alone. I found a small tool bag and filled it up with the seed packs and gun powder.

I found some cases of mason jars and made a mental note. It would be a long way with a pushcart, but probably worth it. I grabbed another three or four of the LED flashlights. I didn't think they would last very long, but they might come in handy. I looked at the battery rack. They were all wet looking and had the crusty blue-green coating on them. I left them alone.

I figured to hide the powder and the seeds and get them on the way back. No sense adding weight to and from Anson.

Walking back to the store front, I saw some bottled water that looked to be in good condition. I opened a bottle and smelled the water. No bad odor was present. I put a couple of drops on my tongue, and it tasted okay.

I found a pack of Dixie Cup Bowls that had not been interfered with by our furry friends and poured Blue a bowl of it to drink. He lapped it up, and I gave him some more. I took another one, testing it the same way. Satisfied it was okay, I drank it down. I grabbed three more to put in my backpack but couldn't fit but two of them. I put the third one inside my shirt.

On the way out the old store building, I saw a sign on the inside of the door, handwritten with a marks-a-lot.

DANNY - IF YOU MADE IT THIS FAR - WE ARE ON OUR WAY TO DALLAS. IF YOU MAKE IT TO DALLAS - COME TO GRANDMA ELLIES HOUSE - LOVE MOM

I would love to fantasize that Danny made it to Grandma Ellie's, but my heart knows the truth.

I pray you are alive and well in Dallas, Mom.

Me and Blue headed out the door and found a Subaru with a cracked back door in the middle of the pack. I looked inside and was happy that it was unoccupied. I stashed the goody bag in the floorboard and closed the door. I checked it to make sure it would open again.

A little late for that if it doesn't, old fart, Baby Girl's voice said inside my head stated. I smiled.

We made our way through the maze away from the store and got back on the highway toward Anson. The road opened up a little as we let the community, and we got back in the rhythm.

The Walkin' man looks into the eye of the sky

Wonders what miracles to view

The various shapes when the clouds pass by

All seem to look like old Blue.

A couple of miles down the road I came up on another road sign. Somebody had shot it full of buckshot, a waste of good ammunition if you ask me. By the looks of it, we had another nine miles to go to get to Anson. We were in hill country now. The going down was okay, but the uphill was a bitch.

If you're going to suck the gravy, son, you've got to chew the bones. Jeremy Singer's voice rang in my head.

Old Blue didn't seem to have any trouble at all, and I sure wasn't going to let him know I was hurting. Like always, when I am pounding the road, I let my mind wander.

Chapter 9: Mr. Angus

It was the summer of 1977, the year after the big bi-centennial celebration. I worked all summer of my fourteenth year for Mr. Angus. He had a ranch and farm about three miles down the road from my house. I would ride my bicycle there and back every day.

He wanted me there at sunrise every morning so we could drink coffee and talk about what we were going to do that day. He was always the most gentle and serene man during the early morning coffee time.

He would turn into the Tasmanian Devil by the time the sun peeked out and the cup was empty. I thought there was a magic spell or something in his old LSU ball cap that possessed him. He would be cussing and jerking and snatching on whatever piece of equipment we were working on or whatever animal that was the focus of our attention that day, but when he pulled the ball cap off for lunch, he became the genteel southern gentleman again.

I know it was the ball cap.

If we were working in the fields, my first job every morning was to fuel up the old John Deere and grease everything. Not just a squirt or two either. "You grease the damned thing?" he would ask and would look at all the grease fittings to make sure fresh grease was hanging off of each one.

"Yes, sir. Ten shots in each one." He would nod and line me out on where he wanted me to disk or bush-hog or cultivate.

I took a great liking to Mr. Angus. He was a hard man, but he was fair.

One time I was out on the lower sixty, that's the sixty acres behind the catch pen. I had been bush-hogging the turn rows around the edge. I ran over an old stump and before I knew what was happening, a swarm of yellow jackets were all over me and the tractor.

I shifted the tractor to high gear and tried to outrun them. I was cornered and trapped within the back fence. They were stinging me all over and I ran right through the fence and out into the hay field.

The yellow jackets decided they had tortured me enough and headed back to their house that I had destroyed. I stopped the tractor and watched over my shoulder as that Ford pickup rounded the barn and was heading across the pasture.

That's it, I'm fired for sure.

When he got to where I tore through the fence, he stopped and got out of the truck. He went to cussing and carrying on and came through the fence like a prizefighter getting ready for the match.

Yep! Tasmanian Devil time.

"What in the hell do you think you're doing?" he asked while he was storming up to the tractor. "Have you lost all your..." He stopped and looked at me.

The Tasmanian Devil disappeared, and he came running up to the tractor and helped me get down off of it.

I was starting to swell all over.

My eyelids felt heavy, and I was squinting within another minute.

He helped me over to his truck, put me in the passenger side and took off with that truck like he was Mario Andretti. We skidded to a stop in front of the house.

When he ran around to the passenger side and opened the door, I almost fell out.

Mrs. Sadie came running out the house to see what was going on. She took one look at me and took off back inside. When we got inside, he started pulling my old T-shirt off, all the time pushing me towards the bathroom.

Mrs. Sadie already had the water running. Mr. Angus told me strip to my skivvies and make sure there weren't none in there. Mrs. Sadie left and came back with a box of meat tenderizer. She poured the whole box in a washcloth and wet it in the sink.

They started rubbing me down all over with the poultice until I looked like I had been in a mud bath. She told me to sit on the toilet and got me a glass of water.

"Drink this," she said while she was taking the back of her hand and laying it on my forehead.

She turned to Mr. Angus, "You know better than to have this baby out there on that tractor."

His magic ball cap was in his hands, and he was wringing it like a chicken's neck. He had the most fretful look on his face, and he was the southern gentleman again.

"Sadie, he is as much a man as any thirty-year-old I know. He did the only thing he could have; it was just too many of them. Hell, I'd have done the same thing."

After he said that about me to her, I would have walked through fire for that old man. Stings or no stings!

After I sat there a minute, I stood up and said, "I'm okay, no need to fuss over me."

She laid her hand on my chest and eased me back down on the Johnny. "You ain't going nowhere for the next little while." She turned to Mr. Angus. "You go fetch the tractor, and I will watch him for a little while. If I think it is going to set, I'll call the doc and we will bring him in." She filled the glass up again in the bathroom sink and handed it to me. "Drink some more."

I said the only thing that would come to my mind. "Yes, ma'am."

He turned to go but had the worn-out look of a man that life had been beaten down so many times that he had come to expect it. I watched him put the ball cap on through the door through my eye slits. I swear his back straightened and he started walking faster.

She sat down on the edge of the tub, turned the running water off, and looked at me. "How are you feeling?" she asked. "And be truthful."

I told her that my face felt tight, but I didn't really feel that bad. Maybe a little weak but nothing I couldn't handle.

She saw the glass was still in my hand. "Drink some more," the anxiety in her voice was subsiding. She eased forward and placed a gentle hand on each side of my face. She gently worked my neck side to side and leaned my head back where she could look at my neck. She brought my head back to where it was.

"I think you are going to be okay, but you are going to hurt later and might even get a little sick to your stomach. Do you feel up to a bath?" she asked.

She got a towel and a clean washcloth out of the cabinet and set it by the tub. I was kind of embarrassed. I was sitting on the toilet leaning forward in my fruit of the looms and trying to hide the manly parts.

She felt the temperature of the water in the tub, "It is going to be a little cool, but that's the way we want it. I am going to be right outside, soak a little, and then wash the poultice off, okay."

"Yes, ma'am," I said. Once again, I was at a loss for words.

I eased into the tub, and she not joking about the cool part. All of my manly parts shriveled up, but I sat there a good five minutes.

She called through the door. "Are you doing okay, Dinky?"

"Yes, ma'am, I am fine," I answered.

I washed the meat tenderizer off, and it turned the water into a grainy sludge. I took the washcloth and started to scrub my face. Bad idea!

I got out and dried off gently with the towel, looked my fruit of the looms over really good for any stowaways and put them back on.

I check the mirror and that's when I started to feel sick, not before. My face was so swollen, my eyes were slits, and my skin was covered with red welts. I didn't even recognize myself. I put my Levi's back on but don't know where my T-shirt ended up. The Levi's felt tight on my legs and waist.

When I opened the door, Mrs. Sadie was standing there with another glass of water and two pills in her hand.

"Here, take these and go lay down on the couch for a while."

I did as I was told but was feeling guilty because I knew Mr. Angus was out there by himself. She must have read my mind and softly smiled at me.

"Don't you fret over him; he has been working this farm by himself for years. I couldn't believe it when he actually hired you. Ever since we lost Bennie in Nam, he hasn't taken a shine to anybody. He must see something in you."

She gave me a look that let me know that I was going to be okay and smiled again. "Close your eyes for a few, and we'll see what this swelling does?" she whispered and patted me on the back of the hand. Miraculously that was the only place that didn't get stung.

I closed my eyes and thought about Sarah Spiney. She sure was pretty.

Lord, if I fall asleep, please don't let Dinky's manly parts come to life.

Before I knew what was happening, I drifted off.

When I woke up, it was after midday, and my mom was there. She came over and asked me how I felt. I had to think about it for a minute. I tried to move but it felt like somebody had taken a Louisville Slugger to me.

"I'm okay," I said, looking up at her. "Where is Mr. Angus? He is going to need help with that fence." I didn't see him, but I heard his gentle voice behind me.

"I got the fence taken care of already," he said, "Your mom is going to take you home. I'll bring your bike by the house later on this evening."

"Am I fired?" I said, starting to tear up.

"Fired?" he raised his voice a little. "Hell, no, you ain't fired. You are more than welcome here anytime you feel like working."

I didn't see it, but I know he put that ball cap back on and went outside. Then the door closed, and the Ford fired up.

The next morning the swelling had gone way down but I was sore all over. I looked outside and my bike was by the front porch. I put on my clothes and headed toward the door.

"Don't even think about it, mister," Mom said. "Not today."

That was one of the longest days of my life until Jason's mom dropped him off after lunch. We had the best time playing in the creek, turning over stones and catching crawfish, trying to catch those tricky little black water bugs, and we even skinny-dipped in the deep hole in the creek bend.

By the end of the day, I was back to being Dinky. Except the welts started to itch like crazy.

The next morning, I was up before sunrise and, with Mom and Dad's permission, was headed to the farm. Mr. Angus was glad to see me, and I thanked Mrs. Sadie for everything she had done.

We drank our coffee and talked about the work he planned for the day. It was a beautiful morning, and we finished our coffee on the porch. He stood up and reached out his hand to me for my cup so he could take them back into the house.

When he took it, he looked straight at me and almost smiled. He stepped back through the screen door and put that damned ball cap on.

Here we go again!

I fueled up the John Deere and hooked up the hay cutter, and he showed me how to cut the hay for making wind rows. Nothing eventful happened that day, and I eventually realized that Mr. Angus was not mad at me for tearing down the fence.

By the time mid-August rolled around, we had put up the hay, got the soybeans laid by, mended what I deemed a hundred miles of fence, installed new gates, cut and stacked six cords of firewood, and drank a whole lot of coffee.

It was on a Friday, and we were having our morning coffee.

He never looked at me; he gazed out over his kingdom when he said, "Dinky, I want this to be your last day. Not because I want you to leave, but because you have busted your ass this summer."

I kept silent and took a sip of coffee; the ball cap was loosely placed on his head.

"You still have a week to ten days before school starts back, and I want you to enjoy yourself."

I was at a loss for words because I had come so accustomed to being here. Not thinking of anything else. "Okay, sir, thank you. I really enjoyed working here this summer."

He still never looked up. "No, son, the pleasure was mine."

I reached out and took his empty cup to take in the house. When I stepped back through, he was halfway to the barn, and the ball cap was reset to business.

That evening I went inside to get my last paycheck. Once that was dispensed with, he stood up.

"Come with me," he said, and didn't reach for the ball cap.

 Mrs. Sadie dried her hands off with a dish rag and followed out behind us. We went to a side of the barn that we hardly ever went in while I was working here.

He opened both doors real wide and inside was a coal black, 1967 Ford step-side pickup. It was obvious that he had pulled the cover off and washed it.

"Dinky, this was Bennie's truck. He won't need it anymore." His voice wasn't just right.

Mrs. Sadie walked up beside him and took his hand in hers.

He collected himself and tried to be stern, "I cleared it with your folks. I won't give it to you because you would not appreciate it if I did. I will sell it to you for fifty dollars if you want it."

I was so excited I almost peed my pants, but I tried to keep all the excitement out of my voice.

 "Mr. Angus, I would love to have it, but are you sure that you want to part with it? I would not ever want to take something that is as special to you as I know this is." I said.

He walked over and put his old rough hand on my shoulder.

"Son, you don't know how much you have helped me this summer, not only with the farm but with my own demons. I would be proud to have you make this old truck your own," he said, with a slight waver in his voice.

My excitement was showing through. I looked him straight in the eyes and shook his hand.

"Okay, sir. It's a deal!" I said and handed him the fifty-dollar check he had just written me.

He pulled the title out of his back pocket. Mrs. Sadie was smiling from ear to ear. A single tear eased down her face.

And that was how I acquired Smokey, although mom and dad didn't let me drive him until I got my driver's license at fifteen and I could keep liability insurance on it with my own funding. Even though I couldn't drive him, I kept him washed and waxed and spent a lot of time in him pretending to drive and listening to the radio.

During the Thanksgiving break, I rode my bicycle up to Mr. Angus's farm and knocked on the door. There was no one at home. I went to ask him if I could work again that next summer, and honestly, I plain flat missed the old man.

I asked Mama if she had heard anything about them and she told me he had the cancer. It started in his prostate and had spread throughout his body really fast. He was in a nursing home and was being kept comfortable until he passed.

"What is a prostate?" I asked Jason.

"I ain't sure, but when Uncle Limen had trouble with his, they had to go through his butt to get to it," Jason told me.

"That can't be good. What happened to your Uncle Limen?" I asked.

"He survived but he doesn't crap anymore. His poop drains in a bag he wears on his side," he said sadly. "He doesn't do anything anymore but sit in the house and drink his beer. It's a shame too; he used to be a hell-u-va man."

"Mama said they have him in a nursing home and kept comfortable," I said almost in tears. "I don't think Mr. Angus is going to make it."

Jason looked at me with sympathetic eyes. "We will pray for him, Dinky, and if the Good Lord wills it, Mr. Angus might make it." Jason reached to hug me.

Mama stopped by to see Mr. Angus and Mrs. Sadie, knowing that I would want to visit, asked him about it. He told Mama that he wanted me to remember things the way it was during our summer. He didn't want to scare me with the way he looked now.

Mama respected that and, honoring his wishes, never said anything to me until I discovered it myself. He passed right before Christmas, and Mom took me to the funeral. They had a closed casket with an older picture of him and Bennie together on the top of it.

They were smiling and looked happy.

It was so many people at the funeral home that it was hard to find a place to sit. I stood in the back and let Mrs. Bailey sit with Mama. Mr. Angus had been a WWII veteran and a respected member of the community. It showed in the faces of the funeral congregation.

When I hugged Mrs. Sadie, I started bawling like a two-year-old and didn't care who seen it. I couldn't help myself. She hugged me tight and whispered in my ear.

"He loved you too, Dinky."

Mrs. Sadie sold the farm to some big farming conglomerate that put up no trespass signs and such. I never went back to it after that. I heard later that she moved to Anson to be with her sister, Mrs. Pearl.

Sometimes when I was all alone in Smokey, I would recall him taking my coffee cup like we were two grown men instead of one and that I almost made him smile.

It gave me a peaceful feeling inside when I did.

Chapter 10: The Thing called Hope

As I put the cold compresses on the red rashes of my legs, I could feel the fever in the angry splotches. My energy level was depleted and it felt like my entire body was on fire. I lay back on the sofa, closed my eyes and prayed for the Tylenol to kick in.

I thought about when Darrel was about eight years old; when a baseball glove and his Daddy to throw a ball to him was all he wanted. He was good too, probably could have made the majors.

I don't discuss Darrel and the babies with Dinky anymore. We have gone through ever scenario imaginable and it only seems to make us melancholy. It was never spoken aloud, but we know Darrel won't be coming home. My one and only hope was that, if he went down with the Pentacle virus, my grandbabies went with him. Any other scenario was unthinkable.

Brenda, his wife, never made it through the early round; the NV-17 virus. 2015, the year of the NV-17 virus, weakened society and bankrupted the global economy. It took lots of casualties, most were due to the virus but some were due to the stupidity of humanity. Brenda was a registered nurse working in the midst of the outbreak. She contracted the virus and isolated herself from Darrel and babies. I respected her for that.

Dinky and I drove over to Atlanta for the funeral.

That was the last time I saw Little Darrel and Sweet Baby Jane. Her name's actually Janet, but we called her Jane. Sweet Baby was a name that Dinky gave her; said she carried a sweet glow about her, like her Maw-Maw.

Sweet Baby Jane held onto me the whole time the funeral affair was taking place. A four-year-old doesn't have the adult knowledge of those happenings, but she had the feeling of it and I did my best to comfort her.

Little Darrel was seven; he knew what the score was and had it all bottled up inside. He reminded me so much of his Daddy; Darrel was always like that.

Darrel was about in the same predicament. They both seemed to be shell shocked during most of the funeral.

The social services were still active then, but the funeral home was so busy that we only got one hour of visitation, one hour for the funeral, and then off to the cemetery. They were running two to five funerals a day through that facility.

I am glad that we did get to bury her. Brenda loved my Darrel; she was a good mom and a good daughter-in-law to me.

I've watched Dinky stop and look at the family picture that Darrel sent us for Christmas 2014, before the NV-17 started. They are all smiling and looked like the perfect American Family. In a way, I guess they were. They were "living the dream" as they used to say. He never mentioned them nor revealed his thoughts about them. He didn't have to, his body language said it all.

I think the not knowing is worse than the knowing sometimes. Not knowing always left room for hope. Hope could be a powerful ally or your worst nightmare, depending on the situation. Hope never dealt me a winning hand that I can remember.

We returned from Atlanta about the time that the newscasters stated the World Health Organization had everything under control. The NV-17 virus was not going to escalate any further. The survival rate was starting improve drastically and a vaccine was ready to go to animal trials. At that time, it had killed twenty-one million people in eighty-six countries.

The news didn't tell us about the NV-17 virus' capability of rapid mutation and that it built resistance to just about every antibiotic known to the medical world. They may or may not have known at the time, but I would bet that they did.

They had never understood why some of us were not even threatened by it, even when directly exposed to it. Had they not tampered around with the NV-17 Virus; it might have just played itself out without the total devastation that occurred. In the first two to three weeks of the mutated NV-17 virus, later dubbed the Pentacle Virus, the anchors were still on CNN and Fox News. There were experts on the tube stating everything from DNA profiles, to antibodies, and of course the hereditary theory.

How can you be automatically immune to a virus that your mama and grandma had never been exposed to?

Dinky and I kept waiting for the bug to hit us, but it never did. I always wondered what the odds of two married people being immune and surely, if there was anything to the hereditary theory, maybe Darrel was still alive in Atlanta.

There is that damned old Hope again.

One of my favorite fantasies was to look down the old driveway and see both of my Darrell's. Little Darrell and Sweet Baby Jane would be waving at me. I can only Hope. The old hymn sounded off in my head.

What a day of rejoicing that would be.

I don't think anyone knows what happened to the Pentacle Virus in the past couple of years. After the pandemic climaxed, there were so few people left. It devastated the animal population as well. It was especially hard on the swine and the equine. Dinky told me that he has not seen a live pig or a horse since Pentacle. They may be completely extinct for all I know.

I removed the compress and got off the sofa. I forced back the fatigue and opened the front door to gaze down the driveway.

All I have left is hope.

Chapter 11: Member of the Country Club

It was getting on late evening and the shadows started to lengthen. We were definitely getting into a more populated, well used to be more populated, area. My old Timex said it was 4:30.

"We should find a place to hold up tonight and get a fresh start to Anson in the morning. Whatchu think Blue?" The sign said, "East Anson Country Club," with an arrow pointing to the left. "Want to go hang out with the High Rollers?"

He looked at me with the, fell-off-the-turnip-truck look, and kept walking. When I got to the road entrance, I hooked a left and Blue had to readjust stride but followed in behind.

It looked like the East Anson Country Club was actually a high dollar subdivision, with big houses all around what used to be the golf course. I figured the first couple of houses would have been used up by pilgrims and by-passed them. I thought about going on to the Club House but decided against it.

A cart path crossed the road. Two houses were visible across the fairway. Well, it looked more like a hay field than a fairway. I took off across the path and doubted anyone had been this far back. I didn't want any more nights like the one me and Blue had last night.

As I came over the hill near the sign for the twelfth tee, sound erupted. They were human sounds. There were people up ahead. I got Old Beulah into the plug-and-play position and stored the walking stick between my back and the backpack.

"Blue, stay close, boy," I whispered.

He came up to my right leg and kept rhythm with my stride. He was on semi pink feline alert.

As I got close, I could see that there were three individuals. There was a man and woman around their thirties and a little girl of about six. They were playing tag and laughing. I stood there a few minutes watching, and it filled my heart with joy to see the little girl playing.

The man noticed me standing there and all activities stopped. The woman and girl ran into the house, and the man reached for a shotgun leaning against the porch rail. He didn't level it at me, but no doubt, knew how to use it.

I kept Beulah pointed at the ground and told Blue. "Sit!" He did and without the hokey-pokey I might add, but he was in full alert just the same. The man stood his ground and eyed us up and down, I guess trying to figure out if we were friendly or not.

I didn't know how I knew the things that I knew, but I was convinced this man did not want any trouble. I was also convinced he would not take any shit either.

I put the barrel of Beulah onto the top of my boot and laid my hand across the back of the stock showing him both of my hands. He didn't flinch. I had enough of the stare down so I said.

"Sir, I am sorry that I disturbed you. I was just watching the baby girl enjoy herself. That is a rare and beautiful sight to see these days. I don't want any trouble, and if you want your privacy, I respect that and will be on my way."

He thought a minute but did not take his eyes off of Beulah or Blue. "Who are you and where are you from?"

"I'm Richard Engelmann," I immediately replied, "but everyone calls me Dinky. This here is Blue, and we live near Barkston. We are on our way into Anson tomorrow to look for supplies."

I was on a roll, so I threw it out there. "I mean you and yours no harm and only hope you have many blessings. I would only ask to have some conversation with you if it suits you. I will not meet nor bother your family unless you deem it safe."

He loosened up a bit.

"I will leave all my belongings at the edge of this path," I continued, "where you can see them if you let me approach."

He thought a minute but did not waiver the semi ready state of the shotgun.

This ain't his first rodeo!

"Approach as you stated."

I started really slow and eased Beulah off my foot and turned the barrel sideways in the opposite direction of him. I took off the old backpack and set it down on top of Beulah. I turned and raised both hands to show him they were empty and said, "Blue, Stay!"

He didn't like it, but he stayed with Beulah as I walked toward the man.

As I approached the man, he kept his stance and readiness. The shotgun was never pointed at me, but it always in a position to do business if it needed to. When I was five feet from him, I stopped and stood there with my hands up. He must have determined that I was not a threat, and lowered the shotgun.

"Name's Benjamin, Benjamin Holmes from Meridian, but I am originally from Belleview," he said, swapped the shotgun to his left hand and held out his right. "Dixie, was it?"

I took his hand in mine and thought how this simple ritual had become almost extinct. I remembered how much respect and good faith a simple jester like a handshake could bestow. Ten thousand words could not describe what was learned about a man from a simple thing like a handshake. I was in the presence of a decent but resilient man.

"No, sir," I said. "Close though. It's Dinky."

He motioned for me to sit down on the porch with him. Whoever the original owners were had four high back rockers with cow hide bottoms in them. I couldn't help but think that they must have been beautiful when they were new. He waited until I sat down and then he sat, leaning the shotgun on the porch rail but still within easy reach.

He looked over at me and smiled, "I apologize about the greeting, but I cannot be too careful these days."

I returned the smile, "Had it been me and mine, I would have played it the same way."

We nodded and understood that we were now well met.

"Is that a Blue Heeler? I haven't seen a domesticated dog since the Pentacle."

"Yes, sir, he is a Heeler, and his name is Blue."

"You can call him in if you want to. I would love to meet him, if he's friendly,"

I pursed my lips and let out a slight whistle. Blue was one the porch in about two seconds.

"Sit, Blue," I told him and he sat down. "Blue, meet Mr. Benjamin," I said.

"Call me, Benjie," he said and eased the back of his hand toward Blue so he could take a sniff.

Blue eased over and sniffed his hand, and then to my surprise, he stuck his head under his hand wanting to get a little scratch. Benjie had no trouble accommodating Blue on this and was enjoying it as much as Blue was.

When Blue had enough, he eased over toward the edge of the porch, did the hokey-pokey, and lay down.

"Meridian! That must be a hundred miles or more. How long have you all been on the road?" I asked Benjie.

"A month or better, it has been two full moons," he sighed.

I nodded, "Have you been into Anson?"

"No, sir, I didn't come through it, came around it on the 620 Loop. I didn't like cities before the Pentacle; damn sure don't like them now."

"I never liked them much either, but I need to check out some of the big pharmacies," I said. "I need some medications for my wife that I cannot get anymore within my normal scavenging range."

I spilled it all out.

"Sarah has a type of Lupus. It is not really life threatening as long as she stays on the Presyscodine. We made it through last winter, but she has been without any for a couple of weeks now. I need to stock up with all I can get my hands on. It has a good shelf life if I can find it."

"Your best chance would be the hospital pharmacy at the Plaisance Memorial Hospital. Do you know if it has a name for a generic pill?" he asked.

"Don't know of a generic pill. Why should I target the hospital pharmacy?"

"It is a medical university as well as a hospital. If they have the one you need, they would probably have a decent supply," he said.

This man is genuinely intelligent!

"Why are ya'll on the move?" I asked. He settled in the rocker and opened up on the story. I settled into my rocker and listened.

Chapter 12: Benjie's Trip Home

I was a certified public accountant in the past life. I had my wife Jennifer and two daughters, Jessica and Brittany. We all survived the NV-17 virus and thought the worst was over.

One of my firm's biggest clients was Quaker's Haven, a farming and food producing conglomerate whose home office was in Bingham, thirty miles away. I normally dealt with only the Belleview branch, but they were scheduled for a week-long audit and wanted everyone there. After a fiscal year of NV-17 which devastated the global economy and seriously impacted my firm, I was obligated to go. The word Pentacle had been around a couple of weeks, and the already paranoid people were starting to panic, but Quaker's Haven was more worried about the bottom line.

They had put me up in a Holiday Inn within walking distance of their main office. We were in the second day of the audit when the airborne infectious phase of Pentacle hit Bingham full force. The sickness escalated, and the panic stricken that wasn't yet infected, was leaving in droves. I am not sure where any of them thought they were going; being outside only exposed them sooner.

I had never seen anything like that before or since. I still have nightmares of the sick, the dying, and the panicking. By the next day, the bottom line didn't matter anymore. The big wigs that were pushing the audit and the auditors themselves were either dead or dying somewhere. All the transportation had shut down, and I realized the predicament I was in. I could not get out of Bingham by car. Car jams were in every exit street going out of the city. I struck out on foot

In a car where the folks in it had already passed on, I found a pistol, checked it to have a full clip and started walking out of there. The people that was still alive were in a state of shock, watching their loved ones die, most on the brink of death themselves. Some were crying, some were praying, some were cussing, but most all of them were definitely dying.

I finally got out of the city and the highway seemed to be a little better, but still congested. I came upon a parked motorcycle with the kickstand down. A man in a leather outfit about ten yards away was already gone.

I took the bike and headed towards Belleview with only one thought on my mind. I knew there was no way that I didn't contract the virus. The only thing I wanted was to get home long enough to say good-bye and die with my girls. I had called Jennifer on the cell phone, and she said they were all right for the moment. No sign of the Pentacle yet. I got on that bike and rode for hell!

By the time I got into Belleview, the cars were so bad I couldn't navigate the bike anymore.

The last mile and a half, I ran.

When I got to the house, Jenny had broken out with the hives and Jessica was sniffling and coughing. I kept praying and hoping all the way home that we would be spared and everything would be okay. They said on the news that recovery was improving and some people were surviving it. What a bunch of crap that was!"

From what I had seen in Bingham and on the road, the news networks were full of shit. I didn't even think of myself and started trying to nurse them. At this point Brittany was fine and wanted to play. I started trying to break the fever in Jennifer and Jessica. I tried cool cloths, fever suppositories, and finally cool baths in the tub.

Jessica broke out with the hives and Jennifer was covered in boils. I could not get the fever down no matter how hard I tried. I pumped them with medications and found some baby antibiotics that Brittany had taken. Nothing worked. We stayed up all night, except for Brittany.

I watched them drift away, and I couldn't do anything about it. I got down on my knees and prayed. I beat the walls and cussed like a sailor. I cried till I couldn't cry anymore and then knew I had to say my good-byes.

By dawn they were to weak to stand. I took Jessica into the bedroom with Jenny and lay on the bed with both of them. It felt like I was wrapped between two electric blankets on the highest setting. I talked to them and told them I loved them.

Brittany announced to the world that she was awake. It broke my heart, but I let her cry that morning because I wasn't leaving Jen and Jess.

Jennifer took in a big breath and looked up at me. She mouthed, 'I love you,' and drifted into either sleep or a coma. Jessica had passed the point of consciousness. Their breath was very labored and raspy.

Brittany was persistent and wasn't giving up. I eased out from under them and went to check on Brittany. She was fine and showed no symptoms. She was just pissed. I changed her diaper and warmed up a bottle for her. I held her for a few minutes, and she decided she could manage on her own.

I went back to the bedroom, and found only silence. I fell to my knees in the doorway of the bedroom and cried. I was lost in my sorrow until I felt a little hand pulling on my shirt.

I wondered why I wasn't sick yet and why Brittany seemed fine. I got up off the floor and picked my little angel up. She smiled at me, and I knew I had to save her if it was my final act in this world.

At that moment I realized I had the hard part. I was going to survive.

I buried them both in the backyard, and by the time I got all that done, I was exhausted. I took a hot shower and fixed a sandwich that I only nibbled on. I fixed Brittany a bottle and changed her again.

It was definitely nap time for her, and we fell asleep on the couch.

At nine o'clock that night five men showed up in full body suits and SCBA's and opened the door. I got up and Brittany went to crying. They told us to get a small pack of belongings together and get in the bus. I was still shell shocked from the three previous days and did like I was told.

Chapter 13: The Three Bee's

We had been there about twenty minutes or so while he told his story. I didn't interrupt and hung on to every word. I had heard variations of this same story, just different names and different places. Old-T and the evening sun confirmed dusk was approaching.

As Benjie collected his thoughts, and I heard the door crack open. Blue was lying in the sun with his eyes closed facing the steps; he raised his ears up but never moved or opened his eyes. Benjie looked toward the door and motioned for them to come out.

A young girl busted through the door. Old Blue jumped up and flew off the porch down to the ground. When he figured he was far enough away, he stopped and turned around.

He seen there wasn't any danger, did the hokey-pokey, and started easing back toward the steps. Benjie and I were laughing as hard as we could because Blue had this dumb look on his face.

The lady giggled as she walked up behind Benjie and around to the other side of him. The girl came straight up me.

"Who are you?" she asked.

I was still giggling a little myself, some was from old Blue and most of it was from looking at the innocence of youth.

"I am Richard, but you can call me Dinky," I said, and I stuck out my hand for a handshake.

She grabbed my hand and turned it sideways and gave me a high five with her version of, fell-off-the-turnip-truck, face.

"Mind your manners, young lady," Benjie said.

She sullied up a second and then a bright smile lit up her whole face. She was the kind that you fell in love with the first second you met her. I bet if it was a shade darker outside, I could see the glow.

"Yes, sir," she said and followed it up with, "I'm Brittany, glad to meet you."

I couldn't help it. I started laughing again, and this time she joined in. Blue came easing up with his what-in-the-world-is-this look, and his ears pinned back to his head.

"C'mere Blue and meet Brittany," I said.

"Brittany, this is Blue," I told the little girl.

With a bit of warning in my voice, I said, "Blue, meet Brittany."

Blue didn't have a tail, but his bob was down and his ears were pinned. He eased up to Brittany, not knowing what she would do. He had never been around many children; most of them around this age were scared of everything, including him.

Brittany wasn't scared of anything. She bent over a little and stroked his head and started smiling at him. Yep, he instantly fell in love with her too. Within the span of a minute, they were laughing and playing, and he was licking her face. She loved every second of it. She bailed off the porch with Blue right behind her.

"Stay where I can see you, Brit," Benjie yelled.

He turned to me and said. "Dinky, this is Belinda."

I stood up, took my hat off, and stuck my hand out again, and she gave me a shake.

"Pleased to meet you, Dinky," she said and straightened her back. She put her hands on her hips, "Can I get you gentlemen something to drink? I have water and I have some tea made."

"Miss Belinda, I would love some tea if it's not too much trouble." I said.

"One sweet tea-coming up." She looked at Benjie.

"Yes, ma'am, me too." She went off to get the tea, and I sat back down.

I didn't take but a minute, and the story started back up. The mood had faded and he didn't get as emotional as he did before.

Chapter 14: The Belleview Crew

They took me and Brit out to East Bell High School where they were setting up a crisis center. Brittany went with the other children, but you could tell some of them were already showing symptoms. We wore face mask and latex gloves but I knew that if we didn't get it from Jen and Jess that we probably weren't going to get it at all.

I pitched in to help with the setup. We did the best we could for that night. Me and Brit got us a place in the corner and bedded down. During the night I heard the moaning, the retching, and the raspy breathing that I hoped to never hear again. When we got up the next morning around 7:00, there were dead and dying all around us. There was me, Brit and about four others that were not showing symptoms.

Belinda was one of them.

We did what we could, just like I had with Jen and Jess, but it ended with the same result. Belinda had taken Brittany away so she didn't have to watch the end for the one's remaining.

The road noise had all but stopped and things got quiet. The only audible sound was the remaining folks hanging onto dear life and losing the battle with every passing second. We fought with them all that day; the last of them succumbed in the late evening hours.

Now the only sound was the humming of the fluorescent lights in the high school gym. It never occurred to me that they made that much noise until that night.

By that time, I had gotten to know Belinda, Hal, Johnny, Ezra, and Mrs. Dorothy. The seven of us found a classroom and set up for the night. Mrs. Dorothy kept Brittany occupied, cleaned, and happy while I did a survey around the outside. I needed to find formula for Brit and would run out of diapers pretty soon.

After four days living in the classroom, we realized that we had to leave. The smell in Belleview started to become overwhelming. Most of the population had succumbed, with the exception of the few individuals that seemed okay, the rest were dead. The older corpses started to bloat; flies and insects invaded the gym

Mrs. Dorothy kept Brittany for me. The four of us, me, Hal, Ezra, and Belinda went on a supply run to stock up for the journey

We walked into the Walmart and found an enormous amount of people decided to make this their final resting place. The visuals were becoming less shocking but still grabbed you by the heart. A young woman sat with her back to the paper towels, holding a baby that couldn't have been more than two months old. It was the sight of a loving embrace; one that still haunts my dreams at night.

I got a shotgun, a pistol, ammunition, and all the essentials that I could think of. We got backpacks and new shoes for walking. Hindsight being 20/20, what we thought was essential wasn't even close. We walked back to the high school and noticed all the dead animals. I recall thinking; it must be the end. We won't even have fresh meat anymore.

By the time we struck out the next day, the smell was getting really intense and the flies had started buzzing everywhere. It seemed like there were already millions of them.

Everything was quiet, too quiet.

We traveled south, hoping the southern wind would blow the smell away from us, but we never got out of it. Sometimes it was weaker, but it was always there. We passed the cars on the side of the road and could see the carnage inside of them. Pentacle had done its damage.

We came upon a group traveling north and told them what was in store in Belleview. They told us the same scenario occurred in the two communities to the south, Donnerville and Briston. We decided to get off the routes and go deep in the woods to get away from it all.

I talked it over with the crew, and they were in agreement. We needed to stop somewhere, and soon. Mrs. Dorothy was tough as shoe leather, but she was not a spring chicken anymore. We went right on the next farm road, and I hoped that it was not a dead end. Three miles into the road we found a farm and decided to stop for a rest. The smell was not as bad there; the house was on the back side of a hill. We stopped, and I knocked on the door.

No answer. I check the door, and it was unlocked.

When I went inside, I found the old farmer and his dog in the den. The dog had a bullet hole in his head and was already a little swollen. The farmer was sitting in a recliner, and the back of his head was gone. His brains and blood were on the wall behind him, and from the looks of it, he probably done himself within the last day.

In the bedroom I found his wife, she had been dead a day or two; she had definitely passed from the Pentacle. It was evident that the old farmer had done everything he could to help her but couldn't stop what happened.

I went outside and told the crew to stay out there a while and asked Ezra to come help me. Ezra kept a level head and didn't look shell shocked all the time. We moved the bodies out the back, rolled them up in quilts, and lay them out together. I found another quilt in the closet and hung it over the wall behind the recliner. We took the recliner and the dog outside and covered up where the animal had died with a floor rug.

I told the others to come in. The second bedroom was empty, so Mrs. Dorothy took Brittany in there, and they took a nap together. I looked around the house, found food in the fridge and pantry, and started making us a meal. The electricity was still on at this stage.

We tried the television and the radio but found nothing except the alert broadcast on the radio telling us to write identification markings on your body and stay in your home. Someone will be coming to assist you.

I wonder how many people still believed someone was coming when they took their last breath.

We had a good meal and the crew rested in the farmhouse, currently thinking that things could be worse. I was thinking we have to go further in until the dead rotted down to a tolerable level. Today we rest, tomorrow will be worse. I headed out back to find a shovel to bury the farmer and his wife; Ezra followed shortly behind me.

I woke up in the early morning and started fixing coffee and eggs. Mrs. Dorothy came in and ran me out of the kitchen with a wave of her hand stating that was her domain. We headed out around 9:00 and started further into the rural road.

You could tell it was a farm road because the houses were acres apart instead of feet. There were a lot of cattle over on their sides, starting to bloat. We passed a deer in the road ditch, and I saw more than one dead squirrel.

Around noon we approached a farm and I asked the crew to stay by the road. I had noticed that there were no stranded vehicles along the way; the miles we had walked since exiting the state highway were open road. Ezra and I walked up to the house and found a decent looking Chevy crew cab. I noticed the electricity was operating, as well. I didn't even knock this time. I just opened the door.

I found a repeat of yesterday, but this time it wasn't by the farmers own hand. It was all Pentacle. I looked around for the keys to the Chevy and was about to give up. Ezra suggested that I check his pockets. It was not a friendly sensation digging in a dead man's pocket, but I found the keys.

I looked in the truck to see how it looked, tried the key, and started it. It showed to have three quarters of a tank of gas. It should get us away from here. I turned it off and went to snooping around the place. I looked in the freezer and found it well stocked. There were two igloo coolers in the shed. One of them was a big one. We raided the kitchen and the freezer, gathered pots and pans, a coffee pot, all the canned goods, and containers of water.

I found a 30-06 rifle and two boxes of ammunition. It had a scope mounted on it, and I hoped he kept it true. I would have bet that he did. We could use it to hunt for food and might need it for protection.

I didn't know exactly where we were but my Dad and I had hunted in this area years ago. I recalled their being some enormous forests further in. This road would eventually end up near Kilpatrick where the National Forest is, just south of Pinto.

We cleaned out the seats, made room for everyone, and headed down the driveway to the road. The crew was all smiles when I pulled up in that truck. We had to get deeper in the woods, away from the populated areas.

Driving down the road, it looked like just another day in rural America, except there was no activity going on anywhere. I knew that, as-the-crow-flies, we could not have been more than twenty miles from Belle View, but we were heading away from it. Soon, we were in deep forest woods with nothing but trees on each side and a few dead animals here and there.

We rounded a curve, and I had to slam on brakes. There was a big Angus Bull lying in middle of the road, and it was starting to bloat. There were two other dead cows I noticed outside the fence, but not in the road. I put the truck in four-wheel drive and eased around the bull

The animals were on the edge of the forest and close to a big pasture. Farther down, I understood why the cattle were out. The gate was open, someone either opened it on purpose or didn't have the strength to get out and close it.

It was not a fast journey; I slowed down for all the curves after the bull scare, but we made about twenty miles. I needed to find something permanent and felt we were close to where we needed to be. We should be centralized here and a pretty good distance away from the larger towns in all directions.

We passed a fair-sized bridge over a running creek in a valley. It went up a small hill that curved toward the left. A pasture fence line started with the curvature, and I saw a nice-looking house three hundred yards away in the right-hand corner.

There were dead cows in the pasture, but there was a cow and large calf still grazing.

I turned the truck into the driveway

There was a grey Ford Truck in the carport. It appeared that a vehicle was missing. I hoped that the previous owners had tried to make it out and were not at home. Thankfully, I was right about that one.

The door was locked when I tried it. I went around to the back door; it was locked as well. I took a piece of stone from the stone path and broke the windowpane next to the door lock and went inside. I tried the light switch; nothing. I walked through the house and opened the front door.

It turned out to be an excellent abode to wait things out. The crew got started with the process of moving in.

Over the next days, I found a tractor in good condition and dragged the dead cows away. Hal was good with tinkering; he got the generator running for us. We ran it six hours a day to keep the freezer and fridge cold and to pump water for us to use.

Mrs. Dorothy made the meals, and we made an amicable existence for about a month, even with the continuous odor and the heat. As bad as it was, we were thankful we were not any closer to the source.

It was obvious that we needed a supply run. It was to the point that Mrs. Dorothy and Belinda washed out dish rags and used them for Brittany's diapers. That project had improved; they were making progress with the potty training.

Our clothes were becoming ragged, and none of us were prepared for any type of winter weather. I called a meeting, and the decision was made. We made a list of the things needed and shut it down for the night.

Me, Ezra and Johnny headed out the next morning in the Chevy and made good time. We followed the farm road north, and ten miles into the trip, we turned left toward Pinto. At eight miles in the parked vehicles started getting thicker.

The smell was almost unbearable, and the insects seemed to be everywhere. Flies, mosquitoes, gnats, beetles, and roaches were all out in force.

We had reached the suburbs of Pinto, soon we would arrive in the commercial area. We never made it that far and found the vehicles jammed to a point where we couldn't go around them.

We stopped the Chevy and got out. Ezra was okay; Johnny retched a couple of times before we moved on. The graphic scenery inside the vehicles was right out of a horror movie, and we tried not to look at them. The smell was bad enough.

About a half mile in, after weaving through the maze of vehicles, we came to a shopping center. I got up in the back of a truck and stood up on the roof of the cab. I could see a Walmart sign several blocks down the street on the right. Navigation was impossible; the street, road ditch, driveways, and most parking lots was filled with vehicles of all shapes and sizes.

About one hundred yards down the road to the left, I saw a Caterpillar sign. I got a crazy idea cooking around in my head and headed down the road.

There were no bodies in the Caterpillar building. They had had sense enough to close up shop when the panic started.

I hoped the keys would be in one of the main offices. I found the keys, grabbed them all and headed out to the lot. I found the biggest dozier I saw and tried keys until I found the right one. The batteries were good, and the fuel level said one quarter of a tank. I fired it up with Johnny looking at me with a dumb look, and Ezra nodding and smiling.

I worked the blade up and down and figured out the gear pattern and started toward the street. It looked like Johnny had caught up with the plan. I started pushing the cars off the middle of the highway.

Now that was something you didn't get to do every day."

"The bad part was when the doors would open or the corpses inside would get jiggled around. Some that were swollen busted and some seemed to have body parts detach from each other. The smell was even worse, and the flies were everywhere.

I kept pushing. I opened the roadway back to where the Chevy was. Ezra backed it down the highway to an open spot. I kept pushing.

I found a little opening, turned the dozier around the other direction, backed up onto a car. The weight of the dozier crushed the car and the corpse of a young woman leaned out the new opening.

Johnny completely lost his cookies.

I motioned Ezra to follow me, and we headed down the main drag. I got back to the Caterpillar place and started pushing the jam toward the Walmart. I cleared the path all the way to the Walmart entrance, turned the dozier into the parking lot, and cleared the road to the front entrance.

We went shopping.

We loaded the Chevy down with everything on the list; the truck bed was full. I walked in and out of the vehicles and looked for another one that was without a corpse and with some keys.

At the end of the parking lot I found what I was looking for, a Ford half-ton with the keys in the ignition. I opened the door and got in. I tried the key, and she fired up.

I giggled to myself because I was going to get to play on the dozier some more, but damned old Ezra beat me to the punch.

The big dozier was pushing a path to me. I didn't fuss; he needed to have some fun too. I pulled the Ford up to the door, and we went shopping again.

With both vehicles loaded down to the top of the bed, we headed back toward the farm. We had one more stop to make, and I hoped it would be successful.

Johnny was in the Ford and Ezra was with me in the Chevy when we got to the Farmers Coop. According to Ezra, the Coop owned fuel trucks. They would haul fuel to the fields and farms to fuel tractors and farmer fueling stations. It was on the outskirts of town; Ezra had brought it to my attention on the way in.

There were a few cars scattered here and there but not to where you couldn't navigate, and we pulled both trucks up to the Coop. We had to break the lock on the door; no one had held up or died in here. It looked just the way it did on the last day of business.

In the warehouse out back; it was very obvious that new residents had already taken up the space. Most of the feed sacks had been chewed into; the feed and seed scattered all over the floor. We looked out the back door and found the fuel truck.

It didn't look like much; I had my doubts on its ability to move, much less haul anything. The key was not in it, so we went back to the office and searched for it. It was in the office behind the door on a key rack.

Ezra smiled his big grin as he grabbed the key and headed out back. In a few minutes, he had it fired up and running. There was a half a load of gasoline in one tank and about three quarters load of diesel in the other. He laughed about always wanting to be a truck driving man and crawled in behind the wheel.

We headed for the farm.

We made it back with our load, and it was like Christmas for everyone. We stocked and inventoried best we could and settled in for the long haul of fall and winter.

I started counting the full moons because we didn't know what day or month it was.

I picked a day four moons later that we called Christmas Day, and a week after that, we celebrated New Years.

The smell was better then, but the reminder lingered in the air. We survived the first winter in that farmhouse.

Chapter 15: Blue's Sleepover

It was late in the day now, and the shadows merged together to form dusk. "I want to hear the rest, but I have to find some shelter for me and Blue."

"Nonsense, you can stay right here with us," Benjie said.

I thought about it for a minute, "Okay by me, as long as it is not an inconvenience."

As much playing as Blue and Brittany had done, he wouldn't be up long tonight anyway. They were winding down a little. Brittany was on the bottom step giving Blue rubs and scratches in all the best places.

The only other person that made him that happy was Baby Girl.

"Do you mind if I go get my gear?" I asked, and added, "You can keep old Beulah safe with you till morning."

"Who is Beulah?" he asked.

I had to laugh out loud. "I'm sorry, I didn't think about it. Old Beulah is my shotgun. She has saved my old butt more times than I can count."

He didn't laugh but nodded in agreement to the terms and conditions. I was learning to respect this man more and more.

When I got to where old Beulah was, I made sure he watched me take all the bullets out and put them in my pocket. I left the pump down and the chamber open all the way to the porch and handed it to him.

He looked almost apologetic but took the shotgun.

"Thank you," he said.

"No, sir, thank You," I said, picked up both the tea glasses, and headed into the house.

Blue and I had the guest room all to ourselves, and I put the backpack and walking stick in there. I reached in the backpack and got one of the little flashlights. When I got back in the living room, I gave it to Brittany and told her to use it only in emergencies and when her Dad said she could. She took it and smiled that big smile that lights up her whole face. Her Dad didn't tell her she could, but she tried it just the same. I hoped I hadn't overstepped my bounds.

Belinda made a meal of Spam and biscuits; I ate like there was no tomorrow. We talked and laughed; I was entertained mostly by Brittany who never seemed to run out of energy. After complete night fall, with the windows up and a light breeze blowing through the screens, Brittany finally gave up and curled up on the couch with Blue right beside her.

They were out.

Belinda said she was going on to bed and asked Benjie to bring Brittany when he came. He said that he would and told her he would be along directly.

Benjie continued the story. I felt like he needed to get it off his chest and I just enjoyed the sound of another man's voice.

Chapter 16: Thank You, Ezra

We made it through the first winter and were thinking about our next move. Did we want to stay there or try to find other people? Could we take a small town and make a community out of it?

It was a late spring morning. Ezra and I decided to make a run south and do some scavenging and exploring. He and I wanted to see what condition the towns around us were in at this point.

Maybe with another dozier and some other equipment, we could establish some sort of society. Pinto was too big, that was confirmed, and I felt that Belle View would be too big as well. We needed a small town in a relatively protective area. The map showed that, if we drove back to US-145 and turned south, there was a little town called Sanctuary. That is where I wanted to look.

We left that morning without a care in the world, just glad to be doing something. We eased back out the way we came that first day. The bull, or what was left of him, was still in the road. There was no sign of human life all the way back to US-145.

I turned right and headed toward Sanctuary. As we got closer there were more cars stranded in the road, but it wasn't until we actually got to the town entrance that it was not passable by vehicle.

We got out and walked. I didn't think I needed to carry a weapon and left the shotgun in the Chevy. When we started walking, I imagined about how this place could work. With some equipment we could make this a nice residence: a sanctuary.

There was a river that ran through the town; water would not be a problem, and it would provide a food source with fish. There was a volunteer fire station, which probably had equipment, and a Sheriff substation. I figured they both carried long range radios. I was in my own world; we could do this, and we could do that, when Ezra grabbed my arm.

When I looked over, he had his finger to his lips. I listened, and I heard it as well. It was people. My heart raced, and I started taking off towards the sound. Ezra grabbed my arm again and shook his head. 'Let's watch them first before we just walk right up to them,' he whispered in my ear. I am thankful for Ezra looking out for me; I would have just run into the midst of them.

I followed his lead, and we very quietly eased up to the side of a building and peered around the edge. There were four men and two women. The two women looked like they had been through hell. The men seemed to be relaxed; the women looked scared to death.

Ezra never said a word, backed slowly out of the area, and pulled me with him. He never spoke until we got well away from them. 'They are bad news. I've seen this type before. We need to get the hell out of here before they spot us.' We started easing away from the area.

"Don't move, don't even flinch," a man with a rifle came right up to us. There were five, not four and he yelled for the other men to get over there.

Ezra grabbed the barrel of the rifle and pushed it sideways at the same time the man pulled the trigger. Ezra pushed him away and took the gun from him, and we started running like hell, through the cars and toward the Chevy.

The others had showed up to where the other man was and started shooting at us. Bullets were flying off of cars and trees. They didn't hit us, but it was close enough to scare the hell out of me.

We kept running and when we made it to the Chevy, I heard combustible engines and realized by the high pitch that they were motorcycles. I backed the Chevy the way I had come in and managed to scrape the paint in places and put some dents in others for my efforts. I was moving too slow and couldn't turn around; they were going to catch up.

I heard Ezra start shooting.

The lead cycle was about to clear last obstacle, and Ezra's bullet caught the rider in the chest and sent him backwards off the motorcycle. Instead of stopping to help their friend, the others swerved around him and kept coming. 'Whatever you do, don't stop!' Ezra hollered.

The other two cycles gained on us. Ezra shot at the one on the right who tried to ride and empty a pistol at the same time. Ezra missed.

The windshield busted from a bullet that ricocheted off the truck frame. I reversed that Chevy like a bat-out-of-hell and looked for a turnaround spot.

Ezra took aim again and fired. The rider laid the bike over on its side.

The third rider was trying to get a pistol out of a shoulder holster and drive at the same time.

"Piss on this," I heard Ezra say. He threw the rifle in the floorboard and grabbed the shotgun. The rider was well within range now. He leaned out the window, and I heard the shotgun sound off. He must have got the rider because, when I glanced back, I did not see him. Ezra eased back into the truck, sat in the seat and let out a big moan. That's when I noticed the blood coming from his chest.

I found a wide driveway coming up and backed the Chevy into it. I threw it in park. "Don't stop, get the hell out of here!" Ezra hollered.

I threw it down into drive and bolted out of there as fast as I could. It was hard to see through the busted windshield and I kept a check on the rearview mirror to see if I was being followed.

By my count there should been five; that meant there were two more somewhere. My count was right; a Dodge Ram was coming up behind us.

I looked at Ezra, who was still bleeding pretty bad. "I need to stop the bleeding," I said.

"Quit worrying about me, if they catch us, we are both dead," he said with a stern look.

The back glass blew out of the Chevy, and I swerved the truck. I kept barreling down the highway. The road was fairly open, and I remembered the lay out pretty well.

The Dodge was trying to catch up and doing a pretty good job. Another shotgun blast came, and I thought he was shooting at the tires. It sounded like the tailgate and fender got the worst of it.

Ezra threw the shotgun into the back seat. I don't know how he done it, but he crawled over to the back.

"Keep it steady!" Ezra yelled.

He aimed the shotgun, and I heard it go off inside the cab of the truck. My ears rang, and I was convinced I was having heart failure.

He nailed the dodge in the front grill.

"Don't let up, Benjie!" he shouted. "Don't look back, just drive!"

I kept the pedal pressure to the floor except for the curves. We had to have been into the second mile, and I hoped the Chevy could keep going. I heard Ezra when he landed in the back of the truck bed.

He had squeezed through the back-glass window. By my count, he only had two shells left. I took a glance; he was crouched down in front of the tailgate. The Dodge gained on us, but it had steam coming out from under the hood.

Another shot rang out that peppered the tailgate. I thought sure that Ezra had to have been hit again.

He lifted up and fired the shotgun; in the side mirror, I saw the truck veer to the left and out into the brush. I pulled the truck over, grabbed the rifle and bolted out of the truck door. I jerked the tailgate down.

"That's the way we do this shit," Ezra said, smiling that big shit-eatin grin. His teeth were stained with blood.

He was hurt bad, but it didn't look like the gunshot wound bled as bad as before. For a minute, I hoped he might make it.

From how it looked, the Dodge had left the road, rolled over in the ditch, and skidded on its side into a pine tree. I saw movement in that direction and prayed I could get Ezra in the front before any more confrontation.

I was trying to get my arms under Ezra and a shot rang out. It was a shotgun but the range was too far and the shot peppered the ground before it reached us.

I got Ezra on his feet.

"Let's get in the truck," I said as I tried to help Ezra up.

He cocked a little smile that was more of a sneer and then his face got hard.

"You have to finish this," he said.

The man coming at me up the road was staggering a little, obviously favoring his left side. I noticed he was bleeding from his head and had trouble with his right arm trying to shift the shotgun.

"Stop, dammit; Stop right there - We don't have to do this!" I yelled as loud as I could. I cried more than yelled, and my voice cracked.

He didn't break stride and was coming as fast as he could.

"Now, dammit, he will be in range to kill you in another few steps!" Ezra yelled at me.

I had never used a firearm against another human being; I put the rifle to my shoulder. I took center of the man's chest in my crosshairs.

"Please, stop!" I yelled.

He was within his range and started raising the shotgun to his shoulder.

I pulled the trigger.

He stumbled backwards and then went down on one knee. He was trying to orientate the shotgun back up again.

I shifted another shell took deliberate aim at this head and fired.

He rolled over; his legs kicked out from under him. He quivered like he was having a seizure and then lay still. I lay the rifle on the tailgate, grabbed the shotgun out of the back of the truck, and took a look at Ezra. He was holding his own at that point.

"There ain't but one shot left," he reminded me.

I walked over to the man in the road; he was dead. I should have felt guilt or remorse, but at the time, I didn't feel anything. I went to the truck and kept the shotgun ready for anything.

The driver was still in the cab and pinned by the air bag. His left leg was broken and jagged bone protruded from his leg. His face was turned left where it was visible; his left arm was limp. He was alive, but there was no doubt that it wouldn't be for long. I walked up to him.

"How many of you were there?" I asked him.

"Eight in total, I reckon three now." He groaned.

He licked his lips which were covered in blood. "I told them assholes they couldn't bully everybody they met. They thought they were gonna rule the world," he said weakly and winced.

He took a ragged breath, and I thought he was passing on. He looked straight at me.

"The little one, Angie, take care of her will you. Don't give a rat's ass for the other two." He closed his eyes. When he opened them and looked at me again, it was with raw determination.

"Don't you leave me like this," he said.

I put the shotgun to his temple and pulled the trigger.

When I returned to the truck, Ezra was sitting on the ground with his back leaned against the back tire. His head was hung low, and he never looked up.

"Finished?" he asked.

"Yeah, it's done." I said and then asked. "How bad is it?"

"It hurts like a mother," he said but never changed his tone.

"Come on; let's get you in the truck," I said.

"No need for that, I ain't going nowhere," he sighed.

He coughed and a trickle of frothy blood ran down the corner of his mouth. In a panic I grabbed him. He winced and moaned from the movement. I realized he was dying.

I eased him back to the tire and just looked at him in shock. I had witnessed a lot of dying, but this kind I was not used to. Pentacle I couldn't help, but Ezra was dying for no other reason than stupidity.

I got the water bottle out of the truck, sat down beside him, and helped him drink it. He was weak, and his eyes glazed.

"Thank you for everything Benjie," he whimpered. "We wouldn't have made it this far if not for you."

"I learned more from you than you ever did from me," I told him.

He smiled that crooked smile and laid his chin on his chest. A couple of more breaths and that was all of that. I put my face in my hands and cried for a while. He was heavy, but I loaded him in the back of the truck and closed the tailgate.

I reloaded the shotgun and headed back to Sanctuary. I was cautious as I walked up to the two women who were there.

"Where is Angie?" I barked.

They looked surprised that I would know any of their names.

"She's tied up in the minivan," the older woman said.

They pointed in the direction, and I went over to it and found a girl of about sixteen in the back seat of the van tied up. All she had on her whole body was a T-Shirt and a pair of socks. Both of them were ragged and stained.

There was a pair of blue jeans near the front seat on the floorboard. It became too obvious as to what had taken place in this van, and my anger rose.

I cut her loose and looked straight into her eyes.

"If you want to live, get dressed and come with me," I said.

She never said a word and got out of the van rubbing her hands to get the circulation back. She put her blue jeans on and headed in my direction as I walked back to the other two women.

"The men that you were with are all dead. You can come with me if you would like, I have other people living with me. If not, you can go your own way," I said.

They both said at the same time. "We'll go with you."

I didn't know it was gratitude or fear that made their decision, but they evidently did not want to be on their own. Angie had still not said a word. She had a dull glaze to her eyes, almost as if there was no soul left inside them.

They gathered what belongings they had and followed me to the Chevy. They shrieked when they saw Ezra in the back. Angie didn't look; she just walked to the passenger side rear door and climbed in.

The oldest one, Susanna, climbed in next to me and began to tell me her story of surviving Pentacle and being abducted by the Three Amigos that ended up being Five Amigos. She had been a slave to them in every way.

I had figured that much.

The one behind me stayed mostly silent, probably because Susanna didn't let anyone get a word in edgewise. However, I did decipher that her name was Sam, short for Samantha.

I still had not heard Angie speak. In the rearview mirror, I noticed see her looking at a cell phone and sliding her finger across it to activate it. It had long been dead, and I figured it was her only device of hope to hang on to.

My heart went out to her.

When I got to where the Dodge was, Angie spoke one word.

"Stop," she said.

I stopped the truck, and she opened the door and got out. I got out of the truck and relived the event in my mind. I held the shotgun and watched Angie approach the man on the ground. She walked all the way around him in a wide circle. When she convinced herself that he was dead, she walked to his head and kicked him as hard as she could.

I watched as she lowered her jeans and pissed on his face. She never shed a tear.

She pulled her pants up and looked into her cell phone and tried to swipe it. She walked back to the truck and got in the passenger side.

I got in the truck and looked at the faces of Susanna and Sam. They were solemn and respectful of Angie.

At least Susanna was mostly quiet the rest of the trip back to the farm.

When I got to the farm the crew came out to greet us, and the happy occasion turned into a sorrowful event. Mrs. Dorothy got one of the new sleeping bags acquired from Wally World. She and Belinda cleaned Ezra up, and we put him inside the bag and zipped it up. Mrs. Dorothy sewed the top of it closed while he was on the couch inside it.

Hal and I went out to a spot on the right-hand side of the barn and started digging the grave. When we got it dug, we all brought Ezra out to the burial site and laid him to rest. They looked at me to say the final eulogy, and I blundered through it. Even Susanna was emotional, and she had never met him.

Angie never came outside; she was still in the recliner where we left her when we got back. She stared into the dead phone and periodically slid her finger across it as if it would magically come back to life.

Johnny went over to her and touched her arm to see if she was okay. She screamed a blood curdling scream and jerked away from him. He jumped back away from her and looked at me.

"Leave her be for now, she has had it really bad," I said.

Mrs. Dorothy prepared the evening meal. We found areas for the three new arrivals to stay. I put Angie in Ezra's old room so she could be alone if she wanted to be.

The crew was on pins and needles for the story of the day's events. I gave them the short and sweet version of it all, and they nodded in all the right places and cried when we got to the part where Ezra passed away.

Brittany wanted to play, and I was mentally and physically exhausted. Mrs. Dorothy read the writing on the wall and told Brittany that she could sleep over with her tonight. Her Daddy needed to get some rest. That was right up Brittany's alley. I said my good nights and checked on Angie.

"Are you okay?" I asked her point blank.

She looked straight at me that time. She didn't speak but nodded her head.

Mrs. Dorothy and Belinda heated water, and I tried to clean away the events of that day. I scrubbed as hard as I could, and I know I got the skin clean but didn't think my soul would ever be clean again.

I went to my room and closed the door.

Sometime around midnight Belinda came into the room and came over to the bed. I looked over at her surprised.

"Is everything okay?" I asked. "Is it Brittany?"

She laid a finger to my lips and whispered, "Everything is fine," and climbed in the bed with me. She held me while I cried myself to sleep and we have been together ever since.

Chapter 17: Time for the Sandman

I didn't know where the time had gone. Old T said 10:15, but it felt like 3:00 in the morning. I stretched and yawned. Blue cocked his ear forward and raised his head a little. I told Benjie we would talk more in the morning, but the old man needed his beauty rest.

I looked at Blue who was giving me an inquisitive look.

"It's up to you," I said.

He got up, did the hokey-pokey, and eased toward the door. I let him out and stood on the porch while he watered the lawn. He went back in the house and checked on Brittany who was sound asleep and trotted towards me.

Benjie blew out all the candles except for one and picked Brittany up. He took the candle and headed up the stairs. In her hand she was clutching the little flashlight, and I smiled inside.

Blue and I headed for the guest room, and I stretched out on the bed. I had found conversation and heard the laughter of youth. Blue had a day in the sun playing.

I thought of Baby Girl and fell asleep that night like every other night, the most fortunate man in the world.

Chapter 18: Day 3, Anson

Early the next morning, Blue and I had breakfast with the three B's. Brittany and Blue ran and played in the yard while Benjie and I sat on the front porch sipping coffee.

My curiosity made me ask, "What happened to your crew?"

He kind of smiled and looked sad at the same time.

"After what happened at Sanctuary, I was afraid to establish anything. All I wanted was to stay out of sight and keep my crew alive and safe. We stayed at the farmhouse for another full year plus."

"Responsibility can be a heavy burden sometimes," I said. He nodded and looked across the yard where Brittney was rolling on the ground with Blue.

"We only went out when we had to have more fuel or something that we couldn't make. We learned to observe and evaluate people from afar, to establish whether to approach them or not. We never threatened anyone, but we were always prepared for defense if it called for it. A group of twelve was travelling to a commune called New America in Meridian. It was rumored that they had modern conveniences and social services reestablished. I asked the leader of the group if it was possible for them to stay in Sanctuary that night, and I would ask my crew if they wanted to come."

"I asked the crew, and we voted on it. The vote was yes. The only two who voted to stay at the farm were Angie and Mrs. Dorothy. I think Angie was comfortable with the crew and didn't want to meet any strangers. Mrs. Dorothy didn't think she was up to making the journey. They decided to agree with majority rule and come with us."

"The next morning the nine of us loaded up the Ford with back packs and essentials and headed for Sanctuary. We met up with the group and started out on the journey. It went relatively okay with no major obstacles. We devised means to push Mrs. Dorothy and Brittany through the open road sections with the use of an old wheelchair."

"About forty days later in midsummer we came to New America. The rumors about the modern conveniences were somewhat farfetched. It wasn't like pre-pentacle days, but it was serviceable. You still could only run the generators for short periods of time, long enough to cool fridges and heat water. The public water system was reestablished, but the water pressure was a hit and a miss most of the time."

"We settled into a fair semblance of life and were expected to share in the labors of the community and vote for amendments and statutes for a governing society. We were not unhappy, but as time went on, the council became more and more centered on the benefits of select individuals.   I overlooked the idiosyncrasies of the hierarchy and succumbed to the live and let live philosophy. The crew was safe and I began to I crave my freedom and hoped there was a place on this earth to raise Brittany to know better morals and values."

"The morning we found Angie; I made my mind up. We tried everything we could to bring her out of the shell. Those bastards had just done too much damage. She was living in a house with Sam and one of the young men in the community approached her. His intentions were harmless when he tried to give her a kiss. Sam found her the next morning, she had hung herself with a bed sheet," he said.

I approached Belinda and she stated she could not believe I had made it as long as I did. "When do you want to leave?"

"We struck out and have been staying in out of the way places while I look for the permanent area that we can call home. That brings us up to hear and now," Benjie said.

"Well, I would love to stay longer, but I have to make it in to Anson today. Thanks for all the hospitality. I will stop back by here on the return, probably late tomorrow or the next day and see if you are still here. If you are, we can visit some more."

He handed old Beulah back to me. "We won't leave for at least two days, unless we have to. Have a safe trip; I hope you find what you need."

"Thanks for everything," I said.

Brittany ran up and gave me a hug, but she about squeezed Blue to death. He loved every second of it and licked her in the face as she giggled.

We struck out.

The Walkin' man struts with a swagger and a giggle
The Walkin' man listens to the birds
The Walkin' man strides with a hop and a wiggle
Whistling all the tweets that he had heard.

We headed into town on the 430 Express Lane which we came to about three miles past the Country Club Entrance. Everything was wide open at first, and we could've run a vehicle. Closer to town was crowded with walking room only. Inside the town the Expressway turned into an over-pass junk yard that went on indefinitely.

Blue didn't like it, and he stayed really close most of the time. I looked for the hospital and Medical University of Anson. I knew from past travels about where I needed to go. From the height of the overpass I saw the larger buildings, the ones near the medical center. I started watching for a hospital emblem on the exit signs.

The medical buildings were on the left-hand side and not far off the expressway. Other than the hospital grounds, the rest of the area looked like an inner-city slum. That would not matter anymore; we're all finally, created-equal. I found the right exit, and we veered off the expressway.

It was close to mid-day with the sun up high in the sky. There was evidence of tremendous looting and destruction in the stores, and my heart sank. William's idea of condition and mine seemed to be of totally different perspectives.

We continued down the street going around cars, trucks, and freight vans. Some of the vehicles had been vandalized as well. Most of the tires were flat and several windshields shot out. There were bullet holes in some of them. It looked like someone used them for target practice.

The hospital was about three blocks ahead on the right. Blue was in his nervous stance and stayed really close to me. He watched his step and footing with all the broken glass and debris littering the street.

His hair was started to raise on his back a little, not full alert but attentive. The little hairs on the back of my neck tickled. I felt like we were being watched and followed but did not see nor hear anything to prove it. I didn't change my posture or stride, but I started consistently looking at all corners.

The buildings were taller here, and I prayed that there were no snipers in the lofts. I also watched Blue real close, readied to reel him in if he took off.

In the next block there was a city park on the left side of the road. As we approached Blue's hair rose up on the back of his neck, and his ears were perked forward. I heard a low growl start in his throat. I watched as the Pink Panther took over, and he eased to the left.

I heard the noise in the park as we got closer and pulled old Beulah off my shoulder. I snuck towards the park crouched down and placing my footing as not to crunch the glass and giggled. The old shit-eater has me doing the Pink Panther, too.

There was panel van up ahead, and we did the feline shuffle all the way to it. Blue was in full alert and moved a little ahead of me. He turned to look at me and wanted approval for the go ahead.

I patted my right thigh with my hand.

He didn't come back to my side, but he stopped to let me catch up. I looked around the front of the van.

There is something you don't see every day.

There was a giraffe in the park feeding on whatever it could find. Blue looked up at me, and his eyes were filled with wonder, but the feline mode had left and he settled back to semi alert. He seemed to be more curious than concerned.

I patted his head and did a quickie scratch behind his ears.

"That is one for the history books, old boy," I whispered.

We moved down the street to get a better look inside the little park. There were two deer in the far corner. Knowing what these were, Blue got excited. I patted the side of my leg again.

"Maybe next time, Blue," I said. "Maybe next time."

The giraffe raised its head up and looked at us, so did the deer. They seemed to get a little nervous and then when back to grazing.

"They don't know about old Beulah, do they Blue," I said laughing.

I looked back at them a couple of more times as we passed. They didn't seem to have a care in the world. Maybe I was wrong about other people being here and the feeling of being watched.

If someone was here, these beauties would have been supper by now.

My golden apple was a couple of blocks ahead of me.

I had seen car jams and had gotten used to them, but this one at the medical center complex was on a scale I had never seem.

There were vehicles of all shapes and sizes in total disarray. They were in the parking lot, on the grounds, in the street, and on the sidewalk packed in like a can of sardines.

The rest of it was the same old story of desperation and hope of the dying pilgrims that tried to seek refuge at their commonly known place of healing. There were the skeletonized and the mummified in all manner of positions and placement. It didn't differentiate between the young and the old. Deciding the sex of the occupant was determined by the nature of the remaining clothing and shoes present.

A hint of that old familiar smell was still present in the air. It refused to let go of its reminder to society that everything decays. The rats and the squirrels were out to pick the best bones to chew on.

It broke my heart when I saw it; it was obvious that it would be an obstacle course.

Blue and I made our way into the maze, and I couldn't shake the feeling that we were being followed. Blue was nervous too.

It was mid-afternoon, and I had resolved to the fact that we would have to stay in town for the night. I looked around at the close buildings and tried to guess where the safest place would be.

Blue was back to semi alert and hung close by again. He found an interesting tire and I stopped long enough for him to sniff it out and hike his leg. He gave me a smug look that said, "I'll show them who is boss around here."

The carnage here must have been bad enough to keep away the vandals from up the street. There was no evidence of any disturbance or damage here. I was amazed at the difference within the five city blocks.

To be honest, if I didn't have to be here, I would avoid this place like the plague. It feels like a thousand ghosts are crowding in around you. Hospitals gave me the heebie-jeebies even before the Flip.

According to Old-T, it was 3:25, and I had not made it to the door.

"We've got to get a move on, old boy," I said.

At times we climbed over the cars because it was easier than finding a way around them.

All the windshields were covered in dust and probably ash. The opaque view of the pilgrims inside did nothing to assist in helping my uneasy feeling. Blue had a little trouble keeping his footing on the car hoods, but he managed to stay upright.

The final push to the front door was all car to car. Most of these had the doors open and the lingered smell was strong as we got closer. I pulled my old bandana out of my pocket and tied it around my nose like an old west bank robber. Blue looked up gave me the, if-you-can't-stand-the-heat, get-out-of-the-kitchen, look.

He really was a prick at times.

Just to prove the point, he did the hokey-pokey and almost slipped on the hood of the old Chevy Impala we stood on.

"That's for being a smart-ass, shit-eater," I laughed.

It seemed like it took hours to get there, but when we got down and to the door, Old-T said 3:40.

I couldn't help but think it; it cemented into my soul. If there were ever was a week of hell on this earth, it happened in this lobby. This was by far, the biggest congregation of lost pilgrims I had ever seen. I thought I had been acclimated to carnage, but I felt tears welling in my eyes just the same. I needed to find some peace in my heart and found a bare spot on the floor, not a big one, but a spot.

I made a low whistle to Blue, and he tip toed around the bodies and came to me.

I knelt down on the bare spot of that lobby with my right hand on Blue. I took off my old ball cap and bowed my head. Blue read my expression and lowered his head. As I gently stroked Blue, I cried the cry of the emptiness in my heart I felt for these lost souls.

When I felt the tension easing up and was able to speak again, I closed my eyes.

"Father, I hope that you can still here the plea of an old stiff-necked sinner. Your will was done then as it being done now and from the beginning of time. I feel the need to pray for the souls of these fallen pilgrims in and around this building. With the vast amount of souls that were here on the final days, I am sure there were good and bad in your eyes. I pray only that, if it be your will, that you let them find peace in your world. Please keep your loving grace upon Sarah and Blue, if it is within your design to do so. Look after Benjie and his family if it satisfies your will. Thank you for each breath we take. Amen," I prayed.

When I opened my eyes and looked up, it appeared to me that the building was a shade brighter. The display of the pilgrims laid before still pulled at my heart, but not near as bad.

I gave Blue a little scratch behind the ears, and he looked up at me with his happy face. I found that I had a little more strength left in me after all. I put on my old ball cap and got to my feet.

"Thank you, sir," I whispered.

I made my way across the lobby and tried not to disturb any of the pilgrims in their rest. I looked for the information sign. Blue seemed to be respecting the privacy of the deceased as well. He perked up a time or two as skittering noises were heard in the emptiness of the great building. I spied some pretty good size roaches darting here and there, but those sounds were from our little pointy nosed fur ball friends.

I found the information desk at the back wall of the entrance hall. There was such a crowd around this desk that I had to gently move a couple of pilgrims a little with my walking stick. I located the sign that showed the different departments.

The pharmacy was on the first floor, which was good news.

I found where I stood, and the destination was down the right wing just beyond Emergency. I let a slight whistle, and Blue came up beside me. I pulled my backpack off and found one of the little LED flashlights and put the backpack back on.

I gave Blue a little scratch behind the ears, and we headed for the Pharmacy. Old-T said 4:00.

We better hurry; I for sure don't want to spend the night in here.

As we started into the wing hall it got darker. We had to go all the way down this wing and then to the right. I hoped the Pharmacy was on the outside wall and had windows.

I tried not to let it, but my mind recreated the happenings of the final days. Each corpse told a story, every open door another chapter. I tried again to block it out of my mind but couldn't. The scenes that came back from the beam of the flashlight made sure of it.

One room had a corpse in the bed, one in the chair, one on the couch, and one on the floor. No doubt this was the final resting place for a family. Even through the complete chaos it appeared that the dying respected the ones who were already admitted. Although the halls were littered with corpses, they did not crowd the rooms.

There is hope for humanity yet.

We made it to the end of the wing, and I shined the light down the right side. The room number in front of me was 1015. It was 4:15 by Old-T. It would be getting dark within three hours.

Old fool; you know you are cutting it too close. If you want to be out of here before dark, you need to hurry.

I checked closed doors as I passed. Found one that was locked and made a mental note of it.

Three rooms down after 1018 the hall turned to the left and by the flashlight beam; it looked like it ran for about fifty feet. We passed room 1019 on the left which used to be the gift shop. It didn't appear to have too many occupants in there. The hallway turned back to the right, and the crowd of pilgrims was back to full capacity.

Room 1020 was the cafeteria, and it appeared that a great many pilgrims settled here during the final day. That meant the pharmacy is past all of this, my hopes of getting out of the city by nightfall diminished.

I could see the pharmacy entrance. Blue and I navigated through the maze of corpses being as respectful as we could and made it to the door of the pharmacy. The place was in total disarray. There were corpses everywhere inside the pharmacy aisles.

This told another story of desperation that pulled on my heart again. I made it through the hair and skin products and reached the pharmacy counter. The roll up door on the Pharmacy was pulled down.

The door into the pharmacy had been busted open.

I am not the first one to come here for medications.

I eased the door open, and to my surprise, there were no corpses to be found inside the apothecary. After Blue got inside, I gently closed the door. Old-T said 4:35.

I pulled off the backpack and got out my cheaters. Old Blue snickered at me when he saw them on my face.

"You'll get old one day, my friend," I said.

I started down the first aisle with the pharmaceutical bottles arranged. Some had been disturbed by the first shopper, but most were neatly lined up and dusty. There were a few spider webs here and there. I felt like the majority had not been disturbed.

I found all manner of different drugs and wished a thousand times that I knew what I was looking at. I found some Viagra and giggled. Baby Girl would slap me with a frying pan if I brought that home. I kept looking for the Presyscodine. On one of the packages it stated, "Better living through modern medicine."

That was then and this is now.

Blue emitted a kind of whine-growl, indicative of a, not-sure-what-I-heard, be-still-and-listen, situation.

I stopped and turned the flashlight off and stood still in the darkness. Old Beulah leaned against the shelf to my right, and I laid my hand on the forearm. I didn't know if it was fear or comfort, but it relaxed me a little just to touch her.

It was pitch black, but my mind's eye saw Blue cocking his ears forward his eyes narrowed to slits. He whined a low yelp; I strained to listen. That is when I heard something. It sounded like someone or something moving through the maze of corpses not too far from us. We were not alone; as someone was creeping up on us to see what we were doing. I strained again and heard another sound that was even farther away. Seemed like whoever it was might be leaving. They had no form of light and was feeling their way through. We stayed in the silent and still for another five minutes and did not hear anything else. Blue did not make any other inclination that he was concerned. I made a mental note to be extremely watchful on the way out and turned the flashlight back on.

I shined it on Blue; he was relaxed and trotted over to where I was, did the hokey-pokey, and sat down. I gave him a scratch behind the ears and checked Old-T. Old-T said 5:00.

I would have thought the pharmacy would put the drugs in alphabetical order, but that did not seem to be the case. The drugs were stored by manner of illness they assisted and not much help to me.

"It looks like we are spending the night, old boy," I whispered to Blue.

He looked up at me with the, No-shit, Sherlock look before standing up, doing the hokey pokey again, and laying down his head on his front paws.

I had to giggle to myself.

I checked the backpack, and I had two more of the LED lights left.

Continue the quest for the Holy Grail, Percival.

I started reading each bottle again.

"You would think they would have made the print bigger on some of these bottles," I said out loud, mainly to hear something in the quiet.

I should have gone back into the over-counter section and found some better cheaters.

"I need to check on some on the way out," I mumbled. I heard Blue let out a heavy sigh.

Nothing I wanted was on this aisle.

I checked Old-T and found out it was after 6:00 and realized that neither me nor Blue had eat anything since this morning. I opened up the backpack and got out the rations that I had brought. Some baked flat bread and a can of SPAM. Just out of habit, I checked the expiration date on the SPAM. It said - Good to 27-June-2017.

"Just a little out of date, Blue, but I'll bet the farm that it is still good," I told Blue as I opened the can.

I didn't get an offensive odor from the can, but the smell did make my old stomach convinced that it needed something in there. I set the can on one of the upper shelves so Blue wouldn't be tempted. I pulled out the water bottle and checked it; almost empty.

I remembered some quart size distilled water on the last aisle and went around to where it was. I opened one of them and shined the light as I poured a little out. I stuck my nose to the top of it and didn't smell any odor, so I took a sip. Not spring water but not bad.

I took two more bottles.

I shined the light around, and on the counter, there was pink colored spit tray that someone used to store pens and highlighters in. I dumped it out and shined the light on it. It will do. Right beside it was an aluminum clipboard, perfect.

I took the bounty back over to the aisle where Blue was and set up the feast. I cleaned off the clipboard and laid the slab of SPAM on it. I pulled my Old Timer folding knife out of my pocket and cut two thick slices from it. I laid the two slices between two of the flatbread pieces.

"A meal fit for a king," I told Blue.

He got up and did the hokey pokey, locked his back legs, and stretched as far forward as he could.

I opened up a bottle of the distilled water, rinsed the spit up bowl out, and poured the rest of the bottle in it. I laid the clipboard and the spit up bowl down on the floor and backed up.

I got my sandwich and eased down beside Blue and placed the flashlight on the bottom shelf to shine out over the aisle. Before I got my butt to the floor, the SPAM on the clipboard had disappeared and old Blue was lapping at the water.

So much for formal dining with Blue!

Old-T said 6:30. I finished my sandwich and drank the bottle of water. The events of the day had caught up with me, and I felt tired.

I told Blue to stay and got up and grabbed up old Beulah.

"I'll be right back, old boy," I told Blue and took the flashlight. I went over to the door and shined the light out into the over-counter section. I was reminded of everything as the light fell over the faces and remains of the pilgrims in the store.

I worked my way around and found two electric blankets on the wall aisle that were still in boxes. I grabbed them and did a quick shine around to see if there was anything else of value. I didn't see anything.

It amazed me as I looked at the things, we used to think were so important. Curling Irons, Blow Dryers, a half of aisle with nothing but make-up on it, cell phone cases, and DVDs. So much time and effort spent chasing the almighty dollar to make totally useless purchases. That was definitely another place and another time.

I headed back to the apothecary.

I came through the door with my boxes and closed the door. I pulled the small aisle next to the door over until it covered it. I dropped the blankets off on the aisle old Blue was in. He looked up at me inquisitively and then laid his head back down.

"Alright, I'll do your job for you," I told him.

I made the perimeter check that night with the flashlight, and satisfied that we were secure, I came back to the aisle Blue was in and opened the two boxes of electric blankets. I lay one of them out and wadded the other beside it. I reached in the back compartment of the backpack and got the blanket that I always carry. I laid down on the electric blanket and positioned the backpack for a pillow. I got the other blanket ready to cover up with if it got cold.

Old Blue came over and nosed the other electric blanket until he got everything in place like he wanted, did the hokey pokey, and lay down beside me.

I turned the LED Flashlight off, and it was pitch back inside the room. I could not see Blue but heard him breathing and reached my hand out and found him in the dark. I gave him a gentle rub and good scratch behind the ears.

When I finished, I heard him shake his head real fast; that was the hokey without the pokey. I heard a big sigh and then everything got quiet except for the rhythmic breathing of me and Old Blue.

My whole body was exhausted, but my mind would not let go just yet.

Chapter 19: Gordon Thompson

It was several weeks since the start of the pentacle wave and a couple of weeks after I had buried Jason and Melanie. Baby Girl and Blue had become the dynamic duo and our supplies were becoming rapidly diminished. I felt the coolness in the morning and evening air. Winter would be here sooner than later and I needed to make sure we were ready for it.

I had obtained enough gasoline to fill the Ford up and then some. I had stored some extra for the generator so we could plug in the refrigerator every day and the freezer every other day for a couple of hours.

We made do with what we had, but we were definitely not in a decent condition to make the winter. The smell was really strong, even around the house. I knew I had to do something about that smell for Baby Girl.

I went into Barkston again and attempted to make it to the hospital in the Ford. I got within two blocks of it. The sight of the corpses at that stage was horrible and looked like the worst horror movie ever written.

There were flies and maggots all over the corpses. There were all manner of roaches and insects crawling over the remains. Ugly liquids seemed to ooze into every crevice in the streets and sidewalks. There were buzzards everywhere pecking and pulling on the most plentiful bounty they could ever conceive. Most of the corpses that were in the open were missing their eyes. It was hard to look at, but I needed to find a path to the hospital.

I was glad that Baby Girl didn't see this sight. Blue was still a puppy and did his part by keeping Baby Girl occupied and happy at home. I was alone with the rotted remnants of society.

I might be able to get to the back of the hospital by the loading bay if I took El Cinco Street over to West Palmer and came in through the back way. It was flat over there, and I could use the 4-wheel drive if I had to.

I had to walk it first to find out.

I got out of the Ford and put on a filter mask, one of the ones that the Volunteer Fire Department gave us when the NV-17 quarantine lockdown began. It didn't help the smell, but I didn't want any extra proteins in the form of insects. I toted a twenty-two pistol and an old ex-shovel handle converted to a walking stick.

I started toward the hospital and took a left on El Cinco Street which is a residential area halfway in from the main street. These were mostly pier type houses built in the forty's and fifty's and were mostly kept up with tendered lawns and flower gardens. On that day they were grown over with scattered litter. Nothing about this scenery reflected what it was three months prior.

When I got to the intersection of El Cinco and Pecos, I looked to the right, back toward the hospital. It was navigable, but I could not get to the back where I wanted to go. I stayed straight on El Cinco which was passable in the center of the street.

When desperation time came the poor pilgrims, their only focus was to get to the hospital; two blocks away it was business as usual.

I remembered the names and faces of the people that resided on the street.

Mrs. Arnold lived in the Victorian on the corner. She held the prize for prettiest lawn and garden at the local fair for three years straight during the 1990's.

Doc Jenkin's place was straight across on the other corner, the two-story antebellum style house with the columns. The doors were wide open, and it looked like someone had been inside. It had to have been a local; no one else would have known he was a doctor.

The third house on the right was Gordon Thompson.

As I got closer to the house, I saw Gordy sitting on the front porch with his head down.

He was not a corpse.

I walked to the gate and opened it. Gordy heard the gate and raised his head. He looked at me and never changed his expression.

"She's passed Dinky. Ellie Belle is gone," he said.

I looked at his face; he was in shock bordering on insanity. It was evident that he had lost weight and probably hadn't eaten for several days.

"I did everything I could, but nothing worked," he said. "I tried everything I knew."

I sat down in the chair next to him.

"Where is she, Gordy?" I asked.

He looked up with glassy eyes.

"She's in the bed taking a rest."

I had thought that to be the case.

"What are you going to do now?" I asked him.

He looked like he was having trouble thinking.

"I know I should bury her, but I can't stand to look at her," he slowly said. He continued without changing his voice tone. "I already dug the grave, but I just can't stand to see her this way."

"I tried a couple of days ago, I really did, but her arm started coming off, and I couldn't do it," he cried.

"Calm down, Gordy," I told him.

I chose my words carefully, not wanting to upset him further.

"Gordy, what if I went in and got her ready where you didn't have to see her? Do you think we could bury her together?" I asked.

He sniffled a couple of times, never changing his tone, "you would do that for me, Dinky?"

I would rather have two root canals done and fight a grizzly bear in the public square.

I placed a hand on top of one of his. "Sure thing, Gordon, I would do that."

He looked thoughtful and appreciative but never made a move to get out of his chair.

"Can I go in there now and see what I can do for her?" I asked him.

 "Please," he said, but he never got up and never looked up at me.

I left him to his thoughts and walked into the house. I was ashamed that, for all the years in which I had known Gordy and Ellie Belle, I had never been inside their house.

We had socialized at town functions, and I saw Gordy a couple of times a month on the lake and at the bass club meetings. We had fished together on a couple of the bass tournaments.

The house was an old-style pier frame with high ceilings, and Ellie Belle had made Gordy a good wife and a pleasant home. Gordy had inherited the house from his grandmother years ago. They had lived by modest means, and the old house was impeccable.

I saw pictures of Sandy and Mike from the time they were babies all the way to adulthood. Sandy had been a school grade under Darrel. Mike would have been about four years under her.

Sandy was such a beautiful girl and I wondered why Darrell never made a run at her.

Gordy had not disturbed one thing in the house and left it just like Ellie Belle had it. He had been sleeping in the lazy-boy recliner. There were water bottles around the end table by the recliner. At least he was drinking some water. The bedrooms were down the hall and all the doors were closed. Generally, the master bedroom is at the end. I heard insects buzzing inside the room; my hunch was right.

I put the mask back on.

The drapes were drawn, and I pulled them open so I could see. A survey of the room showed what was once a vibrant god-fearing woman was hardly recognizable anymore.

I had the urge to retch and forced it back. If that happened, I might run out of this room like Gordy did and never return.

Ellie Belle was in a queen-sized, four-poster bed. The sheet and comforter had been wadded up on Gordy's side, and she had died on her side facing outward.

I looked around the room and saw a patchwork quilt on a rack on the wall. Someone loved them enough to make it for them, and they appreciated it enough to display it with honor. It would be fitting for a burial wrap. I laid it out on the floor and went back to the bed.

I removed the comforter and laid it off to the side. The result was that the mattress had been saturated with fluid and insect excrement. Ellie Belle was shrunken in and shriveled; it was obvious the insects had done their due diligence.

There were maggots and larvae all over her face and in her open mouth. Her eyes were open sockets, and her jaw was agape. I looked at what had the appearance of movement and discovered her mouth was full of insects and larvae. I wanted to run away and scream at the top of my lungs.

I saw where Gordy had tried to roll her over and how her arm was out of place. My body wanted to retch again, and that time my stomach almost won. I got the strong taste of bile in my throat to compliment the pungent smell that surrounded me.

Lord, please help me to get this done, I silently prayed.

I took the top sheet and laid it over her. It was crusted with dried fluids in some areas and soaked in others, but I managed to find spots that I could use that weren't affected. I untucked the fitted sheet on Gordy's side and folded it over her.

I went around to her side, untucked the fitted sheet and folded it up to the other sheet. It took some effort, but I found two unsoiled places that I could grip.

I folded them up together and lifted her up.

Her legs were at an unnatural angle, but I lowered her to the center of the quilt in one piece. I wrapped her up in her burial cocoon and felt better once I got the quilt over her.

I went outside to where Gordy was; I needed to ask him a question, but mainly I wanted some air that was a little fresher than what was inside that bedroom. I pulled my mask off.

"Gordy, do you have a sleeping bag?" I asked him.

He thought for a minute, almost as if he couldn't remember what a sleeping bag was.

"Yeah, there's one in the hall closet on the bottom shelf," he said.

"I have her covered up so you can't see her, but you are going to have to help me with her, okay?" I told him.

He didn't speak but nodded; he slowly got up out of the chair. His eyes seemed clearer, and he was able to focus a little better.

"Sarah?" he asked.

"She is still with us right now."

"Thank God for that," he whispered.

"Amen."

He went to the hall closet and pulled the rolled-up sleeping bag out and handed it to me.

I told him to hand me another one of the blankets that were in there and wait just a minute for me. I went into the bedroom and laid the blanket over the mattress where she had lain so he wouldn't see the saturated mattress.

I moved Ellie Belle over toward the bed to make room for the sleeping bag and then opened the door.

I told him to come on in.

He was wild eyed when he walked in, and he started getting anxiety.

"Unroll the sleeping bag and place it over here," I told him.

He got better as he focused on the task. We spread out the sleeping bag and got on each end of Ellie Belle to lift her over. I watched him close to see if he was going to be able to finish. He struggled, but he held it together.

I told him to grab the quilt and not her. We gently picked her up enough to transfer the body to one side of the opened sleeping bag. I folded the other side over and zipped it up all the way to the top. Ellie Belle was completely inside.

I looked at Gordon and checked his stability; he still seemed to be managing.

"Pick up the bottom, and I will pick up the top a we will carry her out of here," I said.

Again, he didn't speak but just nodded.

We picked her up and started for the door into the hallway.

"She is so light," he mumbled.

In a soft voice I said, "Yes, sir, she is."

We made it through the door and down the hallway. We made a right through the kitchen and toward the back door. Without speaking, we looked at each other and gently laid her on the kitchen floor. Gordon opened the back door leading out onto the back porch. We eased her back up and started out with her.

The backyard was a yard to be envied by all. Ellie Belle must have had a great love for plants and an incredible green thumb.

On the right side of the porch there was a doghouse and food bowl. I didn't ask if Gordon had taken care of that one already.

Over to the left side of the yard, near a large azalea bush, there was a large mound of dirt. I knew what that meant.

He started in that direction, and I followed. When we got to the grave, we laid her down on the side of it and got in position on our knees at the head and foot and lowered her in the ground.

When Gordon looked back up at me, he was closest to normal than he had been since I found him.

It was getting on near mid-morning by now, and I knew I had to get busy.

"Gordon, do you want some privacy?" I asked him.

He looked up at me puffy eyed and stated. "Dinky, I can't thank you enough for what you did. If you need to be going, I understand. Honestly, I don't want to be alone right now."

"Okay, Gordy, where can I find a shovel?" I asked.

"Over there in the garage," he said.

I left him to his thoughts and mourning and went to the garage. The smell was strong in there too. I found where Gordy's old Labrador's final resting place was. He wasn't much more than a sack of hair and bones at this point.

I found a flat and a pointed shovel hanging on the back wall and brought them out to the back. Gordon was on his knees at the head of the grave with his head bowed. I stood there a few minutes to let him make his peace.

Gordon raised his head, and I walked over to the dirt mound, shovels in hand. Gordon reached down with his hand and gathered a handful of dirt, stood up and emptied it into the grave.

"Ashes to ashes, dust to dust," he prayed. "Father, please take care of my Ellie Belle until I see her again."

He looked up and reached out for one of the shovels. I handed it to him. Without saying another word, we filled in the grave as best we could.

Afterward, Gordon stood still by the grave side, but his body language stated that he was returning to reality.

"I am glad you wrapped her in that quilt. Her grandmother made that for us as a wedding gift thirty plus years ago." He took a deep breath, "Damn this smell, you can't get away from it."

I didn't want to tell him that his own smell wasn't much better.

"What are you going to do now, Gordy?" I asked.

He thought a moment.

"Not sure, but I need to see if I can find Sandy and Mike. Sandy was in Shreveport the last time I spoke to her. Do you think I could hang out with you for a while?" he added quickly. "I'll earn my keep."

"No problem Gordy, I would love to have some help at times," I said. "You need to gather up some belongings and some foul weather gear. Winter will be on us before we know it."

"Have you looked around town since all of this happened?" I asked.

He nodded. "I have and I kept thinking I was going to wake up, but I never did."

"Is Palmer Street open to the back of the hospital?" I asked.

"If you take the truck entrance off the side feeder road it is."

"Okay, I'm going to go get my truck. You pack up some belongings," I said, and he got the deer in the headlight look.

I looked him straight in the eyes to let him know I wasn't jerking his chain.

"I will be right back, Gordon."

"Okay," he said, but I am not sure he was convinced.

By the time I got back with the Ford, Gordon had a mid-sized drag bag beside him, a Browning twelve-gauge automatic shotgun and a nine-millimeter in a holster on his side.

I guess he noticed the .22 Caliber I was carrying.

He opened the back door on the crew cab and put his items inside and then climbed in the cab. We headed down El Cinco towards Palmer and made a right. He was correct about the feeder road and truck entrance, and we made it all the way to the back of the hospital.

I got out and told Gordon that he could come or stay. It was his choosing. He sighed a big sighed and opened the truck door and got out.

We went to the back door near the loading dock and checked the door. It was locked.

"I will have to go around to the Emergency entrance and come to the back to open it," I told him.

I started to the truck to get my flashlight when I heard the shot.

After the day I had already had, I almost shit my pants.

I turned back and seen Gordon pulling on the door which was still locked. Before I could yell at him to stop, he aimed the Glock and fired at the lock again. This time when he pulled on the door, it came open. Even from where I stood, I could instantly smell the stronger aroma of confined decay.

He turned to look at me and that was the first time I seen him smile since I found him. He holstered the pistol and motioned for me to come on.

I got the flashlight and followed.

When we got inside, I shined the light around, and it looked like, as soon as we get the lights back on, we will be business as usual. Nothing was in disarray. I looked at the walls to see if there were any maps of the shipping and receiving area. Of course, there was not any. I prayed this next door did not lead into the main hospital and opened it.

Here we go again.

The sight was horrific with dozens of copses in all manners of distortion with all the glory of the insects, fluids, and decay status. It is evident that some type of animals had been in the hospital, probably in the early days and had opened the bellies of some. Their entrails were pulled out and eaten, and one had been dragged down the hall like an enormous piece of spaghetti. It had since dried up and flattened out.

I shined the light back towards Gordon who was wearing his *I can take it* face, but a tear was easing down his cheek.

I knew the layout would require the receiving warehouse to be to the left because of where the loading doors were and proceeded down the hall that way. The hall made a right turn, and there was a door on the left that said Authorized Personnel Only. I thought this might be it and tried the door. It was not locked.

I opened the door and pointed the flashlight in the room and found the supply warehouse. I went inside and there were no corpses on display. Nothing seemed out of place. I went down the aisle with Gordy right behind me until I came to the loading bay door. I was hoping it was mechanical and not electrical. I found the pull chain for the door on the right side and started raising the door, letting the light in. Once I got it up, I turned the flashlight off and moved to the second bay door and raised it.

Over in the right corner wall I found what I was looking for. There were eighteen full bottles of compressed air and six empty bottles in the small rack next to it. I started getting the full bottles off of the rack. There was a dolly by the bay door, and I went to get it. I got a bottle loaded and left the dolly where it was.

"I'm going to back the truck up to the loading bay," I told Gordon.

He nodded.

By the time I got the truck backed up to the loading bay, Gordy had eight of the bottles transferred from the rack to the loading bay. Within twenty minutes we had twelve bottles loaded and were afraid to put any more on the truck.

I told Gordon to go ahead and get outside that there was something that I had to get. He nodded and got in the truck and pulled it a little forward. I lowered the bay doors and switched the light back on.

I made it to the door and went back into the hallway. Thinking about where I was and remembering the layout of the hospital I needed to go to the right. I stepped around the corpses and took in the scenery, each visual display seeming to tell a more horrific story than the last. Every story drilled into my brain, and I felt the sorrow for the lost pilgrims. By the time I made it to the pharmacy, the corpses were almost stacked on one another.

The floor was slippery in places from the fluids and the insects. The flying ones flew away, and the crawlers scattered due to the disturbance. I did my best not to disturb any of the corpses and entered the pharmacy. It was in the big hall next to the emergency entrance which had some windows, and I could see enough to navigate through the store to the pharmacy counter.

I went through the door, and there was only one body in the pharmacy which had a lab coat on. He was diligent to the end, commendable. I found the drug section which was in alphabetical order and looked for the Presyscodine. There were three bottles of ninety counts, but one of the bottles was half-used.

That will get us through the winter plus some.

On the way back through the store, I found Baby Girl's favorite shampoo and got four bottles of it and three conditioners. That should get me in her good graces for a day or two, especially when she finds out she has another mouth to feed.

I worked my way back to the back door and eased out into the light. By the looks of it, had to be around 01:00 or 02:00. We got in the truck and headed for home.

Chapter 20: Goodnight Baby Girl

Blue was sleeping peacefully, and my mind was ready to succumb to the urgings of the sandman. I thought of Baby Girl and how her eyes softened when she started to glow. I blew her a kiss into the empty darkness.

I went to sleep that night like every other night, the most fortunate man in the world.

Chapter 21: Day 4, The Holy Grail

I woke up in total darkness with sounds of skittering and moaning all around me. I could not see them, but I knew they wanted me and Blue. I heard the door to the apothecary being pushed from the outside against the small aisle I placed in front of it about the same time Blue started to growl. He jumped forward.

"Come to me, Blue," I yelled.

Everything was in slow motion, and I was frantic trying to remember and locate the little flashlight that I had laid on the shelf when we went to sleep. The door had been shoved open, and I heard scraping sounds of something dragging itself across the floor. I was in a panic now trying to find the flashlight and old Beulah.

In the darkness I heard a yelping cry from Blue followed by a howl like I had never heard him make before. The next sound I heard was the sound of what I imagined as wolves feeding on a deer carcass.

My fear rose exponentially, and I feared the worst had happened to Blue; along with fear crept in anger. I ran my hands back and forth on the shelf and realized I was touching the second shelf. I dropped my hand down one shelf and immediately located the flashlight. I clicked it on long enough to locate Beulah.

The feeding sound was ongoing, and I got to my feet. I leveled Beulah and placed my hand with the flashlight on the pump action, turned it on and stepped around the end of the aisle. There were at least a dozen corpses bent over and feeding on what was left of Blue and another dozen plus trying to push into the room.

My anger at seeing Blue dead threw me into a rage; I started blasting away with old Beulah. The corpses feeding on Blue turned toward me and started walking and dragging themselves in my direction. They were all oozing a foul-smelling liquid. Some had maggots dripping from their eye-sockets, nose, and mouth. They all had wide grins on their faces as they started for me.

I emptied the remaining two loads of buckshot into them: four of them went down. Two of the four starting crawling toward me, and there were more behind them coming through the half open door. I ran back to the center of the aisle and grabbed my backpack. I went to the corner of the apothecary hoping they could not locate me.

I don't see how they can. They don't have any eyes.

My rational brain tried to tell itself that zombies were not real, but the sight of Blue being eaten ruled out rationality. I had found the shot shells in the bottom of the middle compartment and got old Beulah re-loaded, quietly, in the dark.

I shifted a shell into her barrel and listened. The sounds were coming closer and louder. I took a chance, leveled Beulah, and turned the light on.

I was cornered with at least fifty hungry corpses in the room coming straight for me. My heart was beating so fast that I thought I would have a coronary before they got to me. I let loose with Beulah and tried to flank around the left side to get to the door.

They closed in, and I was trapped.

I emptied Beulah again and started running towards the middle of them using Beulah as a club, but there were just too many. I was trapped, and Beulah was being held down by the arms trying to reach me. I started using my fists, but it was no use. They closed the gap, and I backed up, trying to find an escape route.

I tripped and landed on my back, and they closed in. I felt wetness on my face and knew this was the end for me. It was pitch black, and I fought the beasts for all I was worth. The wetness was still there, but I heard a squealing yelp.

I jerked awake and realized that Blue was trying to wake me up. I must have hit him. My heart was still beating the tom-tom boogie, and I was covered in sweat. I found the flashlight where it was and turned it on.

Blue had got over the punch I'd given him. He was no longer concerned; now he was tee-totally pissed. That was okay; he was still alive. I picked up Beulah and checked the door. Nothing had been disturbed, but the vision inside my head would not go away.

I set down with the light on and told Blue to come to me. He was reluctant, but he did.

"I am sorry, old boy," I said. "That was one of the worst dreams I have ever had."

He looked up like he knew all about it, but I still did not see any sympathy in his eyes.

Yes, sir, he was still pissed.

My heartbeat was finally starting to slow, but I was scared to turn off the light. Old Blue got over his mad spell. He did the hokey-pokey and lay back down on the electric blanket.

I looked at old-T, and if he knew anything at all, it was 3:30 in the morning. One thing was for sure. I would not be going back to sleep there. I might as well try to get what I came for and get the Hell out.

I got the last LED light out of my bag and made a survey of the apothecary. I knew there were probably candles out in the store, but there was no way in hell I was going out there.

I giggled to myself and thought about how many times Baby Girl told me those movies I like would give me nightmares. She tried to watch a couple of them with me and backed out every time. She didn't know it, but some of the books I've read scared me far worse than the movies ever could.

Kudos to you, Baby Girl. You got me on this one.

I found two jar candles on the counter desk, fumbled in the backpack, found the matches, and lit them. I wasn't much light, but it made me feel better. If the flashlight went out, I could find my way out.

I pulled out my cheaters; in my mind, I could hear Blue snickering. I started searching the enormous stock of drugs for Presyscodine.

Man, I wish I knew what some of these other ones were for. If I run across Valium, I think I might take a handful.

I continued the search; this was going to take a while.

Chapter 22: Gordon Moves In

When Gordon and I arrived home and I opened the truck door, Blue tripped and rolled trying to get to me. Baby Girl was laughing heartily until she heard the passenger side door open. She immediately grabbed the front of her shirt and pulled it together. That was a habit she has had for a long time. I guess it was something she watched Mrs. Emily do, and she can't help herself. I don't think she is aware she does it.

When she realized that it was Gordon, she smiled and opened her arms and gave him a hug. She saw the sorrowful look on his face and gave him an inquisitive look.

"No, ma'am, Ellie Belle is no longer with us," he said.

Baby Girl looked over at me, and even in the mid-afternoon sun, I could see the glow when she gazed at me.

"Fire up the generator and the water pump, and let's get Mr. Thompson here a hot bath started while I fix us up some dinner," she said.

And just like that- he was part of the family.

Baby Girl settled him in Darrell's old room, and he showed the respect and gratitude of a southern gentleman in her presence at all times. Once he had a regular bath and few meals in his belly, he started being the old Gordy that I knew.

Baby Girl pinned him one evening and got her scissors out and did a pretty good job with his hair and beard. He was serious when he needed to be, jovial the rest of the time.

I had to admit that he could out work me on most days.

The next morning, we got the air bottles out of the truck and stacked them up against the house. I went into the basement with Gordon, and we strung battery lights inside and ran the wire up to the inside of the house and sealed it off. It was not a very big basement.

We got into the booby hatch where it leads up to the basement door and insulated it. We laid out and installed a solid metal door to the bottom of the basement and completely sealed it off where it would be airtight. We worked on the door jamb of the top basement door and placed weather-stripping seals all the way around.

I drilled a hole through the washroom and into the basement through the booby hatch and installed PVC hard pipe from outside the house all the way through the basement where it was open ended.

I fitted a hard rubber balloon with a low-pressure gauge assembly inside the basement. We cleaned it up as well as we could and put a few chairs down there to rest on. We brought one cushioned armchair down there for Baby Girl.

I hooked up one bottle and opened it up and purged the basement area with positive pressure. We went into the staircase and closed the upper door to let it equalize and opened the lower door.

We went inside the basement, and for the first time in almost three months, we did not smell the strong essence of decay. The only scent of decay was when someone got close enough to you that you caught a slight drift from their clothes.

It was better than Christmas, and Baby Girl was happier about the basement than she was about the shampoo and conditioner.

When things got rough over the next two to three months and as fall set in, we would clean up and go down into the basement. I would purge the room and we would breathe the compressed air from the cylinders. For a few hours we could minimize the constant odor that stifled and threatened to smother us.

Gordon and I raided the stores and shops of all tangible goods and stockpiled them.

We collected gasoline in a large farming transport tank and set it up for use.

We located about fifty, five-gallon propane bottles and filled them all with propane at Dewey's Grocery and brought them home.

We cut numerous trees for firewood and stacked it in rows behind the tool shed.

We found three trailer houses and removed the standalone fireplaces from them. We installed two of them in the bedrooms and the other in the shop building.

We hunted, although there was very little game to be found.

We fished on several occasions and caught a good many. I would get out the fish cooker and fire it up when we did.

In one of the trailer houses, we found a long-range communication radio set up and brought it back to the house. It took a while, but we thought we had installed it properly. Every so often we would turn it on and see if anything or anyone was on the emergency broadcast station of the radio. We would not stay on it constantly because it was difficult to charge the twelve-volt battery.

During the runs for supplies, we would be happy sometimes and melancholy sometimes, but we always had each other's backs, no matter what.

On one run into town, there was a group of pilgrims headed west toward Dallas. We struck up a conversation with them and told the leader about the radio setup. He had heard that channel 19 was being monitored by all the citizen bands and others trying to communicate. It was the old truckers' channel, and everyone was used to it.

When we got home, we switched from the emergency transmission station to channel 19 and found chatter in all kind of places. Baby Girl was beside herself to be able to talk to another female, even if the rest of the world could hear the conversation.

Gordy started conversing with a man from Shreveport, Harley Swenson, about the area and whether he could get out and about in the area. After several days of conversing back and forth, Harley went to 3189 Anderson Lane in Shreveport to see what he could find in the house.

Harley was excited to report that either someone in the house had survived and then left or someone had looted the place and took only clothes and essentials with them.

Shortly after that, one night in the basement, Gordon looked at me and Baby Girl with a solemn expression.

"I love the both of you and cannot repay the kindness you've shown, but there is a chance. Not much of one, but a chance. When the dogwoods bloom in the spring, I am going to leave for Shreveport," he said.

The first winter was not all that bad; we survived it with grace and dignity. Gordy and I made a couple of more outings during those cold months.

On the last one, I had a specific chore in mind, and Gordy smiled when we walked into the Honda dealership. It took a while, but we got him a four-wheel drive side by side all-terrain vehicle running and full of fuel. It was cold, but he drove it all the way to the house.

"I had to break it in," he said.

Over the next few weeks, we installed a CB Radio with a whip antenna, a CD player, an extra battery, extra fuel storage, a four-thousand-pound winch, and a siren into the buggy.

We also fabricated a back panel with Plexiglas and silicone sealed the back of the buggy. Baby Girl made him a paint stencil, and he painted, *Dream Weaver,* across the back of the tail gate.

When the fruit trees started getting buds on them, I realized he wouldn't be around much longer. He was true to his word; it was the end when we saw the dogwood blooms.

"Dinky, I am going to head out in two days," he said.

Baby Girl spent the next day cooking flat bread for the road and a final meal to share with us. Me and Gordy and Blue spent the day getting spare fuel cans, extra drinking water, tarps, sleeping and cooking equipment, along with tools loaded into his vehicle.

Blue didn't know what was happening, but he made sure he got in the middle of whatever we were doing. Everything was ready except for his personal belongings which he will store where the passenger seat used to be.

That night we had a wonderful meal of pink salmon patties and angel hair pasta. Baby Girl opened a bottle of wine; we had a great evening.

We never spoke of whether he would find Sandy; it was not a place any one of us wanted to go. Baby Girl cleaned up the kitchen while Gordy and I went in the living room and relaxed. Blue came in and ran back and forth between me and Gordy.

Gordy smiled, looked down, and shook his head. He looked up, and for the first time in a long, while I saw tears in his eyes.

"Mr. Engelmann, I can never repay you or thank you enough for what you did for me and mine." He choked up a little but stated, "What you did that day for Ellie Belle was something most men would not have even considered, much less offered."

He was trying really hard to keep it together. He sniffed a couple of times.

"After all that, you took me in your home and saved me. You did save me, you know. I had already stuck that Glock in my mouth a half a dozen times," he said. He was starting to get it together. "In a few more days, I would have pulled the trigger."

He was silent for a minute, collecting his thoughts.

"I have nothing I can give you except that I will always love you and your family and would do anything I could to offer assistance if you are ever in need," he said respectfully.

I could tell he was sincere and didn't want to end the evening melancholy.

"Mr. Thompson, I pray that you find everything you are in search of, but I want you to know that if you ever feel the need and you are able to make it back, you have a home and family here," I said.

I realized just how much I was going to miss him. I cracked a joke to hide my feelings. "That is, as long as you will admit that I am the better fisherman."

"Never!" he said and laughed.

He left before daylight the next morning, and I'm guessing he pushed the buggy down the driveway before he cranked it. He called on the CB about 10:00 and told Baby Girl goodbye and that he would be out of his range before long. He bragged on the buggy and how good it was working out.

He had already had to go off road in two places but was making good time and thought he could make ten plus miles a day. Baby Girl told him to be careful and to return some day to see us, but we both felt we had seen Gordon for the last time.

Gordon Thompson was and always will be a friend of mine. I hope and pray that someday our Lord and Maker should see fit that we meet again.

Chapter 23: The Mother Lode

On the next to the last aisle after thinking I had wasted all my time and efforts, I found the Presyscodine.

There were eight bottles of one hundred eighty counts on the shelf with only one bottle being opened. I opened the lid and the tablets did not seem to be melting together or distorted in any way.

I closed the lid and let out a big, "Wahoo."

I heard Blue get up and trot over to where I was being careful in the dark. He looked up at me with the can-we-go-now look, and I reached down and gave him a great big all over scratching. I made sure I hit that sweet spot that made his back-leg quiver. I wanted him to be as happy as I was.

"Old boy, Percival has found the Holy Grail," I said and laughed.

When I finished the scratch, he stood and stretched, did the hokey pokey, and moved off. I guessed he went to look for a fire hydrant in the apothecary.

Reminder to self: watch for puddles and Hershey bars on the way out.

I loaded up the booty in my backpack, thinking I would need a bigger container and should look for one when I can. Maybe one of the backpacks on wheels. When you get tired of toting it, you can drag it awhile. I ended up with my jacket tied around my waist, and my blanket got left behind. The pack was too full. I grabbed old Beulah and my walking stick, whistled for Blue to come on, and went over to the little aisle.

The dream rushed back to me, and the images of the corpses were instantly vivid again. I pushed them back into the recess of my mind and bade them to stay there. I needed nothing to spoil the elation of the discovered bounty.

I really wanted to get away from this place and into the sunlight. Old-T said it 9:30.

I moved the small aisle and opened the door. The scene inside the pharmacy store was the same as I left it. I reminded myself that I really should quit reading those booger books.

We eased out of the store the same way we came in and made it to the hallway. It was obvious that some of the corpses had been disturbed since yesterday. My Sixth Sense was tingling. There was no doubt that we had been followed and watched.

"Stay close, Blue," I whispered and continued down the hallway.

I noticed the lock on the door that I checked yesterday had been busted, further evidence we weren't alone. The hair on the back of my neck was standing straight up now. I leveled old Beulah and opened the door.

In the glow of the flashlight, I found that this was a utility closet. Someone had spent the night in it. Whoever it was evidently meant us no harm but was probably watching our every move.

I eased the door back to and started down the hallway to the lobby. My steps were not as careful as before; I needed to get where there was light, telling myself to calm down and quit being so paranoid. When I got to the main lobby and into the window light, I felt better. I stopped at the edge of the hallway entrance and surveyed the area for signs of the living.

I found nothing but the dead staring back at me. We started for the door; every nerve in my body told me that I was being watched.

We worked our way through the maze of corpses and made it to the door. I was still paranoid but felt better. I needed to get outside; Blue had a nervous look about him as well. We made it to the congestion of vehicles and had to exit the same way we came in; up and onto the cars. Further into the parking lot we got to the area where we could navigate the maze from the ground.

I felt better and stopped to empty the old bladder. Blue saw me taking care of business and decided to moisten a couple of tires in the process. We worked our way on through the cars and toward the street entrance.

Blue looked like he was trying to find a vacated piece of ground; I stopped and looked the other way. Blue finished his ritual because he came up beside me, did the hokey pokey, and looked up at me with an inquisitive face.

"Okay, old boy. Let's go home," I said. "I'll bet Baby Girl has had enough of being by herself."

We made it to the street still weaving in and out of the vehicles, but it started opening up, allowing us to move a little faster. Old-T said it was 11:40.

"We're making good time Blue; we might get to see Miss Brittany again," I said. "How would you like that, old boy?"

I could have sworn that he nodded his head yes.

We were about three blocks from the park. I decided that if the deer was still there; I was going to kill one and take as much meat as I could handle to Benjie. I tried not to kill many animals at this point. Over the years since the Flip, I have discovered that only some of the offspring are in the immune category.

But if I could see that little girl smile with a full belly, I could die a happy man.

I told Blue to be on the lookout for game, and he sensed my meaning and went on ahead. He was staying out of sight and moving silently.

I might call that one Pink Alert Mode.

I heard something in the alleyway to my left that sounded like someone had tripped over some garbage and landed in it. I heard cussing and immediately looked for Blue. He switched to full alert mode but stayed where he was and tried to locate the source of the noise. I checked to make sure old Beulah was ready and set her up for quick shouldering if needed.

"Lord, please let this meeting be a friendly one," I prayed in a whisper.

Two men came out of the alleyway and were dressed in robes. The taller of the two was slender with long stringy hair and a beard. Even from the distance, I could tell that he had striking ice blue eyes. As he walked up, I noticed he carried what looked like a .357 magnum on his hip.

His companion was shorter and stockier. Other than being filthy, he had no discernable qualities other than a pistol in a shoulder holster and a sawed-off double barrel.

I glanced toward Blue without moving my head and seen that he had left the open and found a place to hide. I imagined that he was in full pink panther at this point.

"Stay hid, Blue," I whispered and kept my eyes on the gentlemen approaching.

"That's far enough, my friend," I said loudly.

The taller one laughed in a nonchalant way.

"There is no need for alarm, my son. I am the reincarnation of Jesus Christ," he stated with his voice soft and soothing. "Let me welcome you into the body of Christ."

He continued walking forward.

"That's far enough, Jesus," I said. "If you will be so kind, please go back where you came from. I will move along, and there will not be an issue here today."

He smiled and continued forward.

"I mean you no malice, but you will kneel before me and make offering to me in the manner that I see fit. It is God's will, and I am the representative of God."

I realized that it was the deity want-to-be practicing with his .357 that caused the damage I saw down the street. Another thing that I am pretty certain about was the second coming of Jesus. Jesus was going to return; he never said anything about reincarnation. Lastly, I could not imagine a world, not even this one, where Jesus Christ would need a .357.

I change to my stern voice.

"If you come any closer, I am going to find out if my Lord and Savior can bleed, I said. "If you are Jesus Christ, I must be long-lost son of Zeus."

I heard a window open in the building behind me; I was outnumbered. I hoped that I could get Jesus, and Blue could get the disciple before the sniper got me.

Jesus changed his voice to a harder tone.

"My son, there is a rifle on you right now. You will do as I command, or I will have to give your soul to Satan." He raised his voice, "Put down the gun and kneel before me."

"Okay, Okay!" I said, pretending to kneel. I went into to a sideways roll toward the cover of a Chevy pickup truck.

A rifle report rang out. The bullet missed me by inches, ricocheted off the pavement and plowed into an old Buick. Jesus was trying to get his .357 out of his holster. I prayed that Blue had the disciple.

From the ground, I raised Beulah and fired.

Jesus took the buckshot load in the chest and propelled backwards, his back landing on the fender of a BMW. He slumped down to a sitting position with a stupid look on his face.

Another report rang from the window; I was pinned down behind the Chevy.

The sniper positioned his body outside the window to try to get a better sight on me.

I heard a rifle shot from across the street.

The sniper dropped his rifle, clutched his chest, fell face first out of the window, and splattered on the sidewalk. It reminded me of the old Wild-West movie shoot outs where the one on the roof pitches forward and falls in the wagon load of hay. It would have been funny at any other time.

I never seen him, but I heard William's voice.

"I got him, D-D-Dixie," William yelled.

Damn Fool, you should be halfway to Langston.

"Get down, William!" I shouted as the disciple fire off the smoke pole.

That was the opportunity Blue had waited for. The next sound I heard will haunt me for the rest of my life. The disciple found himself knocked down with a bear trap placed on his throat.

He had time for one blood curdling scream before he no longer had a voice box.

When I peeked around the corner, he was on the ground and flopping like a fish out of water. Blue had another jaw grip and was holding the disciple down while trying to guard himself from the blows which didn't seem to have enough force in them to inflict much damage.

Blood gushed in and around Blues mouth, but he would not release his grip.

"Blue, away!" I hollered. Blue jumped back out the way and stationed behind the man's head to maintain watch.

The disciple was still pumping blood; there was nothing that could be done for him. He was diligent to the end and began to reach for the pistol in the shoulder holster. I moved in closer and leveled Beulah at him.

"Don't do it. Don't fight it; let it happen," I said.

He tried to raise his head to speak and realized he could not talk. With the amount of blood around him, I didn't see how he was still moving. I moved over to where he was, pulled the pistol and threw it out of reach.

His eyes started to glaze over; he would soon leave this world. I hoped he had something set up on the other side. I knelt beside him.

"For God so loved the world, he gave his only begotten son that whosoever believeth in him should not perish but have everlasting life," I prayed. "Do you believe that Jesus Christ is your Lord and Savior?"

He could not speak and very weakly nodded.

"You are absolved of your sins and can enter the glory of heaven," I said.

He was gone, but before the gurgling and blood flow stopped, I thought I saw him smile.

"Father," I prayed. "I sure hope and pray that I didn't just overstep my boundaries. If I did, I pray that you can forgive me." I glanced at Blue. He was still alert but relaxing and I stood up.

I heard a moan over to my right and remembered William. When I got to him, he was sitting with his back to the panel truck; blood oozed out of his upper stomach and chest. He had been shot with game load, but at that range it was just as deadly.

When I got to him, he looked at me and smiled.

"You said if you ever laid eyes on me again that you would kill me," he said with a shit-eating grin.

He laughed and coughed up a wad of blood and spit it out.

"You damn fool, I told you to go to Langston. What are you doing here?" I said.

"I followed you. I had never had anyone show me the kind of man I needed to be before. I did like you said and buried Byron, but when I got back to the road, I knew I had to find you again and thank you for what you done. I think it was that one 30-30 bullet sitting on the table that did it," he said tenderly.

He started to hitch in gulps of air and bloody froth started to form around the edge of his mouth. I knew what was coming; I let him get everything off his chest.

"I caught up with you when you came out of the store building at Good Falls and followed you," he said.

He snickered and looked up at me.

"I still can't believe I actually hit the sumbitch," he laughed, which caused another coughing fit.

"You nailed him good, and by the way, my name is Dinky," I said in a lowered voice.

He started to laugh again, and an enormous coughing fit followed. He blew pink bubbles like a baby now. He was fading away.

"William, do you want to pray together for your soul?" I asked him.

"Naw, Dinky, I made my bed and will leave it to the powers that be," he said.

"William, I thank you for the sacrifice you made you here today, and I will pray for your soul," I said.

"Dinky, if you want to help me, bury the girl," he said, barely making voice.

"You have my word, William," I said.

He seemed to be content with the decision he had made. I guess William will forever be a follower, even in the afterlife. I stayed with him. Within the next couple of minutes, he drifted off to the sleep that you don't wake up from.

His soul is free, and I hoped he'd make it to a good place. Blue walked over and sniffed William trying to figure out why I was being kind to him. He looked at me with the inquisitive sad eyes.

"It's okay, Blue; he wasn't a bad man, just misguided," I said.

I thought about dragging him to the park and burying him but didn't have a clue as to where to find a shovel. If I wanted to make it back to Benjie's, I had to leave.

I opened the back of the panel van and found it mostly with tools and trash. I lifted William up until I got him inside. Just because I wanted to, I recited the Lord's Prayer and closed the doors on William.

No one but Blue and I will ever know the story of William, but he had found his own place of honor in the end.

I walked over to where Jesus lay to see if he was still with us. He had gone over, but I felt the person he impersonated wouldn't take kindly to his impression. I left him next to the Beamer and hoped his ghost could still hear me.

"Tell Lucifer that I said, hello."

I picked up old Beulah and the walking stick, situated my backpack for comfort and looked at Blue. I had to find some water to wash the blood off before Brittany saw him. We headed down the street side by side this time toward the park. I am sure with all the commotion; the animals are long gone.

It never hurts to try though.

When we got to the park, I noticed there was some water in the fountain base. It wasn't pretty, but it would do to clean Blue. Blue and I were in the pink feline mode as we snuck up on the park entrance.

There were four does in the right side of the park, about in the same place they were the day before. There was an entrance to the park on the left-hand side, and it looked like there was fence everywhere else. We moved through the entrance, and I went toward the right to keep limited sight of me while I crept upon the deer.

Blue went to the left toward the left entrance and as he approached, they started to get really nervous. The lead doe threw her head forward and wheezed a warning to the others. She through her tail up but did not run. She started moving toward the left entrance. Blue blocked her path, and she wheezed again.

She took off toward the main entrance followed by the other three. Blue came in behind them but not enough to crowd them. When the third one got broadside to me old Beulah roared. The doe rolled up, and Blue was on her in about one second.

He grabbed her throat and clamped down.

She tried to get back up but could not get her feet under her with Blue in the way.

How he knows where to stand when he is doing this amazes me.

He clamped even harder, locked and braced his legs, and started shaking his head really hard. That's when the flesh, jugular, and windpipe came out with one large pull.

I was not going to have to use another shot on her.

She was bleeding down rapidly now and was just kicking and twitching every so often. Blue stepped back to watch her making sure it was over. It was.

I did a field dress and removed the tenderloins and a hindquarter. I let Blue have whatever else he wanted. I wrapped the meat up in my jacket and hoped that the weather stayed mild. I took the bailing wire and secured it to my backpack; we started forward again.

By the time we made the front entrance, there were three or four cats moving in on the carcass. Old Blue turned around with his hair rising up on his back.

"Not this time, boy. We have to go," I told him. He made a low growl to show his disappointment and then turned around and caught up with me.

I stopped by the fountain and moved some of the debris from the top of the water; it wasn't as bad as I thought. I cleaned Blue's face and neck and removed most of the blood. He gave me the stink-eye and did the hokey pokey right next to me to make sure I got some of the water on me too.

We got back to the street and restarted the maze travel through the street back out to the highway. Old-T said it was 3:40; we had to hook it up if we were going to see Miss Brittany tonight.

We got back to the highway and the lanes opened up enough to start a good pace. We headed toward the Country Club.

The Walkin' man struts with a swagger and a giggle
The Walkin' man and Blue is bringing home the meat.
The Walkin' man strides with a hop and a wiggle
Venison gravy and mashed potatoes are hard to beat.

Nothing else got in our way and the weather was pleasant for the walk. We made it to the Country Club at 7:30 according to Old-T. I went back to the path where Benjie was staying and about to give up and turn around when I heard a voice say.

"Dinky, is that you?" Benjie asked.

I turned toward the voice and shined the flashlight in my own face to let him know that it was me. I shined the light, and Benjie was behind a red oak tree with his firearm at rest.

"I come bearing gifts," I said and laughed, taking the blood-soaked backpack off. "I hope you haven't had supper yet."

"You're a day late and a dollar short," he said. We both laughed like old friends.

The screen door opened, and Miss Brittany was on the porch with her little flashlight. Blue let out a bark and took off like a rocket toward that little girl. Benjie picked up the backpack, and we headed toward the house.

Belinda was excited about the fresh venison.

"Put it in the kitchen, Dinky," she said, "and get out of those clothes. There's warm water and towels in the bathroom." She brought me a pair of bib overalls, a flannel shirt, and underwear to put on. I took it all to the bathroom, did a fair clean up, and put the new clothes on.

It wasn't a bad fit if I have to say so myself.

When I got back to the living room, Brittany and Blue were having a ball. I stopped in the hallway for a minute just to watch the two of them. Benjie saw me watching them.

"It does the old heart good, doesn't it?" he said.

"It sure does that, my brother." I nodded.

We went in the kitchen where Belinda was cleaning up and slicing the tenderloin into medallions. She looked over at us.

"Well, Dinky, you clean up pretty good." She then put her hands on her hips and said laughing, "Get out of my kitchen, both of you."

We got us each a glass of sweet tea and headed out of the kitchen. We ended up on the porch again and within a matter of minutes there was an odor. A smell that my Dad would have said could make you, "slap your grandma." I didn't realize that I was hungry until my nose got a whiff of that venison being seared.

"Figured out where you are going, yet?" I asked Benjie.

"No Sir. Not yet," he said.

"I'm not one for butting in another man's business, but there is an abandoned farm next to my place." Before he could butt in, I said. "I have good stock of food, more than enough for you and your family to make it through next winter. The offer is open if you have a mind to come."

He thought for a minute and said he would talk to Belinda about it tonight and let me know in the morning. We talked and laughed at Brittany and Blue until she got tired and went inside. Blue looked at me, and I nodded so he followed her.

In about an hour Belinda brought us both a plate of venison medallions and gravy, two wine glasses and a bottle of Merlot. It was better than I could imagine, and I made a complete pig out of myself. The time was spent with good food and good people.

It was better than any Old Milwaukee commercial I had ever seen.

She saved old Blue a bowl and put it on the porch for him when he wanted it. He inhaled it on his next visit outside.

We ate and had some more conversation while we finished off the Merlot. I recited the story of Jesus and the disciples and how William had saved my butt when he shot the sniper. I gave him the condensed version of how I had met William and why he was there. I let him know that my quest was successful, and I got an extremely good supply of Presyscodine.

He stated that he had heard an engine earlier in the day and that was why he snuck up on me when I came back.

We did the same routine except I had to get Blue off the couch with Brittany before he could pick her up. I took him outside, and we both did our relief in the darkness. I bedded down in the comfortable linens. Blue did the hokey pokey and jumped up in the bed. I blew out the candle Belinda had left for me.

I went to sleep that night like every other night, the most fortunate man in the world.

Chapter 24: Day 5, Greetings My Lady

I got up the next morning before the rooster crowed. Old Blue shook himself out and stretched; he was ready. Inside the bedroom door, my clothes and jacket were folded up nice and neat. They had been washed. Belinda had been up all night to get this done.

The house was still asleep, and I wanted to get an early start. I pulled the map I had found in the camper and laid it on the table. I dug a writing pen and my flashlight out of my backpack and circled the town of Barkston and put an "X" on where my property was.

I wrote Benjie a note:

This is where I am heading. You are welcome here anytime. I cannot thank you enough for your hospitality. You will remain in my heart and in my prayers. Give Brittany a kiss from me and Blue ……. Dinky.

We eased out the door and towards the entrance to the Country Club Road. I was ready to see my Baby Girl.

The Walkin' man steps with the knowing in his heart

My Baby Girl; she sure is a good'un

The Walkin' man yearns for the glow of love to start

And wishes for a bate of Shaky pudding.

With my backpack and old Beulah across my shoulders and the trusty old walking stick, we headed south on the highway, and I struck up a pretty good rhythm. Old Blue was full of piss and vinegar and headed on up a way. He investigated this and that but never got out of my sight. He had to let me catch up a time or two and this irked him.

If I wasn't in a hurry to see Baby Girl, I would have slowed down even more.

The spring morning was perfect, had the right temperature for walking, and there wasn't a cloud in the sky. It would probably be a warmer one later in the day. I figured I could make it to the country store at Good Falls.

Maybe one of the vehicles would crank on the back side of the traffic congestion. If I could find a truck, there are a few items in the old store I would like to bring home, or at least closer to home. The chance of that was doubtful. If the battery was good enough to turn it over, most engines would have gummed up carburetors.

I walked through forest on this stretch and looked at the canopy of the oaks and the hickories. They were so beautiful when they started putting leaves on.

I must have slowed down a bit more because Blue was parked on his butt in the middle of the road and looking at me with his worried face.

"Okay, okay," I said.

Before I got to him, he stood up but didn't do the hokey pokey. He was more focused than normal, but not alarmed. He stepped in front of me and made me stop.

I reached down and scratched him behind the ears.

"What is it, boy?" I whispered.

He started into the woods and stopped and turned around to look at me. That was his sign for me to follow. I took old Beulah off my shoulder and started easing toward the woods. Blue stayed in the lead but stopped to let me catch up every few feet.

We came to a clearing about eighty yards into the woods. Blue kept easing forward and then stopped. I eased up toward him when I heard it, a low faint crying. On the edge of the clearing, near the creek that runs on the backside, there was an animal in distress.

I instantly got in the Pink Panther mode and started easing toward the sound. Blue stayed close by my side but didn't seem to be on alert. I crept up to a large white oak trunk and peered around the other side.

There was an old fence running the edge of the clearing and the creek. It was long ago abandoned but the wire was visible in places. About twenty yards down was a dog that was wrapped up in the loose wire and could not get away from it.

From the looks of it, the poor animal had been there a couple of days and was completely exhausted from the struggle of trying to free itself. The ground around where it lay was clean down to the bare earth.

It was coated with dirt and spots of blood from the cuts, but by my guess, it was something close to a mountain cur. Other than weak and entangled, it seemed to be intact.

The thought crossed my mind to put it out of its misery and keep walking, but there was no way I was going to do that with Blue watching.

Blue eased toward the animal; it noticed him and started a low growl in its throat. Blue whined and approached the dog, cowering down to let it know it meant no harm. He made sure he kept his distance enough not to let it start struggling and stayed in front so it could see him.

I eased up and knelt down beside Blue and started stroking his fur and his head. The low growl was still rumbling, but I sensed the change in the growl tone.

It was too tired to put up much of a fuss, but it would if it had to.

I removed the backpack very slowly and eased it to the ground and took the water bottle out of it. I poured some water in my hand and offered it to Blue who lapped it up immediately. I was not foolish enough to stick my hand in front of this one yet and looked in the backpack for something to pour some water in. I found the last can of Spam.

"How bad do you want to do this?" I looked at Blue.

He looked up at me, and I knew this was going to happen. I opened the can of Spam.

I took my Old Timer folding knife and cut a sleeve off my old jacket and poured the contents of the Spam can onto it. I cut me and Blue a piece of it, and Blue's disappeared like a dust bunny in a vacuum cleaner.

I got down on my hands and knees and started easing the meal towards the poor animal. I made eye contact the whole time. The low growl increased as I got closer, but it did not try to move yet. When I got close enough, I took my walking stick and pushed the meal close enough for it to reach it with its mouth.

It sniffed the Spam and immediately started gulping it down. Well, it was more like the same vacuum cleaner that Blue used. When it was gone, the dog started licking the sleeve. I took the Spam can and poured it half full of water and pushed it to the sleeve, getting a little closer this time.

A closer look determined the dog was a gyp with a white face, three sock feet and blue eyes. She was definitely a type of cur, probably mountain cur.

The growl had stopped when the eating started, and she didn't see the need to start up again. It looked to be painful, but she repositioned where she could lap the water in the can. When she repositioned, I got a little closer. I was within reach of her, but I didn't attempt it.

When she finished with the water, I talked to her in a soft cooing voice and eased my hand toward her palm down to see if she would sniff it. She jerked back and then looked straight into my eyes. I looked straight back at her.

"If you want get out of this, my lady, you are going to have to trust me," I told her.

It took what seemed like ten minutes for her to come around, but she finally sniffed my hand and let me stroke the top of her head.

She seemed to give up and allowed me to gently rub her head. I got a little closer.

If knew if I hurt her with the wires, I might get bit. I continued to talk and rub and moved a little farther down her body until she got used to me.

She had gone through a rusted part of the fence net that constricted her after her front legs and before her back legs. The movement of the struggling only made the constriction worse. There were cuts on her in multiple places from the wire around her mid-section.

I eased away from her and went to the backpack and rummaged around in it. I retrieved my Leatherman Tool from the front zip pocket. I took the tool out of its case, unfolded it, and tried the functionality of the pliers.

I hoped I could cut the wire with it.

I eased back over to her and put some more water in the Spam can and rubbed on her while she drank. I started talking to her again and told her this might hurt in a couple of places. I rubbed and soothed with one hand as I worked the pliers under the wire with the other.

The old wire was pretty rusty, and I was able to cut the first piece of net from her. She sensed what I was doing because she became still and laid her head down. She was looking toward Blue. He sat like a statue and gazed back at her with his sympathy eyes.

The second piece was tight on her body. It hurt her when I worked the pliers under the wire. She whimpered and lifted her head back toward me but did not struggle. I looked straight into her blue eyes.

"I'm sorry, my lady; I have to do this," I cooed to her.

The second section cut and eased the tension enough that I could work the pliers under the rest of it.

I slowly worked until I had all the wire cut away from one side. She should be free at this point.

I eased my hands under the top of her back and started easing up on her.

She got her feet under herself and stood up on shaky legs but stood up. I continued to stroke her and talk to her.

Blue eased up a little more towards her so she could take in his smell for approval or disapproval.

She stepped forward out of the fence.

I poured more water into the Spam can and offered it to her. She drank some and then turned away from the can. I offered the rest to Blue who got what he could.

I rubbed her some more.

"My lady, if you can make it, you are welcome to join us," I whispered to her. "If you can put up with the old shit eater, that is."

Blue gave me the stink-eye, but he was content with what we had done. I stood up and placed my backpack in position.

 "I hope it was worth it, that was our supper and most of the water," I told Blue.

He didn't comment either way. I picked up old Beulah and the walking stick and eased back toward the highway.

Lady looked exhausted and confused, but Blue got close to her. They sniffed each other and communicated in the way that dogs do. I don't know what he told her, but she made her decision to follow along with us.

I wanted to tell him that it was my Spam and not his charm that brought her along, but I didn't. We made it to the highway and struck out south again.

The Walkin' man creeps, brought the stride to a crawl
The Walkin' man is waiting on a lady
The Walkin' man hopes he can make Good Falls
And for Blue to quit acting like a baby.

The pace was slow, and Blue helped her keep up.

So much for making a good distance today; we might have to hunt for our supper tonight. On top of that I have to explain to Baby Girl why I now own a jacket with one sleeve.

We made about a mile, and Lady started to lag behind. Old Blue would run up to me and run back to her. He was covering twice the ground that I was, so I stopped in front of an old drive way by a big mailbox made into a brick column.

I cleaned off a spot on the ground, took off the old backpack and settled in with my back to it. Blue was nervous and brought Lady to where I was.

She didn't get close until I brought out the water bottle and the Spam can. Blue and Lady drank until the water was gone.

I started to open the last bottle we had. It occurred to me that we might better hold off on that. I could tell she was stiff, but she was a fighter, and I hoped she would make it.

She laid down about five feet away from me. Blue did the hokey pokey, of course, and lay beside me. I rubbed his head and scratched behind his ears.

He didn't fool me. He did it to show her that I could be trusted, the old shit eater.

Old-T said it was 10:35, and I closed my eyes for a few minutes and just listened to the sounds. There was no rumble of engines from a vehicle. There was no hum from the power lines over my head. There was no sound of a jumbo jet flying over. No sound at all of the old society that we had grown so accustomed to.

I kept my eyes closed and smiled.

I philosophized that Mother Nature and the Big Man had seen enough of what humans could do to this planet. I don't think there was anything that could have been done by the experts and the doctors. This fate was written and now recorded as history. They put in their hand of cards enough humans to repopulate if the human race can learn from its mistakes and become humble.

I opened my eyes and looked up to the heavens.

"Whatever your will is Father, I will try my best."

A reckoning enveloped my heart; Blue and I were destined to find Lady and take care of her. Much like Tennyson's charge of the 600; the reason why was not mine to ask, just to do. I looked over at her and my old heart just melted. I started thinking about some type of wagon I could carry her in, if I had to.

She slept, a much-needed rest, so I closed my eyes and let her charge her batteries.

I allowed my mind to drift to a happy place. One of my favorites, the summer I was sixteen and headed into my junior year at Barkston High.

Chapter 25: Skinny Dipping

"Jason, get over here," I whispered, waving for him to be quiet. Shh!" I put my finger to my lips.

He plowed through the bushes and sounded like a herd of elephants to my ears. When he got beside me, he saw what I was looking at and got as quiet as a church mouse.

We heard the giggling and the splashing and decided we would sneak up on them and surprise them. What we didn't know was that they were in the middle of Big Rocky skinny-dipping.

It was Sarah, Melanie, Angie Buxton, and Carla Spencer, four of the eight girls on the Barkston High cheerleading squad. Jason looked like he was going to have a heart attack right there on the spot. His eyes were kind of glassy, and he was like a statue behind those bushes. He looked over at me, and the biggest grin came across his face.

I knew in that moment that whatever it was he concocted was not good.

I shook my head but that didn't faze him. He had developed a plan in his brain and nodded his head. He motioned for me to back out, and we eased back toward the trail.

When we got out of hearing range, he looked at me with immense excitement in his eyes.

"Let's sneak up on them and jump in the water." Getting more excited, he said, "We can climb around to the cliff back side and jump in at the same time. That should scare the hell out of them for sure"

"Let's just leave and come back later making a lot of noise so they will get out and get their swimsuits back on. I really don't want to piss Sarah off," I told him.

"Man, you are such a wuss. Do what you want to, but I am going to jump off that cliff right in the middle of them." He laughed, low.

There was no way I could talk him out of it, and I damn sure wasn't going to be left out. Jason would have told everybody, and they would have harassed me for the rest of the summer, probably half the semester too.

"Okay, let's do it, but I am keeping my suit on," I said.

"Okay, wussy, as long as it is your birthday suit."

We took our time and were very quiet as we eased around to the other side of Big Rocky. We heard them splashing and laughing in the pool.

"When we get there, we strip down and jump at the same time, got it," he whispered.

"Got it," I said, but I had no intention of jumping from ten foot in my birthday suit.

The moment came and by-golly, he stripped down to the Good Lord's Glory.

"Come on," he mouthed.

I stripped down to my swimsuit, and he pointed for me to take them off, and I shook my head no. He rolled his eyes and shrugged his shoulders. I caught hell about it later.

"On three," he mouthed at me and stuck his hand out to show one finger. I hoped that we didn't land on top of one of the girls, especially old nut sack next to me.

He stuck his hand out with two fingers and made a fist and stuck his hand out with three fingers, and we both took off for the edge.

No turning back now and leaped as high in the air as we could.

I could see the shocked look of surprise in the girl's eyes before I hit the water and heard the high pitch squeals that I know fulfilled all of Jason's dreams.

When we came up three of the four girls scrambled for the bank, Jason whooped and hollered. "Ya'll come back now, ya hear!"

The only one left in the pool was Sarah; she was shoulder deep and had a stern look on her face.

It was a certain look that I became somewhat accustomed to in years to come.

She brought one hand out of the water and gave me the index finger, come-here, wiggle. The laughter and joy that I felt turned into an Oh-Shit, in my mind.

I eased toward her not knowing if I was going to get slapped or cussed or both. Didn't matter, I had made my bed. When I got directly in front of her, she reached both arms around my neck and pulled me close to her. I could feel her breasts pressing into my chest when she kissed me in the middle of Big Rocky.

Jason and the other three girls on the bank were dumb struck at what was happening. She gave me the Old-Frenchy, and my blood was about to boiling point. She pressed further into me, and I was getting into the kiss. There was no mistaking she felt the growing protrusion that was between us.

When she reached her desired objective, she pulled both arms from around my neck and backed up, slow enough that I got a good look at those beautiful floatation devices she carried around with her.

She looked straight at me with those Baby Blues.

"Go get my suit for me, please," she said. It was not a question nor was it avoidable. I lowered my head; I didn't have a choice.

Her friends were going to laugh and talk about the Boner for days to come. I hoped it would calm down before school started back up. I headed up and out of the water acting like I carry a tent pole with me everywhere I go.

 "Is this the one?" I asked. Sarah was turning beet red in the face, but she kept her composure.

"Yep, that's it," she said.

I eased back into the water, still at full extension, and started walking towards her.

It might take a week before this thing goes back down.

When I got close to her, I threw the bikini bra over my shoulder and held the briefs in front of me on both sides and walked around behind her instead of coming straight at her.

She understood what I intended to do, and the beet red turned into fire engine red. I came up behind her, laid her bikini bra over her shoulder and pressed against her to let her feel the extent of her shenanigan's one more time and then took a giant breath and went under water.

I opened my eyes and pulled up on her right foot and placed it through the brief, pulled up her left foot and put it in the brief. She did not move to assist so I pulled them up to above her knees and come up for air. I reached down and pulled them on up to the proper placement.

No, it will be a month before the circus tent comes down.

I eased around to face her and took the bikini bra off of her shoulder and opened it up for her to step into. I reached my arms around her and hooked it in the back, again making sure she again felt the result of her actions.

When I was done, I lowered my hands to her waist on both sides and drew her to me and kissed her like the world was coming to an end in the next ten minutes. I withdrew and stepped back and asked in a voice loud enough for the onlookers to hear.

"Better now?"

"Better," she said in full blush.

The three girls on the bank were recovering from the Sarah-Dinky show and turned their attentions to poor old Jason.

"Go and get your suit on, Jay. We are not getting in this water until you do," Melanie said.

Jason turned and looked at me with an inquisitive look, and I read his mind.

"Not a chance in hell, Jay!" I said laughing. I got behind Sarah and wrapped my arms around her.

He glanced downward and started for the cliff. He made his way to the cliff side and started finding nooks and crannies to put his feet and hands into to make the climb. His back was to us, but I could see the girls checking him out. Melanie was beaming while never taking her eyes off of him. She really did like him, even though she tried not to show it.

From the looks of the climb, old Jason had to be dragging his ding-a-ling on the rocks, and I thought I saw him wince a time or two.

I know without a doubt that when he dragged that hairy ass over the top, he scraped the jewels.

He disappeared behind the top of the rock face, and I was happy just being there with my arms around Sarah.

"Thanks for keeping your suit on," she whispered to me.

"Thanks for letting me put your suit on," I said and gave her a tighter hug.

I didn't show her who was boss, but I didn't get the blunt end either.

About the time I released her from the hug I heard a mighty yell of, Geronimo, followed by a splash. I thought he was going to knock all the water out of the pool. He came up out of water and flashed that big old shit-eating grin at Melanie.

She started wading out into the water towards him.

They didn't get as intimate as Sarah and I did, but they did some playful touchy-feely stuff in the water, and we all had a blast for the next hour or so.

Sarah kissed me again before they left. "Come see me when you can," she whispered.

"Yes, ma'am. Would Friday night be too soon?"

"Call me tomorrow" she said and kissed my cheek.

That was the day my life started, without Baby Girl, I would be nothing.

Melanie gave Jason a hint of a kiss, and you would have thought he made the game winning touchdown.

I did go over to Sarah's house a few times before school started, and by the time Charlie Brown rendezvoused with the Great Pumpkin, we were inseparable.

Chapter 26: A little Rest for Lady

I must have dozed off during my trip down memory lane. Old -T said it was 12:05 and I felt like I was super charged. Blue picked his head up and looked at me and then turned to look at Lady who was not stirring at all. I sat back down beside him.

"We'll give her another ten minutes and then we have to go," I whispered, stroking his head.

He looked at me with what seemed to be total understanding of what I meant and laid his head back down on his paws. He didn't close his eyes though, and it looked like he was in deep thought. I reached over and gently stroked him and scratched behind his ears, which always made things better. He let out a great sigh.

About ten minutes later, I told him we had to go.

I got up and started getting my things together. I put on my backpack and old Beulah but left the walking stick leaned up on the mailbox. I walked over to Lady, who heard me coming and lifted her head. As I approached, she stood up and moved backwards while keeping her eyes on me the entire time. I slowly eased up to her and placed my hand out palm down for her to sniff.

She seemed nervous but smelled the back of my hand. I gently started to rub her down, checking for swelling and open cuts. She seemed to be in pretty good shape except for being hungry and weak. I got out the Spam can and opened the last bottle of water looking over at Blue. He had the big eyed worried look on his face.

I had to giggle to myself.

"Old boy, I do believe you are twitter-pated," I told him.

Lady drank what she wanted, and I gave the rest to Blue. I took one little sip and felt I had better save the rest. I can get some more in the old country store at Great Falls if we ever make it there.

I headed over to the mailbox and got the old walking stick and eased out to the highway. Lady was reluctant at first but started following me. Blue started his forward and back routine again making sure she stayed up with us. I figured that I was about five miles to Good Falls with another four to spend the night with Mrs. Balderdash again. Nine miles is doable if Little Lady can keep up. I got settled and took in the stride.

The Walkin' man steps with the knowing in his heart
My Baby Girl's the greatest of the women
The Walkin' man yearns for the glow of love to start
If only I could get her to go swimmin'.

I got into rhythm and started pounding the road. I glanced back at Lady from time to time and she was holding her own. I was more worried about Blue and his persistent zig-zag between me and Lady. He was travelling twice as far as me and Lady were.

I began to drift back in time again.

Chapter 27: The Piggly Wiggly

The smell was still lingering but not as rich as it had been except for an occasional strong whiff that would drift by. Baby Girl decided to come into town with me, so I fired up the Ford and left my wagon in the shed this time.

Baby Girl had been out before and had seen the horrors of the Pentacle Virus firsthand, so I didn't think twice about it. I loaded up my favorite shot gun and placed it on the seat next to me. I went in and told Baby Girl and Blue to load up, and they got in the truck. Baby Girl sat next to the passenger window and Blue in the middle, looking like a bobble head doll trying to look at everything at the same time.

The old shit-eater could be so comical at times.

I eased off down the driveway in the late morning light on a still day with very few clouds in the sky. We had the windows rolled down and was letting the breeze blow through the cab of the truck. Old Blue got in Baby Girl's lap and had his head stuck out of the window to get even more wind across his face. Even the trees that had put on new leaves seemed to be smiling. I knew this would not last when we got closer and the corpses started being visible.

I was content to be happy for the moment, and I reached over and placed my hand under Baby Girls hair on the back of her neck and gently rubbed. She turned her head into my hand in the jester of a hug, and my heart was filled with love all over again.

"We are almost to Big Rocky, want to go swimming?" I looked at her.

She blushed and gave me a hard stare before she broke out into a grin.

"Never again, Mr. Englemann," she said. "Never again."

I laughed and gave her my poochy-lip.

Everything was as good as it can get as we travelled towards Barkston. We talked and laughed and played touchy-feely for another couples of miles, and then the cars on the road shoulder started getting packed. The drive became the obstacle course I had become accustomed to with the slow down for the stranded vehicles in the road.

The talk and play ceased, and the attitude become somber. Even Blue had settled down and lay in the middle of the truck seat.

I got the Ford to within a half a block of the Piggly Wiggly and turned it around in a NAPA Auto Parts driveway. I backed it up as close as I could get to the Pork House.

The parking lot at the Piggly Wiggly could have been navigated if not for the cars in the main street that blocked the driveway. It began as a fender bender during the last days and escalated to a comprehensive free-for-all vehicular pile-up.

When the wreck happened, the panicked drivers in the other cars never stopped and never quit making attempts to get around it. There were vehicles that had scraped each other and blocked each other off until there ended up being a total pile up of cars. The pile was so compacted that they couldn't have opened the car doors.

The pilgrims were trapped inside and that is where they stayed for the most part. There were some windows rolled down. Some had climbed out of a coffin that moments prior was their means of escape.

The Flip

The solemn stare and misty eyes told me that the gears ground in Baby Girl's mind. She deciphered the final moments of this catastrophe as well. We walked around the pile up and made it to the fence bordering the Piggly-Wiggly and Jacobsen's Hardware. I had cut through the hurricane fence on earlier trips with me and Gordon. We went through and made our way to the door.

I tried to make light of the visual surroundings.

"Buggy, ma'am?" I said in my best Salesman Sam voice, pushing a shopping cart in front of her.

"Here at Piggly-Wiggly we strive to provide the best products and service in the South," I said and flashed a big old Salesman Sam grin. She was not overly impressed but played along.

"Thank you, kind sir!" she said. We giggled a bit and headed into the store.

The automatic doors had already been pried open and wedged. We rolled on through.

I noticed animal droppings in the second aisle that did not look like it came from a small animal. There were tracks on the floor that looked like a large dog but from the skid marks it was dragging one of its legs.

"Baby Girl, you and Blue come back outside for a minute," I said.

All I had with me was my .22 pistol, and I didn't want to take the chance.

"Blue, watch Baby Girl."

I headed back to the truck, got the shotgun, and rechecked the magazine. I went back to Pork House and stuck the shotgun in the buggy. We started for the direction of the can goods which was what we were after.

The rotten food and decayed corpse stench of the building had diminished but was definitely not extinct. We planned to be in and out as quick as possible. Most items had been picked over, predominantly by me and Gordon. We wiped out the remainder of the veggies and the canned meat. We checked the expiration dates on them, but it would not have mattered.

I brought a flashlight, but we didn't need it until we got in the back of the store. Baby Girl wanted some toiletries that were on the back wall.

I was thankful that the pilgrims that expired in the Piggly Wiggly concentrated near the checkout and not in the aisles. We went back and forth through the aisles like we did before the Pentacle and loaded the buggy with anything salvageable.

The only difference was the absence of the checkout line.

Baby Girl didn't talk or smile; she went straight to the business at hand and wanted to be finished with this chore as soon as possible. She was shining the flashlight on the toothpaste and shampoo when I heard a low growl start in Blues throat.

He immediately got in between the end of the aisle and Baby Girl. I could not see it yet, but something was growling back at Blue in the same tone.

I moved up beside Baby Girl, took the flashlight, and shined it towards the end of the aisle with my shotgun leveled. Blue was on point but did not proceed any further. I started easing down the aisle.

"Stay with her," I whispered to Blue.

I got close to the end of the aisle that at one time was filled with rice, sugar and dry beans. I shined the light toward the last place I heard the sound. I saw the poor animal. It stood close to the end of the rack on the left side.

The light did not bother the poor thing, and it did not shy away nor leave. I tried to decide if it was a threat or not; it was obvious that it was in a bad way.

At one time this was probably a prize Labrador, but now it was a bag of bones in a skin shell. There were hair patches missing on its back and side. The back-right leg had been broken.

I couldn't stand to see it suffer any more and took aim. The sound of the shotgun within the building was deafening. I had not thought about that.

Baby Girl screamed, but I didn't hear it until she screamed again. I heard the sounds coming from the other end of the aisle. I ran toward Baby Girl and got in front of her. Blue and a Doberman Pincher were fighting and going at it full bore.

I raised my shotgun. I could not get a clear shot without hitting Blue. I started towards them and was yelling at Blue to come to me.

Blue was protecting Baby Girl; no amount of yelling was going to stop him until the Dobie was dead or he was.

I closed the distance to determine how to get Blue away from the Doberman.

Blue pinned the Dobie down on the floor and went for his throat. I got in between Baby Girl and the dogs to keep her from seeing what her little boy was about to do. It didn't matter. It happened too fast, and she watched as Blue clamped down on the Doberman's throat. Blue shook his head powerfully, virtually ripping the Dobie's throat out.

There was blood everywhere. Baby Girl looked shell shocked at what Blue, and I had just done.

"Get me out of here, Dinky," she said.

We headed for the front door.

Baby Girl was crying by the time we got outside. I was pissed off at myself more than anything else because she was with us. I should have left her at home and knew something of this nature could happen at any time.

"My ears are ringing, that old gun sure is loud," she said.

I don't know why I said it, but I replied, "Yep, she's almost as loud as your great aunt Beulah."

This got a smile out of her, but not an all-out laugh like I wanted.

That was it, from that day on, my old shotgun was Beulah.

"Come here, Blue," she said, and he trotted up to her with blood all over his mouth and face. She looked at him and smiled.

"Thanks, Blue."

I wondered what she meant until she told me that the Doberman came around the corner and started running toward her. Blue had been watching me and when he looked back, he sprang into action. He met the Dobie about two feet in front of Baby Girl and drove him backward. That was when she screamed the first time.

I figured the Doberman used the poor Lab as bait but can't figure out why the Doberman didn't eat the Lab. Some things are just not to be understood.

With the praise and attention he received from Baby Girl, Blue strutted like a rooster. The dried blood on his happy face looked creepy, but he was walking on air.

I pushed the cart to the truck, and Baby Girl seemed to be much better. We loaded the back of the truck and left the buggy in Johansen's parking lot. We got in and headed toward home.

About a half mile out of town on the two-mile stretch, I looked, and there was a man and woman walking down the edge of the road. The man was armed, and I stopped the truck a fair distance from him. I opened the truck door dragging old Beulah to the edge but not where he could see it.

"Hello, neighbor," I shouted and waved at him.

He stopped and took up a defensive stance. He waved back but did not change his stance. He was ready for anything.

"We mean you no harm and will wait here until you pass, if you want us to!" I yelled.

"That would be kind!" he yelled back.

I got back in the truck and waited, but I took the .22 out of my beltline and had it held loosely in my right hand. They started walking toward us again. When they got to within talking distance, I stuck my head out of the truck window.

"Where are the two of you headed?" I asked.

"We are looking to make it through Barkston and on to Sheffield," he said.

"Have you eaten anything?" I asked him.

The woman was walking with her head down and had not looked up or spoken.

"Not since yesterday," he said, all the while he was steadily walking.

"When you come by the truck, reach over in the back and get you some of these canned goods to take with you."

He looked surprised but said, "Okay, thanks," and walked toward the truck.

The woman was still walking and had her head turned toward the ditch like she did not want us to see her.

"I'm Dinky, and this is my wife, Sarah."

He reached over into the truck and got three or four cans and put them in his pack.

"I am Boyd, and my wife's name is Judy. Thanks again."

Judy looked up, and we instantly knew why she was looking away. Her eye was a swollen black bruise, and it matched her swollen busted lip.

Baby Girl was through the truck door and around the front of the truck before I could say anything. Boyd looked nervous at me and started to reach for the rifle he had propped up against the tailgate.

I through my door open and leveled the .22 at him.

"No need for that, Boyd. Let's keep this peaceful," I said.

Blue had made it to the left side of the truck and was within leaping distance of Boyd if he tried anything. Boyd didn't try anything; he was scared of his own shadow but had no problem with beating someone who was defenseless.

Baby Girl pulled Judy to the front of the truck and talked to her in a low voice.

What I call, The-Ugly-Side, of Baby Girl came around to my side of the truck.

She looked straight at Boyd and growled. "You, sir, can be on your way."

I still had the .22 leveled at his head. "Leave the rifle and step away from the truck," I said.

He stepped back, and Blue got between him and the truck. Boyd was definitely concerned about Blue and why his mouth was covered in dried blood. That bothered him more than the .22 pistol pointed at him.

I reached and got the rifle and told him to hand me the backpack and empty his pockets on the ground. When he did, I had him to lift his shirt and slowly make a circle. He did not carry any weapon other than the rifle that I could see.

Baby Girl loaded Judy in the truck. I took the rifle and the backpack and placed them in the truck bed.

"When I get about a hundred yards or so up the road, I will put these on the ground, and you can come get them, understand?" I told Boyd.

He said nothing but nodded. As I backed away from him, he cried and yelled.

"I'm sorry, Judy. I love you," he bawled.

I got to the truck and reached my hand behind me until I found the latch on the tailgate and pulled it open and lowered it. I hollered at Blue to load up. He jumped up into the truck bed, and I closed the tailgate still facing Boyd with the .22 leveled at him.

I kept the pistol on Boyd who looked to be in shock at the latest turn of events. I found the truck door latch without looking and opened it. I jumped in the seat, cranked the old Ford and took off as fast as I could down the highway.

A hundred yards down the stretch I stopped. Judy was crying, and Blue looked at me with wonder through the back glass with his What-the-Hell-is-Happening face.

I put the rifle and the backpack out on the road like I had told him and got back in the truck. Before I rounded the curve and lost sight of him, I saw Boyd sitting in the middle of the road with his head in his hands. I did not make it completely around the curve and Judy yelled, "Stop."

"Please go back," she said. She looked up at me, crying.

"Are you sure, honey? You don't have to put up with that," Baby Girl said.

"He really is not a bad man, and he has so much pressure on him trying to keep us alive and fed. Please, go back," Judy said.

"Okay," I said and stopped the truck. I put the old Ford in reverse and backed up as I tried to see around Blue who thought we were playing a game. I reversed around the curve and down the straight stretch until I got to where the backpack and rifle was lying in the road and stopped.

I got out of the truck, and Boyd looked up from where he was sitting and started to stand.

"Don't come any closer than you are, Boyd," I yelled at him, and he didn't.

Judy got out of the truck with Baby Girl, and they walked around to my side of the truck. I put another six or eight cans of soup and vegetables on the highway with the backpack. In the glove box, I found a box of .22 long rifle bullets and gave the bullets and the pistol to Judy.

"Defend yourself, or one day he might do more than give you bruises. Scare the hell out of him, and he will leave you alone," I told her.

She looked at the pistol like it was a rattlesnake, but she took it.

Blue pranced back and forth in the truck bed and couldn't decide whether to get out or stay in. Baby Girl hugged Judy and asked her one more time if was sure about this.

"I can't help it, I love him," Judy said.

Baby Girl had tears in her eyes when she got back in the truck and closed the door.

Judy picked up the cans and put them in the backpack, picked up the rifle, and started toward Boyd. He shuffled back and forth and wanted to come toward her but was afraid to.

I got back in the truck and put it in drive. I did not look in the rearview mirror that time.

The past is the past; good luck, Mrs. Judy.

A mile or two down the road, Baby Girl scooted from the window sat close to me. I put my right arm around her and drove with my left, just like I did in the old days. She laid her head on my shoulder.

"Thank you for being you, Richard," she said.

I saw the glow, even in the evening sun.

Blue was in hog heaven in the back of the Ford with his head hanging over the side and his nose in the wind. I was content but also knew that Baby Girl had seen more of the new reality than I had wanted her to.

Chapter 28: Baby Girl's Anger

I had let Blue out for his morning ritual and giggled to myself because she treats Blue like a child. She will not talk serious business in front of him. He might go blabbing her business to the canine gossip society.

"How long were you going to keep me in the dark about what is going on out there?" she asked. She had poured us a cup of coffee, and we sat at the kitchen table.

I took a sip and set the cup down and reached over to lay my hand on hers.

"It is my job to protect you. Part of that is keeping your dignity and sanity at a livable level. Some things you were better off not knowing. We are going to survive, Baby Girl, we are going to survive whatever the cost. The rest of the world will have to do what they think is best but the old man still has some skills."

I looked at her with the come and get me grin. She blushed and rolled her eyes but the tension had lessened a little.

"Is that all you ever think about?"

I got a serious as I could get and told her.

"We are part of the chosen few, by design or by fate, the Good Lord seen fit that both of us should see life after Pentacle. I made you a promise many years ago that I would love you through any and all manners, good and bad. I will make the life we have as good as I can make it and that is all I can promise you. What you witnessed is only a drop in the bucket as to what is out there. The world as it was is no more, and the old bindings that made a man moral are no longer confined."

I could see tears forming in her eyes and I wanted so bad to remove her sorrow.

"What you have to do is to get tough, Baby Girl. We have to adapt to the environment that we are in and be thankful of every day that we are free and have each other."

She knew I was right, but it didn't make it any easier for her. She had not conformed to the world being flipped.

"I know men have beat their wives and have gone to jail for it, but that was a time when women and men were spoiled and could pick and choose mates on a dime," a tear eased down her cheek. "In this depleted society, I don't understand why a man would even contemplate treating his wife that way."

"In the depleted society, there's nothing to stop him from it," I said.

She looked up and me and crossed her arms over her breasts. The tear was gone, and a hardened reckoning had taken its place.

"Richard Engelmann, you don't go anywhere alone again. If me or Blue ain't with you, you don't go," she said in her commanding voice as she opened the door to let Blue back in. This signaled the adult talk was over and she had the last word.

"Yes, ma'am, Mrs. Engelmann; I love you, too."

Chapter 29: Good Falls

I looked back and Lady was still staying with us. Blue had settled down now and kept stride with me, but he constantly looked back to make sure she was coming. Every once in a while, he would lag back and wait up a little for her. The cars started to become congested; we were close to the Good Falls community.

Lady kept coming but her tongue was hanging out; it was evident that she was tired. I looked at old-T; it was 3:15 and I needed to make a stop at the store. I hoped to find something to clean Lady's wounds and perform an assessment on the scratches and cuts on her. I wanted to make it to the Winnebago before nightfall.

She needed a collar as well, but I won't try to put one on her today. Over the hill I saw the car pile in front of the store. I looked for the Subaru I had put the powder in and spotted it. Nothing had been disturbed since we left three days ago. The walk slowed down to a weave in and out of the vehicles. Lady kept up with us at this point but was wearing down quick.

We got to the parking lot, and I made it to the Subaru and checked the back floorboard. My items were still on the floor where I left them. We weaved on through to the entrance of the store.

I fantasized that little Miss Penny Queen is somewhere in the world sporting her crown and laughing at her court jester. I noticed an open spot on the ground.

"You and Lady rest here and I will be back in a minute," I told Blue.

I opened the water bottle and got out the spam can and poured Lady some to drink. She came right to me and started lapping the water. I poured the rest in the can and gave it to Blue.

I hoped what was left in the store was still good.

Lady made a semi-circle with her body, laid down and let out a big sigh. Blue didn't want me to go in there alone and looked anxious to follow me.

"I will be alright, Blue; get a little rest while you can," I said. "You are on guard duty tonight."

He settled down, and I opened the door to the store and walked in. I was greeted by the same pilgrims that were here last time. I didn't have time to allow myself any reflection or speculation. I had to get what I needed and go.

The water was still on the rack, and I reminded myself to get it on the way out. I went back to where the animal supplies should be and looked around. I found the LED light rack on the way back and turned one on to look around in the dark areas. I found the dog collars and picked what I thought was a pretty one that had some pink in it. I grabbed one for old Blue as well. His was getting a pretty old; he needed a new wardrobe too.

In the tool section I found a fairly large canvas tool bag. It should be sufficient for the powder and supplies. On the way back I shined around to find the toiletries.

I got a bottle of Johnson's Baby Shampoo and put it in the bag. Close to the toiletries, I found rolled gauze, gauze patches, peroxide, mercurochrome, and anti-infection cream.

I looked around the food aisles and found some cans of dog food. I fished my cheaters out of my bag and looked for an expiration date on the cans and found they were good until August of 2018. I was pretty sure we were in the spring of 2021.

I grabbed seven cans of it and hoped that it was still good. In the food aisles I didn't find any Spam, but I did find some potted meat and deviled ham. Just as good. I got a couple extra for Mrs. Balderdash in case she wanted to join us.

There were some candles two aisles over, and I threw them in the bag for Baby Girl. With my thoughts on Baby Girl, I went behind the counter and took the rest of the lottery scratch tickets that I could find and put them in the bag. Baby Girl liked to scratch the tickets.

One day, she was going to hit it big time and make us rich.

On the way out, I found gallon jugs of water and grabbed three of them. When I got to the bottled drinking water, I put six of them in the bag. That would leave enough room for the gun powder. I thought of the Dixie Bowls that I had used the last time and picked them up and headed for the door.

Blue and Lady was out front in the shade where I had left them. I checked old-T and he said it was 4:45. We have to get a move on if we want to see Mrs. Balderdash.

I set the bag and the water down. Then, I turned and went back in the store. I looked up and down the grocery section and found what I needed. I grabbed the key style can opener. Close to the can opener on the rack was a bundle of dish towels, and I grabbed them too. I headed back out the door.

Blue and Lady must have thought that I had gone crazy.

I looked in the bag and brought out two cans of dog food. They actually looked better in the outside light. I opened them both and dumped the contents on the concrete in two piles. Christmas had come for the dynamic duo, and they chowed down. I filled up one of the Dixie bowls, and the Spam can with water for them.

I opened one of the cans of deviled ham and smelled it. It smelled like I remembered it should smell so I dug into it. I hoped that I wouldn't get food poison.

It tasted as good as I remembered it, or I was just that hungry, one of the two. That meal went down so well, I opened another can and ate every bit.

Lady had lain down again but had stopped panting; her tongue was not hung out anymore. I got the supplies I needed from the bag and went toward her. She immediately got the troubled look on her face, and I stopped and offered her the back of my hand to smell. She accepted who I was and even licked my hand that time.

"My lady, I am going to try to clean you up a little if you don't mind," I whispered to her. She didn't comment one way of the other.

I knelt down and opened one of the gallon jugs and poured some onto one of the dishrags. I slowly started wiping the grime off of her. She was passive so I poured a little water on the rag while holding it over her back. She looked up at me inquisitively but did not resist. I worked the water into the fur and kept wiping the grime away.

I noticed that she had a few fleas crawling on her skin, but she didn't seem to be overly infested.

I put some of the baby shampoo on her and lathered it in. She enjoyed the scrubbing and stretched here and there to make the skin tighter where I rubbed. I rinsed the dishrag and wiped her until most of the dirt and grime was gone.

The scratches were not as bad after they were cleaned up. I decided to let it go until we got home together.

If I had put mercurochrome on her, she might have taken off and never come back. I know I would have!

I opened the other gallon and trickled it over the soapy skin. I dried that off and poured some more until I got all that she would let me get without a fuss. Blue lay like a statue and kept eyeing me. I guess he thought I would leave him be if he stayed invisible.

If I had had more time, I would have soaked him just for spite. I stepped back, and Lady did her version of the hokey pokey and shook it all about. She got most of it on me, and Blue smiled.

I started laughing, just because.

I got everything picked up. Blue and Lady looked ready to start out again. We stopped by the Subaru, and I ditched the last gallon of water and put the gun powder in the bag.

We eased out through the maze of cars and toward the highway. Blue was on point, and Lady stayed close with her ears cocked forward. She took in every sound for analysis. We made it through, and the highway opened up.

Old-T said it was 5:30; the shadows started to get longer.

We can make it to the Winnebago by dark if we hump it. "Let's hump it, Blue. Stay with us, Lady," I said. I got the If-you-are-waiting-on-me, your-backing-up, look from both of them.

I accelerated a little and smiled.

And the Walking Man moves like a lightning flash
The trio struts with a ready, set, go
We hope to visit with Mrs. Balderdash
If we make to the Winnebago.

We pounded the pavement in the best stride that I could muster, and Lady seemed to be keeping up better than before. In a few days and some decent meals, she would be good as new. I was exhausted but maintained pace when I rounded the corner and saw the outline of the old Winnebago at the bottom of the hill.

The extra bag I toted made a difference. I swapped arms often and had to put the walking stick on my back with old Beulah because it kept getting in the way.

I sure was glad to see Mrs. Balderdash.

As we approached, Blue and I fell into the same routine. I stopped and got old Beulah down. Blue made a perimeter check. No issue presented itself. I leveled old Beulah and opened the door. Blue jumped into the camper and made his survey of what was in there and came back to the door to give me that, "All Clear."

Lady looked at both of us like we had fallen off the turnip truck. I smiled at her.

"You can't be too careful these days, Lady," I said.

She still looked as if I had lost a marble or two. Blue came over to her, and she started wagging her tail.

I went into the camper with Beulah and looked around. The light had faded fast, but there was still enough daylight left to see that nothing had changed since our last visit.

We had just enough time make a final meal before full darkness fell upon us, and I took the fixings out of the bag. I opened the windows in the old camper on both sides to try and get a fresh breeze going. Anything was better than what was present on the inside. It wasn't over whelming, just a little unpleasant.

I made my proper greeting to Mrs. Balderdash and took everything outside. I put a can each of ALPO in the Dixie bowls and poured another one full of water for them to share.

I opened a can of Vienna sausage and potted meat and went at them like they were rib-eye steak.

When they had their fill, they milled around, and Lady eased off by herself behind the Winnebago, and Blue looked real nervous.

"Don't fret it, Blue; every lady has to have a little privacy," I told him.

In a minute she came back around the edge of the camper with her tail wagging. Blue went over to his favorite tire and rinsed it off a little. I went around to the front of the Winnebago and took care of my bladder so I wouldn't have to get back up later, or so I hoped.

I walked on into the Winnebago and pushed the door wide open. I let out a low whistle.

"Come on," I said, and they both came into the camper, Lady first. Blue seemed to have become a gentleman in her presence.

I settled on the table couch and propped my feet up while using what was left of my jacket to cover the old throw pillow. Blue did the hokey pokey and got on the bench seat behind me. Lady looked for a place in the center aisle of the camper.

I took the back cushion from the bench seat and laid it in the floor for her to use. She did the full circle thing, almost twice round, and curled up in the middle of the cushion.

A slight breeze blew through the windows. The crickets and the bugs were singing their night song for me. Jiminy was at the podium again. I pondered the probably of having to get Mr. L'Amour and my light out, but I was more exhausted than I thought. I felt the relaxation coming on, and it brought the lazy mental feeling that only sleep can provide.

I had gotten up really early that morning after all. It had been a good day; I have a new daughter.

I drifted off that night like every other night, the most fortunate man in the world.

Chapter 30: Day 6, The Toll Bridge

I woke up to the sound of rain beating on the top of the Winnebago and a moist breeze coming in through the windows. I closed the one next to me and lay there for a few minutes. I had to piss really badly but didn't want to get up.

Come on, Mr. Sandman, knock me out again.

Mr. Sandy didn't show up, and I knew I'd have to get up.

I'm sorry about this, happy campers, I thought as I eased my way into the little closet that serves as the toilet on this vessel.

About halfway into the stream, I succumbed to the fact that there was going to be more to this than emptying my bladder.

Ding, Ding! In the Red Corner, we have the Poo-Poo Monster, a real heavyweight…….

I went back to where my backpack was to retrieve my greatest commodity and my LED light.

"Really, really sorry, folks," I said under my breath to the next happy camper that arrives.

I looked at old-T and found out it was only 1:30.

It occurred to me to put a caution sign on the door, and it made me giggle. In the far corner of the LED light, Lady looked to be totally convinced that I was bonkers.

I giggled again as I made my way back to the couch and tried not to shine the light directly at either one of them and disturb them anymore than I already had. Blue had pretty much the same look on his face as Lady did. He watched me a few seconds more and put his head back down.

I lay there thinking that I would be completely exhausted tomorrow afternoon by being awake this early and not able to get back to sleep. As I was laying there, convinced of the inevitable, the light rain on the roof was just enough that I dozed off again.

I awoke to the grey morning light that come through the window. I had gone back to sleep but now felt like someone had worked me over with a Louisville Slugger.

I stretched and worked the kinks in my shoulders and sat up on the edge of the couch. Blue jumped off the seat and stretched. He did the hokey pokey and looked up at me. The rain had stopped, and the wind had died down, so I went to the door and eased it open enough to let Blue out.

"Perimeter check," I whispered.

He squeezed through the opening I had made and went around the camper. He looked and smelled to see if anything was amiss. Satisfied, he stopped at the back tire and hiked his leg.

Lady had awoken and stood behind me. She wanted to go out as well. I opened the door a little wider for her, and she left. I went back and sat on the couch.

I felt the need to go, but I was not about to venture into the hazard zone again. I waited until I got outside.

I had three cans of ALPO left. I opened one and halved it in the Dixie bowls and poured another bowl with water for them. I put Beulah on my forearm, picked the bowls up and carried them outside.

Blue and Lady hurried my way when they saw the bowls. I went back inside and shouldered the backpack and walking stick. I picked up the new tool bag and stepped out the door.

"Thanks again for the hospitality, Mrs. Balderdash," I whispered as I closed the door.

They finished breakfast in micro-seconds. We cleaned up the dishes and started toward the highway. I was stiff at first but felt the tension in my legs and calves limber up.

I probably made two miles that night from the farmhouse to the Winnebago, maybe three. I had walked all that day except for a couple of rest stops. If Lady holds out, I could be partaking in that shaky pudding that I was promised later on tonight.

That spurred me on even faster.

Truth be known, I would pass out on the couch, and Baby Girl would have to get me to come to bed later. My mind can always imagine more than this old body can back up.

One foot in front of the other, that's the way to get there. Lady was not lagging behind anymore, but she was already panting a little. We'll see how it goes.

We made good time, and Lady kept up with us. She seemed to be getting stronger. I stopped twice and gave them some water, and we kept on trucking. We passed the old farmhouse we stayed in the first night; I thought about William. We passed the railroad tracks. We were close to the crossroads and would turn south in a mile or two. The houses were starting to become more frequent, and the new growth was from abandoned lawns and pastures, not the old wooded forest. There were visible strips of forgotten fence lines along the pastures.

I bet Lady will stay well away from them.

Blue and Lady had moved ahead and were investigating the smells along the highway. They didn't seem to be particularly interested in any one thing. I had not seen a lot of wildlife sign nor evidence of domesticated animals, either. We should not be that far from where we saw the cows on the way in.

At the end of the straight stretch, a wood line came together on both sides at a small bridge going over a creek. I remembered crossing this bridge many times and knew where I was.

Past the bridge up on the rise was Teddy Newman's house.

Teddy had considered himself a good fisherman, but I never seen him do anything but drive that fancy boat of his up and down the lake. To the right, on this side of the bridge, was Terrence McAllister.

I had never gone into these houses on the scavenging missions. It was out of respect because I'd known them before Pentacle. There were very few houses that I went into in the Barkston area where I'd considered the prior owner an acquaintance.

As I approached the bridge, I got a whiff of that smell. The smell that never completely left me. The smell was growing stronger near the bridge and I did not remember the smell being there on the trip five days ago.

There is probably a dead animal close by, either got in the creek and couldn't get out, or got hung up in a fence.

I got to middle of the bridge. A sting in my right shoulder instantly turned into a burn. Someone had taken an invisible Louisville Slugger and hit me on the right side that made me spin in that direction. I lost my balance and was falling over the low bridge rail when the sound of the rifle shot rang out.

My brain recorded that the shooter was in Teddy's house. I landed in a soft spot in the edge of the creek. If I had fallen three feet to the left, the rocks and boulders would have done me in. The fall was probably twenty feet.

As I did a mental check on my body parts, a zip and ping hit the bridge followed by another rifle report. When I looked Blue and Lady were running flat out back towards Terrence's property. I didn't holler at them because I wanted them to get away.

My shoulder was on fire, and it bled openly. My right arm didn't want to work like it should, but with effort, I moved my fingers and made a fist. Evidently it had missed the vitals.

I might survive the shot if I survive the creek.

I looked around and discovered the source of the smell. It was a young man, looked to be in his thirties. He was swollen, bloated, and stunk to high heaven. He had not been robbed or anything. His backpack was still attached, and he carried what looked like a Colt .45 on his hip. I worked Beulah over my shoulder to see if she had been damaged. The movement told me that the shoulder did not like that at all.

I needed to get the bleeding to stop.

It was all that I could do to get the backpack and old Beulah off my shoulders. I was sweating, and I knew my blood pressure had to be through the roof. I have always had a decent tolerance for pain, but this was getting to me.

There was a splashing noise behind me, and I turned my head too fast which caused the world to swim out of focus for a second and the pain to extend a little further. Blue and Lady were running up the creek toward me.

Lady stopped and watched the corpse for a second, but Blue never checked up until he got to me. He licked my face and pranced around looking guilty. It was almost as if he was more afraid of letting Baby Girl down than he was about my welfare. In spite of the pain, I giggled a little. He calmed down a little at that.

"Settle down boy and stay out of sight," I whispered to him.

I needed to move. If the shooter walked out to the driveway and down the highway, he would have his finishing shot right in front of him.

"Blue, Lady, come here," I whispered, and they came.

I tried to stand and fell back onto my butt the first time. My left leg did not cooperate. I rolled over and crawled to the poor pilgrim that had been ambushed and pulled the Colt from his side.

The pain shot down my right arm; I prayed it was the bullet and not my old ticker. With the .45 and old Beulah, I crawled toward the bridge at the edge of the creek so I would at least have some cover. I waited until the pain dulled a little and looked inside my shirt.

There was a pucker hole in the right shoulder but not too much blood around it. I took my left hand and tried to feel the back side.

This ain't good.

I felt the shattered and torn flesh at the top of my shoulder. I would bleed down if I didn't do something.

Blue pranced around and wanted to do something but didn't know what to do. I had left the backpack where I had fallen and needed to get it. I had to stop the bleeding but didn't know if the ambusher was halfway down the hill.

I hated to do it with all my heart, but I looked straight in Blues eyes.

"Perimeter Check, Blue," I whispered.

He immediately went on point and looked out from under the bridge and went farther out. He got into the full alert mode and eased over to the side of the embankment and started climbing up to the top.

Dirt flew up right beside him followed by the rifle report. Blue jumped back down into the creek bed.

Whoever this guy is, he has not left the house.

"Come here, Blue," I said, "Don't go out there." I crawled out from under the bridge, grabbed the backpack, and dragged it back under the bridge with me.

Opening the bag, I got out my folding knife and the shirt that Belinda had given me. I cut a long strip to tie with and cut a pad to put into the wound opening. Reaching the wound was the hard part. I laid the pad on as well as I could and tried to sling the long piece over my shoulder.

It took a lot of effort and when I finally got it around the patch, I had to figure out how to tie it. I found a rock on the bank that looked to be about as clean as I was going to find, and I leaned back onto it pressing the patch in place and holding the tie strip.

I worked the tie around itself and held one side in my teeth and pulled as hard as I could with my left hand. I almost passed out but the knot bit and stayed in place until I could make another knot and repeat the process.

I laid there and breathed in and out for a few minutes thinking that I have to do something. I couldn't leave Baby Girl in this world alone. She was too special for that. The more I thought about it the madder I got. With the blown-out shoulder and the busted left leg, I hoped the ambusher would peep his head around the corner.

With renewed energy, I inspected old Beulah. She was still in a position to do damage. I checked the cylinder on the .45; it had five bullets in the six chambers. One of them was empty to keep me from blowing my own foot off. The kid had been smart.

I started to get chilly in the shade of the bridge with my body halfway in the water. I worked up the strength I had left and moved up under the bridge a little to get out of the water.

Once I got there and allowed the pain to work through its cycle. I watched and listened for the ambusher. Blue would let me know where he was before he could get there.

Lady came and lay down as close to me as she could get, even touching my leg. I reached over with my left hand and gave her a scratch and listened for any indication that the shooter approached.

I looked at old-T and eased out a gentle sigh. The busted glass and the deformed hands told the tale. The old soldier had been with me a long time and was a true patriot if there ever was, a hero and a casualty of war. I took him off my arm using my right hand. I could not lift the hand, so I put the band over to it and held on that strap while I worked my left arm free. I took my left hand and dug as far down into the wet sandy soil as I could and placed old-T in it face up.

 "Thanks for the years of service and your great sacrifice," I simply said and covered him up.

Those words brought a flooding memory of Bart and caused a little tear that streaked down my face.

"Such a waste, Heavenly Father," I whispered, "such a waste."

Lady looked up at me with a look of pure love and devotion and then laid her head back on her paws. Her ears never went back though; she was tuned in to the sound channel better than I was. Blue paced back and forth under the bridge and tried to find a way out where he would not be seen.

There was at least four more hours until it became dark. It felt like the bleeding had stopped, but there was no way I could check it. There was blood all over my back and a little on the ground behind me. My left ankle had swollen inside the boot, and although it hurt like hell, I could still rotate it. It isn't broken but will be hell to walk on in its weakened state.

If the ambusher has not made it down by nightfall, maybe we can sneak out in the cover of darkness.

I had put Baby Girl's medication in the bag, and it is still on the bridge. I will either die or bring it home to her, but I am not leaving here without it.

"Settle down, boy," I told Blue and patted my leg with my good hand.

He came over to where we were but agitated and anxious. He lay down beside Lady where he watched me as well as the creek embankment.

Pain is a funny associate to have. Sometimes he can wake you up and bring you to reality, and sometimes he can be smooth and suck you into the darkness. My pain was such that I couldn't tell the difference. I knew it was bad, how bad I didn't know. It would ease back to a dull ache, and then it would escalate to new heights and hang out there a while. I could feel that my old body was working hard.

I felt extremely tired and had stiffened up. That was not from the fall, but I expect the sudden stop had a lot to do with it. I didn't recall ever going into shock, but I figured that was what happened. I had the two alarm clocks if the shooter wanted to claim his prize. They would awaken me before he got there.

I only wanted to take a little nap. I needed strength to slip away during the dark. I eased the backpack behind me where my head was and ever so slowly positioned myself where I didn't put much pressure on the shoulder.

I laid Beulah in my left hand next to the trigger guard. I had to shoot one-armed and left-handed.

The right one was useless. The pain was all down the length of the arm even though that was not where the bullet passed.

I closed my eyes, and my mind denied the sandman. It crossed my mind, and I mumbled it out loud.

"The Lord is my Shepherd; I shall not want. He maketh me lie down in green pastures; he leadeth me beside the still waters. He restoreth my soul; he leadeth me in the paths of righteousness for his name's sake.

"Yea, though I walk through the valley of the shadow of death, I will fear no evil; for thou art with me, thy rod and thy staff they comfort me.

"Thou preparest a table before me in the presence of mine enemies; thou anoint my head with oil; my cup runneth over.

"Surely goodness and mercy shall follow me all the days of my life; and I will dwell in the house of the Lord forever."

This reminded me of the Ten Commandments, and I pondered on how many of them I had broken. The one that resounded in my mind was the same one that almost drove me mad during the summer of the second year A.P.

"Thou shalt not kill," I said, weakly.

Prior to the first pilgrim that I killed, I had never entertained the thought of it. I had not been in a physical fight since the time Jason got me in the middle of one at the Langston High School parking lot after the football game that we lost. I hung with him, but I got worse than I gave.

The first kill, that one was the one that haunted me. There have been others since, but they did not hold the impact of that first one.

It was the one that changed me into a survivor. I never told Baby Girl what happened, but she knew something was wrong. It took me a long time to come to grips with what had happened.

Chapter 31: The Turning Point

It was a pretty summer day that was dry and still. My Papaw would have called it one of the Dog Days. Me and Blue had been scrounging around in town in the Ford and found a few good supplies. I looked for butane bottles and more can goods to stock for the winter.

Gordon had been gone for a few months, and I missed him. I never would admit that to anyone, but I always thrived on conversation and fellowship between men.

The great Will Rogers once stated he never met a man that he didn't like. I was cut from the same mold as Will.

I wasn't quite that enthusiastic; there were still some men that I liked better than others. Gordy had been one of the great ones.

In those days I would normally take my shotgun, but I would leave it in the truck when we went on the scavenging missions. I guess I was naïve, but that was my nature then.

I thought everyone was like I was, so when I saw the man coming towards me, I raised my hand to wave and started toward him.

He stopped and let me come to him.

I could see that he had a gun with him, but I didn't think much of it. I was heading toward him with my hand out for a handshake.

 "Stop right there," he yelled.

I stopped where I was because I was looking down the barrel of some kind of rifle.

"I mean you no harm, sir. I only wanted to meet you," I said. "I don't get to talk to many people anymore."

He looked at me without any facial expression.

"Get on your knees and put your hands behind your head," he said.

I did what I was told and tried not to panic at this point. He came behind me, and I could not see him anymore, but I felt the cold end of the rifle when he laid it on my neck at the base of my skull.

"You are going to tell me what I want to know, and you are not going to lie to me, understand?"

"Yes, sir," I said.

"I didn't give you permission to speak," he said and jobbed the barrel a little deeper.

I didn't say anything this time.

"How many do you have in your group?" he asked.

"There are only two of us," I said, "me and my wife."

The barrel stayed where it was and I didn't move a muscle, but my knees were starting to bark at me from being on the loose gravel.

"How old is your wife?" he asked.

"She's the same age as me, mid-fifties."

"Is she good looking?" He kind of giggled and asked. It was donning on me where this conversation was going.

"She is ugly as sin but makes a mean pawn of cornbread," I said.

At that he jobbed the barrel again, and I figured that this was it. The feeling in my fingers from being locked together was going numb, and my knees were howling. I might die right here, but I'll be damned if I would ever take him close to where Baby Girl was.

"How did you get here?" he asked.

"I walked; I live on Sycamore Lane about a mile away," I said, breaking one of the commandments. "I can take you there if you want."

"There are some people behind me trying to catch up with me, and I need to get out of here. I have no problem with killing you and leaving you here for the buzzards and flies, but I don't want them to see your mangy carcass." The gun barrel eased away from my neck, but I knew it was close enough to blow my head off. I waited until he said. "What did you have in the bag you were toting?"

 "Some canned goods and few candles," I told him, and that was the actual truth.

"Get up," he said. "Let's go get it."

I unlocked my fingers and placed my hand on the ground and was trying to push myself up when I felt the roundhouse kick of a steel toed boot catch me right below my right-side rib cage. I rolled forward and attempted to breath and found that was near impossible, but somehow, I managed to push up on my right hand and rolled back over to my knees.

I could see his face now and what I saw was worse than any horror movie I ever watched; his eyes were narrow and his demeanor was set.

 "I ain't got time to fool with you; I think I will leave you for an example to the ones that follow."

I was so scared that I pissed myself.

Just when I thought I was going to hear the shot; Blue came out from behind a parked car and launched himself at the man. He swung to aim, and the shot rang out about the time Blue latched onto his fore arm, and they both went to the ground. In the process he dropped the rifle and started to beat Blue with his fist. Blue continued to hold on and caused severe damage to the man's arm.

I grabbed the rifle and bolted another shell into it.

"Get off Blue!" I hollered.

Blue released the man's arm and jumped back away from him but stayed ready to move in again. I leveled the rifle at him.

"Don't move," I said. He took one look at me and started laughing.

"You ain't got it in you, old timer."

He tried to get up on his good arm. He got to his knees and then his feet. I began to believe that he was right. Everything in my existence wanted to throw down the rifle and run like hell. He started toward me reaching across his body with his left hand and pulled a scabbard knife out of its holster.

"Put the gun down, or I am going to carve you like a Christmas turkey and then find Sycamore Lane and your old lady," he sneered.

I didn't aim; the rifle was already pointed at him.

I just pulled the trigger.

The bullet caught him in the upper belly right in the middle, and he went down like a sack of potatoes. His legs were at an odd angle. The bullet had shattered his spine. He was groaning in pain but was still alert and croaked out.

"You shot me, you old bastard," he moaned.

Something washed over me at that moment. I would like to say that it was the devil or evil or anything other what it was. I knew I was going to survive, and I knew that he was going to die by my hand. I felt my heart get hard, and I was angry almost to the point of rage.

I growled at him more than spoke. "Why are they after you?" I yelled. "What did you do?" I shifted another shell into the rifle.

"I had a fling with a woman in the commune," he said through the pain, "a consenting adult woman, but the sister of the Grand Chaplain. She lied and said that I raped her and the fine upstanding members of society beat me to a pulp. When I healed, I escaped. I took care of that bitch and her brother, once and for all."

He was hurt bad, and I did not get close to him because I did not see where the knife went.

"Well, you deserve to let them find you," I said and turned to go back to where the bags of salvaged supplies were. "C'mon, Blue," I said leaving him there in the summer sun.

"You can't leave me like this, it ain't right!" he yelled

I kept on walking. I made it to the bag, picked it up and walked back to where the Ford was. I tossed the bag in the truck bed.

I was scared, and my hands shook. I had crossed over to the land of stress and anxiety. I was thankful to be alive, but guilt ridden with what I had done.

"It ain't right," he had said. Even a rabid dog had the right to be put out of its misery. I threw the rifle off to the side and pulled my shotgun out of the cab. I started back toward the man and Blue started to follow.

"Stay here, Blue," I said.

I walked back to where the man was. He had drug himself about six feet and rolled over when he heard me coming. Now he, faced me. He never said a word, only looked at me and nodded his head.

I shot him in the face with double ought buckshot. I got the shakes and doubled over to puke. I had nothing in me; the dry heaves were so hard that my abdomen knotted in pain. I knelt back down on the raw knees and cried.

No one was around to hear except Blue, so I screamed. I screamed until the shakes passed. From that moment on, I was never the same.

Chapter 32: The Creek Bed

I was trapped in the realm between worlds, not asleep and not awake. The pain targeted my brain enough to not allow the drift away that the sandman can provide. It was still daylight when I came fully awake again. I felt better than before but was really sore and weak.

My ankle was swollen and had filled the space in my boot. The shoulder had a burning sensation mixed with punch pain. I called it punch pain because there was no other way to describe it. It was like you feel when you have been punched really hard or hit with something.

After more evaluation, I felt my side was really sore where I landed on old Beulah during the fall. Thank the Lord, it was the opposite side of the shoulder that had the hole in it.

Lady had not moved and raised her head and looked at me. I locked eyes with her for a minute. She seemed to be satisfied that I was holding my own; she laid her head back onto her paws and watched the side of the bridge.

Blue was nowhere to be seen. I thought about calling to Blue but that would let the ambusher know that I was still kicking.

I could not figure why he hadn't come to claim his prize.

I looked at my surroundings and thought this would be a pretty creek bank to walk down beside. It had the entire hard wood canopy that an old country boy loved to be in. From the looks of it though, after a heavy rain, the water can rise to a pretty high level.

I was glad that it wasn't raining.

Baby Girl's livelihood was above me on the bridge. It was sealed, but I still would not want it to get wet. I checked out the pilgrim who I smelled with every breath. I guess that my nose had gotten used to it during the Pentacle because it did not bother me as much. The flies and bugs had settled on him and worked their job in Mother Nature's demolition team. The buzzards will be at him by tomorrow.

"That's enough of this dicking around, old man," I mumbled to myself.

I put my good foot underneath me and put the butt end of old Beulah on the ground and hoped I wouldn't blow my other shoulder off. I took the weight on my good leg and was able to get upright but held onto old Beulah.

I tried to put weight on the other foot. It barked really loud and hurt like hell but held me up. I had to work through it. I needed to be ready for when night came. I had to get out of this ditch.

I might have to find an area downstream to get out. It was pretty steep near the bridge.

I took a step on the bad foot and put the weight down.

It held until I tried to pick my other foot up. I went down face first on the side of the creek bank. I braced myself with my hands and felt the shock wave in my right shoulder. The pain was so intense that I got dizzy and almost passed out.

Lady stood and looked really concern about my activities. She gave a slight whine as I laid there groaning.

I had to get higher up the bank. I rolled over on all fours and crawled toward the narrow part of the bridge where it met the embankment using the two appendages that worked.

There was a flat landing up there if I could make it. I pushed Beulah in front of me, dragged the backpack as far to me as I could and pushed myself toward it.

I moved at a turtle's pace, but I made ground all the same. I finally arrived and saw that I had left a trail of fresh blood here and there. I had busted the wound open during the fall. I was sure the patch had long ago saturated.

Lady came up to the landing. She did not know what to do with herself, but she knew she needed to stay with me. I wasn't able to look around the side of the bridge from where I was, but the ambusher had to come under the bridge to get a shot at me.

In the old west, they would have called that a standoff.

I got back to my backside and sat up. I wiped all the dirt off of my left hand and tried to reach around to the wound. It was wet and sticky, but the patch felt like it was still in place and the knot held. I was too tired to worry with it.

Old Man, you haven't been in a pickle like this in quite a while.

"Thanks for hanging out with me, Lady," I whispered, and I reached over and stroked her neck. "If you and Blue are able to make it back home, tell Baby Girl that I love her with all my heart, and I will be waiting for her."

The daylight faded fast, and Blue had not made it back.

He had better get his ass back here.

She didn't hear my thoughts and didn't know what I was saying to her.

"Tell the shit-eater that I love him, too." She cocked her head sideways and gave me an inquisitive look.

I couldn't help it and chuckled a little; even that hurt.

The ground was fairly flat, this would be a good spot to try to rest and let the foot heal a little.

I will have to make it work tonight or forget the whole deal.

The shade and the breeze under the bridge made the temperature cooler. I pulled what was left of my jacket out of the backpack and tried to cover with it. I laid back and tried not to put any pressure on the shoulder.

Didn't matter, the pain had set in in. My Dad would have said, "Like a dying-robin's ass." I rationalized with myself, pushed the pain back, and tried to rest.

My little trip of about twenty feet had exhausted everything I had.

How in the world could I make it another six miles? Why didn't the ambusher come and see what he had done?

I felt like I was about to pass out and mumbled to Lady.

"Keep a watch for me, Lady," I said and drifted off.

Chapter 33: I Dream of Misty

I was at the desk in the back of the Maintenance Office when Jason walked in.

"Come on, Big Daddy, its Friday," he laughed and said, "if you keep this shit up, they will give you another promotion."

I looked at him with the shut-up look.

"Go ahead and get gone. I will see you before daylight in the morning and tell Melanie I want some of her apple fritters to take with me," I laughed, "if she doesn't mind, that is."

"You better say that," he chuckled. "I'll bring the fritters if you let Baby Girl make the coffee. I almost fell out of the boat when I tried to drink yours." He slapped the side of the door, and I heard him laughing as he was going down the hall.

I grinned as I returned to the report.

I should have never taken the line foreman's job. Hell, I had it made and blew it. What the hell was I thinking?

I was about to wrap up the report to put on Derek's desk when Misty Presley walked through the door.

"You okay, Misty?" I looked up and asked her.

"Never better, could you give me a lift home?" she asked, being very much flirtatious. "My little truck is not cooperating this evening."

The red flags went up, and I wondered how I was going to explain a twenty-four-year-old, drop dead gorgeous, *I don't have to do anything because the boss wants into my panties*, woman being in the cab of my truck on a Friday night after hours.

"Sure, no problem," I said, "give me five minutes and I'll be ready."

"Okay," she said but didn't leave. She came over to the desk and leaned over from the other side. This displayed the wonderful cleavage that we generally didn't get to see on the shop floor.

I continued to work on the report, but my train of thought had moved to something else. I felt a stirring in the lower region and mentally beat it down. I concentrated really hard and got focused on finishing the report.

She came around to same side of the desk that I was on and moved in really close to me, close enough that her jeans brushed against my arm. She looked real intent on figuring out what I worked on.

She enjoyed being a distraction way too much for my comfort.

"Let me work on this and get it finished and we'll be gone," I told her without looking up from my report. She backed off, and I got back to filling in the production section for the week.

She was quiet as a church mouse. When I looked over at her a couple of minutes later, she was naked as a jaybird and sitting on the couch with her legs crossed. The stirring couldn't be batted down this time, and she knew it.

I turned back to the report like I was not interested in the side show on the couch. I prayed she would put her clothes back on, but she didn't say a word, and she didn't get dressed either. Sweat broke out on my forehead as I tried to get the production numbers in the right place with a raging buffalo stampeding in my boxers.

I never let on and finished the report. I took the carbon copy pages off and put the third copy in the file drawer in my desk. I put the other two together and stood up to take them to Derek's office.

It was obvious that I was reacting to the side show whether I acted like it or not.

While in Derek's office I pushed the buffalo down and rearranged him a bit so he wouldn't be so noticeable and went back. I opened the door.

"You ready," I said, to the sight of her laid back on the couch, spread eagle.

"Yeah, I'm ready, are you?" she said in a husky voice.

There had been temptations in my life, but I never succumbed to them. I told myself I would not do so now. I looked at her.

"Number one, I am old enough to be your daddy!" I said sternly. "Number two, I don't think the Good Lord, nor my wife, would appreciate it. Number three, if you still want that ride, you better get your knickers on."

She pooched her lip out and gave me a slow and seductive movement from the laying position to the sitting position. When I stayed standing by the door, she shrugged her shoulders and shook her head.

She stood up and started putting her clothes on. She got dressed, picked her purse up, and started toward the door.

When she got to me, she reached down and grabbed the buffalo.

"This is too nice of a toy to keep all to yourself. Dinky. You really should learn to share," she whispered while she squeezed the toy and then released it. She almost got a wet spot for her efforts.

"Okay, then, come on; let's get out of here." She laughed.

When we got to the parking lot, she walked to her little truck and got in. I watched her sway that pretty little swing all the way to her truck.

I guessed the mechanical difficulties had sorted themselves out.

I turned back and locked the side door to the office hall and shook it to make sure it latched. She pulled out and drove up beside me while I was walking to my truck.

"I'll see you Monday morning, Dinky," she said, winking at me.

"Okay, Misty," I said and smiled.

I sat in my truck and thought about what had just transpired when the little truck came back and stopped.

The door opened and out stepped Misty.

She was all bloated with boils and puss pockets all over her. She looked to be a cross between a grey and a pale green. She walked toward me in that sashay that drove the shop floor crazy.

As she got closer, I saw that her eyes were nothing but sockets. When she smiled, flies flew out of her nose, and maggots dripped from her mouth.

I tried to start the truck, and it would not fire.

She was getting closer.

"I want my toy, Dinky!" It was more like a slur than a voice saying. "Give me my toy!"

Chapter 34: The Embankment Navigation

My eyes sprang open and I must have squirmed because the pain was intense, and my heartbeat was like a flock of blackbirds that took off all at one time. Lady sensed my distress and whined. I heard her, but I couldn't see in the darkness underneath the bridge. I don't know how long I was out but it was well into the night.

All that was confirmed was that my shoulder hurt like hell, the right arm was now totally useless, my injured foot was on fire, and I had an erection.

"Well, old man," I said out loud. "It's time to root-hog or die." I put some pressure on the bad foot to see how it was going to react.

I closed my eyes and let the pain wash over me and breathed as evenly as I could until it passed.

"No more "moon walking" for you, old man."

I chuckled and Lady whined; that made me think about Blue.

Where is the old shit-eater?

My eyes adjusted to the dark, and I looked closely in all the places he could be, from the ones with a hint of moonlight to the pitch-black areas, but I couldn't see nor hear Blue anywhere.

I let out a low whistle that usually brought him coming. No sound except for Lady stirring before she came to check me over. I felt her nuzzle me on my cheek and reached up with the good arm and loved on her all little.

I put the pressure on the good foot and used Beulah as a brace. I managed to get up on the one foot. That took a good bit of effort, and I had to rest up a minute. I checked Beulah again and took the shells out of the barrel and magazine so I would not blow the other armpit to smithereens.

With my good hand, I jobbed the Colt into my beltline in the middle of my back. I patted old Beulah on the side.

"Sorry about this, old girl. Please forgive me," I cooed.

I turned her over to stick her barrel in the dirt. It was a sacrilege to do so, and I felt like I was breaking a cardinal sin. I used her as a crutch with the stock under my good arm.

I hopped forward on the right foot and found I could navigate a little in this manner. I only hoped I could get out of the embankment and onto the bridge.

Oh Yeah! I also hoped Mr. Sniper was sleeping and didn't have night vision.

I hopped the one step back and picked up the backpack. There was no way I could put it on, but I couldn't leave it either. I threw it forward about three feet and then hopped to it. Picked it up and repeated until I got to the edge of the bridge as close to the top as I could.

The easy part was done; the fun part starts now.

We reached the briars and sticker bushes that I had to crawl over. It was going to be ten feet of hell on a steep incline to get over the top.

"Well, here goes," I muttered and threw the backpack up and over the top; close to the side of the road. That caused a definite rebuke from Mr. Pain.

I stood there and let Mr. Pain finish his latest drum solo.

Breathe, old man. Just Breathe!

I could feel clammy sweat all over my body as I got on my knees in front of the embankment brush. I used Beulah as a club, another cardinal sin, and beat down the briars to get them as close to the ground as I could. With Beulah as a push pole, I eased into a crawling position. Breathing heavily, I lay Beulah in front of me, using my weight to crush the briars, brambles and bushes: cardinal sin number-three.

I crawled forward.

In order to make ground on the steep incline, I had to put pressure on the left foot which did not like it whatsoever. The pain shot up the left leg now, but I knew if I stopped that I would never get out of the ditch. I kept pushing, even though the pain was unbearable. My heart pounded in my chest and the sweat poured from my face like Niagara Falls.

I pushed forward and gained about five feet; halfway there.

"Don't you give up now, dammit," I groaned and kept pushing.

My left elbow was catching the brunt of the briars. I tried to push with my right leg and only used the left one for stability.

I made another couple of feet.

Lady had exited the embankment and nervously paced in front of me. She was in the open; the shooter was either asleep, or his night vision goggles quit working. Lady was wide open for a shot if he had the ability. She didn't seem to care; she was too worried about me.

I was almost to the backpack; she grabbed it with her teeth and dragged it onto the road shoulder.

"Good girl, Lady," I grunted.

She pranced back and forth wanting to assist somehow. I had exhausted everything I had left to get to the top.

She reached and grabbed my shirt collar and set her feet. When she got a firm grip, she started backing up. I gritted my teeth and made the equivalent of Custer's Last Stand. I cleared the bushes and lay on the side of the road shoulder.

I was thankful for the assistance of Lady. If it wasn't for her, they would have found my raggedy old bones on the embankment about a foot from the top. I lay there breathing heavy as the internal battle with Mr. Pain reached its crescendo. Lady came and washed most of the clammy sweat from my face with her tongue.

"Thank you, Lady," I said and stroked her head.

Where in the hell is Blue?

The bad foot cleared the embankment, and I dragged myself another yard or so to the edge of the pavement, pushing Beulah in front of me. That was cardinal sin number-four, scratching her all up in the gravel. I lay on my stomach for a while longer, doing the breathing thing, and trying to calm my nerves.

I was drenched with sweat and hoped that the wound had not reopened. My heart seemed to settle down from the hard-rock solo to a reggae beat; my breath had receded from pant to heavy.

From the looks of things; dawn was in its infancy. I noticed a lighter shade of darkness tinged the eastern horizon. I had watched this phenomenon many times; on the lake, in the woods, and mostly from the back porch. I loved watching morning approach. It had always been one of my favorite times of the day.

That was enough of the daydreaming. Truth was, I could not get across the bridge and out of sniper range in the time I had left. I had enough time to retrieve the bag and get back out of his line of sight. I prayed that he didn't have a night vision scope.

Using Beulah, I got to my knees and then upright by extending my right foot and pushing up with my left arm. It was almost a circus acrobatic act, but I got upright.

With Old Beulah under my arm as a crutch again, we did the bunny hop out toward the bag in the center of the bridge. If I took another round, it was Katy-barred-the-door for Old Dinky. I got to the bag, reached down, and picked it up with the good arm. Using Beulah like a crutch and holding on to the bag at the same time was another act to the same old circus, but we bunny hopped back to where the backpack was.

I had a good grip, so I kept going until I was sure I was out of sight of the ambusher. I dreaded having to go back and get the backpack. The haze of darkness revealed Lady with the strap in her mouth dragging the backpack.

"Thanks, girl," I said.

We needed to find a close place to get out of the way. About fifty yards back toward McAllister's place, there was a depression in the ditch slope. If the shooter ventured out, we could stay out of sight until he got closer.

I didn't know how far I could hit with the pistol, but it might come to me finding out. Five bullets are all I have if I don't use Beulah. We wobbled toward the ditch, the Lady and the Energizer Bunny on a dead battery.

We got there; it was all I could do not to fall down. I was amazed at how weak I was, and there was a trickle of fresh blood running down my back. The feeling was almost nothing in the right arm; I could only move my fingers a little. I couldn't make a fist. I had not coughed up any blood or found bloody froth; the bullet missed the lung.

With the aid of Beulah and under the watchful eye of Lady, I got to a sitting position in the soft grass on the edge of the ditch rise where I could watch the bridge and also the road back toward Good Falls. After the wooziness and the heavy breathing subsided a little, I opened the bag and checked the supplies in it. Everything was still in there. I found the ALPO and the opener.

A small and insignificant chore with two hands became a struggle and battle, but I won. I got the ALPO open and shook it out with my left hand, getting most of it in the Dixie bowl. Lady didn't waste any time making short work of the meal, so I filled the bowl up with water for her. She looked up at me as if to say it was my turn.

I smiled and said, "I will in a minute. I have to rest up a bit first." The first of the orange glow could be seen toward the eastern sky. It would not be long before full visibility would arrive. Any other day, this would have been one of those beautiful mornings.

What I wouldn't give for one of Baby Girl's cups of early morning coffee and a shot of shaky pudding. I had to giggle a little at that, and Lady looked totally convinced that I was a brick shy of the full load.

I positioned the pistol where I could reach, eased back on the incline, and tried not to put much pressure on my right side. I closed my eyes again and let the gentle wave of emptiness come over me.

"Where in the hell is Blue?" I mumbled into the dawn.

I came instantly and fully awake in a state of complete panic.

If he made it back to Baby Girl, they would be getting back here this morning. The ambusher would shoot her as soon as she got to the bridge, if not before. My adrenaline kicked into high gear, and I sat up. I was at least five hundred yards away from the house and had to cross the creek again to get there.

I opened the chamber on old Beulah and turned the barrel around to look down it. There was some dirt in the end of it, but otherwise it was okay. I cleaned the dirt out until the bore was completely open. I looked in the backpack and found six shells left; two of them buckshot. I loaded Beulah to the max with the buckshot in the chamber. All I needed was one if I got close enough.

Chapter 35: Day 7: Judgment Day

Once settled, I unlaced the walking boot of the left foot and let the pressure off for the first time since the Humpty-Dumpty event. Thousands of needles rushed forth. I had either done them a favor, or I had screwed up-royally. I hoped for the first one.

With the toe of the right boot, I hooked the heel of the left boot and pushed it until it started to move. I gritted my teeth and pushed it even harder until the boot came off and I sat there in an effort to ride the wave of pain and not be wiped out by it. I examined the foot. It was terribly swollen; I needed to know the rest. I took the sock off as gently as I could. In my years on the shop floor, I had seen several injuries and sprains. Some were mine and some from other workers.

Old Dinky W.D., the bona fide Witch Doctor, made a complete diagnosis.

I wasn't the ankle that was broken; it was the side of my foot.

The ankle was swollen, but it was from the break below it. I grabbed my foot on the opposite side and tried rotating it. It was painful and resistant, but it would rotate. I could walk on it without doing any more damage, but I would pay a painful price if I did.

I sure do miss old-T. It must be 06:30 by now.

I shook the sock out, replaced it gently, and started pulling on the boot. I took a deep breath, closed my eyes and pushed the swollen foot into the boot. I performed the rapid breathing technique again hoping the throbbing pain would subside.

I laced the boot up as tight as I could get it with one hand. Tying the bow was impossible so I tied a granny-knot and tucked the rest of the laces in the boot.

One job done and one to go; don't pass out, Old Boy!

I rummaged in the bag and got the supplies I had procured to doctor Lady with. It wasn't much, but it beat nothing at all. I had a small roll of gauze, the hydrogen peroxide, the anti-infection cream, the mercurochrome, and a bottle of water left.

In the backpack there was an old T-shirt that I had not used yet. On the back were two fish with a baited hook in between them; the caption read, "I'd Hit That." Baby Girl bought it for me at a big sporting goods store before the Pentacle. I cut strips out of the shirt and cut both arms off to make pads.

I cut the old bandages I had used and let them fall. It was not pleasant, but I worked the button-down shirt over the right shoulder. I tried to get the limp arm out of the sleeve. It was exhausting work, but I did it. I didn't have strength left to take the shirt off; I let it hang on my left shoulder.

I shook off the dizziness and over whelming sense of fatigue, took the water bottle, and rinsed my left hand. I reached around and felt the wound and tried to analyze with my fingers what it looked like.

What-chu think, doc?

The witch doctor exited stage-right and reality crashed into view. There was a jagged hole in my shoulder, about the size of a golf ball. It was swollen and tender around it, but it didn't seem to bleed openly. I soaked the T-shirt strip with hydrogen peroxide and cleaned around it without getting into the wound cavity itself. If it had clotted, I didn't need to disturb it.

I cleaned as far down as I could and then reached under my arm and tried to get the rest. I soaked the next one and did it again.

I folded gauze into the cut arms of the T-shirt, coated it with anti-infection cream and readied the gauze roll. I leaned as far forward as I could and placed the pad onto the wound. I started under my armpit and clamped as tight as I could to roll the gauze over the pad. It took several tries, but I finally got it in place and tight.

I made as many wraps as the gauze roll allowed and tied the tail. I hoped that it would stay. I returned the limp arm back into the sleeve and pulled it over my shoulder.

I was in the throes of extreme heavy breathing, but I needed to hurry; Baby Girl would be almost at a run if she thought I was hurt.

The daylight started to break; the faint light had now brightened from the east.

It must be at least seven o'clock.

With a new determination, I stood on the good foot and got my balance. I placed the left foot on the ground and set it there. Just the pressure of being on the ground sent pain up my leg.

I pushed it hard onto the ground, and the pain did not get noticeably worse. I put more weight on it; I could stand on it. For how long, I didn't know. One positive realization: pressure on the foot minimized the throb of the shoulder.

I took a small step with the right foot; the left one held when I transferred the weight.

Don't come with Blue, Baby Girl, please don't come.

I looked more like a drunken Herman Munster than a man stalking a killer, but I was determined to try. The thought of Baby Girl coming across that bridge brought terror into my soul.

I was mad and that was exactly what I needed, so I let it happen. I started to walk better.

The pain was there, but I didn't care at that point. I had my mission, and I was bound by my vows and Baby Girl's love to embark. I felt pretty proud of myself until the woods got thick close to the creek. I needed to get beyond the house before I tried to cross the creek. I picked my feet up and placed them over the briars and the vines. It was hell, to say the least. I stumbled on occasion but maintained upright.

Lady trailed close behind me and had to jump over obstacles in places. I was all out panting at this point; we were joined together in that respect.

Another hundred yards opened up, and I found a game trail that led in the direction I wanted to go. We arrived at the creek; I could see the roof line of the house.

We needed to go another fifty yards before we crossed. That was the best decision that I had ever made in my feeble existence. Fifty yards down the creek, I noticed a small walk bridge over the creek.

I had to take a break and eased down beside a big sweet gum tree. I watched the back yard of the house and caught my breath. I opened the water bottle, took a big gulp, and let it set in my mouth for a while before I swallowed. I gave Lady the rest.

"That's it, My Lady. The next sip comes from the creek," I whispered and stroked her neck.

The adrenaline had left; I was too-pooped-to-pop as Papaw used to say. All of my being and soul wanted to close my eyes and let the emptiness cascade. I could not allow that to happen.

I checked old Beulah again. She was ready. I checked the Colt again. He was ready. I thought about what John Wayne would have said, "We're burning daylight." I got on my feet again. Mr. Pain was still in the house and rushed back by to let me know it.

I eased toward the walk bridge and was in the Old Blue, Pink Panther mode. I couldn't help it; the theme song reverberated and helped me be silent and stealthy.

We came to an old fence; Lady stepped back and let out a low whine. I kneeled down and stroked her but didn't say anything. I pushed the net fence down and made her a hole that she could easily pass through. I lay Beulah over the top strand of wire and pushed it down where I could swing my leg over to the other side.

I put my full weight on the bad foot and rotated to get the other leg over.

Let us never do that again.

After, I stood there on my good foot a moment, the pain subsided a little. We eased on toward the walk bridge moving as silent as we could.

We crossed the little bridge without much effort and moved into the backyard area. It had grown up a bit, but we were in the open as we approached the house.

I was only going to have one chance with Beulah, and I had to do it lefthanded. I tried to take aim with the right arm and that was a no go.

It is what it is; we eased on toward the house.

Lady was so quiet that I lost sight of her for a minute. She was past the back door in a crouched position. I crept forward until I got to the door; it was wide open.

Holding Beulah left-handed in front of me, I entered the kitchen. It was obvious that the residence was occupied; the occupant was not a tidy individual.

My heart pounded to a ten-piece band; it wasn't from pain this time. Every nerve in my body that was still capable of signaling was on full pink feline alert.

The house was silent.

Beulah had point guard, and we eased forward. I stopped short of the entrance to the living room and listened for any sound: nothing. I looked into the living room and located where the sniper had his set up; the rifle was leaned on the wall next to the window.

He was in the house somewhere, maybe he was still asleep.

I imagined what the layout of the rooms would be. There would be a hallway at the end of the wall I was behind leading into the bedrooms. Lady was still outside, and to be honest, I preferred it that way.

I eased around the door opening and into the living room with Beulah ready. I looked at the hallway, exactly how I imagined it, and started toward it. I saw all the bedroom doors were open.

The pink feline played with a full symphony and kept perfect harmony with the cardiac tom-toms as I crept into the hallway.

I passed the first bedroom door. I looked into it and found nothing out of the ordinary. If ordinary is a skeleton with patches of leathered skin hanging off it lying on a bed. I didn't attempt to analyze the final moment, just moved on down the hall with the feline orchestra.

The next room was on the right; I figured it was another child or spare bedroom. If I remembered correctly, Teddy had two girls. There were no skeletal remains that I could see, just what a teenage girl's sanctuary was once. What remained was the open left door on the right and closed door on the left.

The closed door should be the bathroom, the open door the master bedroom.

I crept toward the right, Beulah on point, and the Pink Kitty Hard Rock Band in full concert. I entered the room and found nothing. I could view the entire room, and he was nowhere to be found.

Maybe he ran out of ammo and left. God, I hope not. He might run into Baby Girl on the way.

I backed out into the hallway and started slowly turning around to start back down the hall. The adrenaline rush was leaving again, and I felt the fatigue coming back over me. I maneuvered down the hall the same way, stopping at both rooms, just in case.

When I got to the last room, I looked again at the poor pilgrim that had breathed her (I assumed she was a girl) last breath. A tingling started at the back of my neck, and I realized it before I heard it.

The bathroom door busted wide open, and the ambusher came rushing toward me at a full run with a knife that looked big enough to be a sword. I swung the barrel of Beulah toward him and pulled the trigger about the same time he slashed the knife and barreled into me.

We both crashed into the door facing of the bedroom and bounced off, landing in the hall.

I scrambled to get to the Colt until I realized that the back of his head was missing and noticed the blood and brain matter dripping off the ceiling.

My eyes were blurry, and I started processing a new pain; I realized the knife had made contact with my face.

I felt the blood ooze down my cheeks. It added to the flow I felt from the shoulder wound that had broken open.

I wrestled my way from under the dead weight of the ambusher. I got the Colt out anyway and started trying to get up.

I heard Lady whining; she stood in the doorway to the kitchen. When she saw me moving, she came running and stopped and looked at me when she got close. I would have freaked just about anyone out about then.

"It's alright, Girl," I said, and she wagged her tail, "old Beulah saved me again, Lady." I was tee-totally drained, couldn't go anymore. I was on the verge of being unconscious, probably from shock.

I finally got to my feet, stepped over the ambusher and limped back to the living room. I made it to the window.

He sat right here and did a sniper routine on me on that very bridge. Good shot too, had to be at least three hundred and fifty plus yards. If he had aimed another inch lower, I would be adding to the stench of the unlucky pilgrim in the creek bed.

Everything is Okay now.

If Blue brings Baby Girl to look for me, she won't be ambushed. Blue will find the tool bag and the backpack and bring Baby Girl to it. That is all that matters. I hope he can find my corpse for Baby Girl so at least she won't have to wonder like she does with Darrel.

I made it to the recliner and sat on the edge of it, knowing what would happen next.

"That's it, folks!" I muttered in my best Porky Pig voice and settled into the chair. I reclined it back, allowing the footrest to come up and take my feet with it. Lady came over and nuzzled my hand, and I stroked her head.

"It's okay now, girl, you and Baby Girl are safe," I told her softly.

The sandman took quick aim, and I never reached the in between place that I like to go. It was a straight black out with the knowledge that this might be the last time.

I fell asleep in that chair like every other time I had fallen asleep, the most fortunate man in the world.

Chapter 36: Blue in a Panic

When my baby, Blue, showed up at the house without Dinky, I almost died right there on the spot. It was late, and I woke up to the sound of him barking at the front door. He never barked; I understood something was wrong.

My heart and soul knew that something bad had happened. I jumped out of bed and ran to the front door in my night gown. He was nervous and anxious and pranced back and forth. He ran toward me and stopped; he turned and ran toward the driveway. He repeated this several times. He would not come into the house.

It dawned on me that I was supposed to follow him. I sat a bowl of water and a couple of pieces of flat bread out on the porch.

"Be still and wait a minute, Blue, let me get ready," I said.

I grabbed the back pack that I used when Dinky and I ventured out on a supply run. I lit an oil lamp to make my way around the house. I did a quick inventory of the backpack, filled two water bottles from the kitchen and put them in the side compartment.

I took the lamp into the bedroom, took off my nightgown, put on some jeans and a flannel shirt. I grabbed my jacket and just because he told me to never to be without it; I got the .38 snub-nose pistol and checked the cylinder. It had bullets in five of the six chambers, just like Dinky taught me.

I made it to the door, stepped outside, and blew out the oil lamp.

"Okay, Blue. Let's go, boy," I said, and he took off towards the driveway.

He did not get too far ahead that I could not see him, but he seemed to keep up the point of urgency in his movement. The night sky was starting to lighten up to the east.

At least I would be able to see soon.

I was as anxious as Blue was, but I had to pace myself. The Lupus had my strength drained and if I pushed too hard, I might be on the side of the road with a coronary. We had travelled four or five miles by this time. The morning skies were grey and wind blew in the trees with a pretty good force; I hoped Blue knew what he was doing. I didn't bring any type of rain gear.

A noise like a gunshot sounded a mile or so ahead, but it could have been thunder. Blue kept pushing. In about another mile we rounded a curve. Blue stopped and came towards me. I tried to continue to walk and he stepped in front of me, blocking me from moving forward.

I didn't get the memo on how to behave around a Blue Heeler, and he got in front of me and barked loudly. He was not going to let me go any farther. I sighed and lowered my backpack.

"What do you want me to do, Blue? Where is Dinky?" I cried.

He turned and looked back at the road and then back at me. He moved straight toward me, making me step back. He turned his head back, cocked his ears, and then took off running wide open down the road. Another dog entered the road from the old drive-way and headed straight toward Blue.

It looked like it had missed several meals but seemed to be energetic. When it seen Blue coming its way, it turned and headed back up the road, and I lost sight of both of them.

When I just about could not stand it anymore and started to get a little scared; Blue came out of the driveway toward me acting in the same manner he did at the house. This time the other dog was with him.

I could tell that it was a female dog but couldn't make out the breed.

She looked to be a cross between a mountain cur and a running walker, if memory served me. My dad loved cur dogs and had some running walker hounds that he used during deer season.

I knew the signal this time and put on the backpack and followed behind him.

About a hundred yards from the driveway entrance, I saw the little bridge in the curve of the road; I knew where I was. This was Terry and Juanita's house. Juanita worked at the beauty salon in the mini mall out on Jefferson Street. I remember them having two girls that would have been in their late teens before the Pentacle.

I kept going up the driveway. The front door was closed but the window was open on the right side and the curtain was pulled back. Blue didn't go for the front door and brought me around the back of the house. We entered the house from the back door; I trusted Blue and knew there was nothing to be afraid of.

When I saw the individual in the recliner, I screamed. I didn't recognize Dinky until Blue went over to him and started licking his hand. The other dog came beside Blue and was nuzzling the hand as well. All I could see was the blood from the gash across his face.

I looked over toward the hallway and saw the mass of piled flesh, the blood on the ceiling, and the wall: I realized what had happened here. I ran over and checked Dinky, praying that he was still alive.

He was still breathing, but he was not hanging on by much. I grabbed the backpack off my shoulder and tore the tail off the front of my flannel shirt. I soaked it with the water bottle and started cleaning Dinky's face and talked to him, trying to wake him up.

I could tell that his right arm was lying funny and that there was more blood on him than the cut on his face should have lost. I kept cleaning his face and noticed the hole in the button-down shirt. I pulled open the collar and realized what the major problem was. I kept wiping the dried blood off the facial laceration and tried not to open it back up.

"Wake up!" I yelled at him. Blue and the cur backed away a bit. He came alert long enough to raise his hand.

Chapter 37: Jason's Camel Hair Robe

It was the longest dream that I could remember ever having. I heard engines but didn't see vehicles. I heard talking but didn't see faces. I heard barking but couldn't find Blue. Everything I looked at was fuzzy designs of darkness, with the predominate feature of blackness. My mind didn't let me drift into the better memories stored in my brain. It was more like a nightmarish version of Peek-a-Boo, where I only got a glimpse every now and then. I felt my chest going up and down, and the heartbeat in my chest. I wasn't dead; yet, I was dreaming.

It wasn't until Jason came into focus that I discovered something was genuinely amiss.

He was at the other end of my bass boat beckoning me to join him. Every cast he made, he hooked and landed a big fish. It was too surreal, and I told him that I could not leave my station.

I had to keep one foot on the trolling motor to keep him where the fish were. He looked straight at me with that crooked grin.

"Dinky, I love you as much as the day is long," he said. He got too serious for my taste, and I was getting nervous. "You have got make a decision, here and now. The people on the shore love you and want you to come back."

His voice was getting deeper and very gentle, and when I looked at him again, he was wearing a camel hair robe and sandals. His hair was long, and he was sporting a beard. He had become my mental version of Jesus, but with the face and voice of Jason. There was a glow starting to form around him like the glow I sometime saw around Baby Girl.

"You have suffered enough and can come with me, if you want to. If you don't, I understand, but the time is now Dinky. You have to choose."

I started to lift my foot off of the trolling motor and the boat started drifting.

I couldn't leave my best friend, and as much as I loved Jason and was really impressed with his Jesus outfit, Baby Girl was my best friend.

I put my foot down on the control and steered the boat toward the setting sun. I saw Baby Girl, Blue, and Lady on the shore of the lake beckoning me to come to them. With my foot still on the control and leaning against the front boat seat, I turned back to look at Jason.

He had walked out onto the water about ten feet away from the boat and was waiting for me. I didn't say a word; I didn't have to.

"So shall it be," he said.

He streaked toward me without making steps on the water. As he approached, he changed into the last image I had of my childhood friend and soulmate.

His body seemed to grow larger as it took on the greenish hue of the corpse I buried, and when he was three inches from my face, he yelled like booming thunder.

"Wake up!"

I did.

I took a big gasping breath and immediately wished I was back on the lake. My entire body felt it was on fire except for the coolness I felt on my face and neck.

Baby Girl was rubbing me down with a cool wet cloth that felt like heaven. I tried to raise my left hand and found that it was all that I could do to move it. Then I heard the most beautiful sound in the world, my Baby Girl's voice.

"Dinky, are you back with us?"

I smiled and nodded my head.

"Stay with us, Dinky, stay with us," she cried, and this time I did. I was headed back into the darkness again, but this time I took the pain with me.

I heard Blue bark. He only barked one time, but I knew it was him and knew he was here. Whether I am still earth bound or somewhere between Jason and Jesus, Blue was with me again. There was just enough light left on my journey into the darkness to allow for rational thought. Before this light faded completely away, I felt my lips curl upward.

Thanks Blue, Thanks for bringing my Baby Girl to me.

Chapter 38: Dinky's Been Hurt

"Dinky, are you back with us?" I asked him.

He nodded his head.

"Stay with us, Dinky, stay with us!" I cried.

He drifted back off again.

"Okay, Sarah! What do we do now?" I said out loud.

Calm down and think.

I went back to the kitchen and looked in all the drawers until I found what I was looking for. I knew Juanita had to have a pair of scissors in there. They were in the bottom drawer with folded up dish towels. I grabbed these, just in case.

I went back to the recliner.

As easy as I could, I cut the shirt away from Dinky's shoulder. He had wrapped gauze around the shoulder and the arm pit.

"How in the hell did he do that one-handed?" I mumbled.

The gauze was blood soaked with dried blood. I cut the gauze and started peeling it back. I had to wet the flannel rag again and rub it with the water to get the stuck gauze away from his shoulder.

I found the bullet-hole as a tear started running down my face. I continued to wipe and pull until I got to the top of the shoulder and cut the excess gauze away and threw it over in the corner of the room.

When I tried to roll him over the get to the backside, he groaned loudly but didn't regain consciousness. I knew it had to be hurting him, but I had to get to it.

I got on the side of Dinky and with all my strength pushed him toward the other side of the recliner. He moved a little and settled into the seat. He was not completely sideways, but I could get to what I needed to. I found the blood soak patches he had made and felt pride for the man that I married.

He could be so resourceful and so incredibly stupid at the same time. I wonder what the hell this fight was all about in the first place.

When I got the gauze and the patches removed, I was shocked. I don't know how he stood it. There was a gaping hole in the top of his shoulder, and it didn't look like this had just happened either. He had been like this for a while.

"Think, Sarah, think," I said; Blue looked at me and whined.

Get a grip or you won't be any good to Dinky at all.

"Calm down," I cried, "Juanita is bound to have some medical supplies in this house somewhere."

Bathroom! She would have it in the bathroom.

I started down the hall trying to find a place to step around the corpse. I saw Dinky's blood-soaked shotgun laying there, the one he named after my Aunt Beulah. It looked like it had been dragged through hell. As proud of that old thing as Dinky was, I could never imagine it being in that condition.

I made a mental note to get it later and made it to the bathroom. I looked in all the cabinets and gathered up everything I could think of. Someone had placed a flashlight on the lavatory. I picked it up and was surprised when it came on. I noticed bedding in the bathtub and a five-gallon bucket of water by the toilet.

Now that's strange. The guy must have been some kind of mental case.

I found a bottle of rubbing alcohol, a bottle of hydrogen peroxide and a small tube of antibiotic cream. There was a Band-Aid kit that had some butterfly strips in it.

I'll need those.

There was some over the counter pain reliever but nothing prescription that I could find. There were a couple of rolls of gauze and some large gauze pads in the back of the cabinet, jackpot.

I took that all back to the living room.

Dinky had rolled back to the original position, and I could see pinkish clear fluid coming out of the bullet hole in the front. I had to get him out of that chair.

I grabbed the lever and put the footrest down. I got in front of him and placed his feet on the floor. I was crying, talking, yelling, and screaming for him to wake up.

He moaned and opened his eyes for a minute. He was trying to come around, and I kept on talking to him, telling him that he had to help me. I couldn't do it by myself.

He didn't speak but he nodded, and when I hooked my arms under his, he winced and groaned again.

Chapter 39: A little Help from my Friends

I was still in the darkness but the total darkness was fading. I could see two men coming toward me and as they got close, I recognized them both. One was Jason and the other was Bart. When they got to me, they were smiling and told me not to worry.

"We are only here to help," Bart said.

When they touched me, the world became light and I was sitting in a wheelchair. I knew I couldn't get up by myself. Jason got on one side and Bart got on the other and hooked an arm underneath mine.

Bart said. "When Jason yells "Three"; I need you to stand up."

Jason started "One, Two, and Three," and I tried with all my might to stand up.

I knew these men that I knew and loved would not allow me to fall, but we almost did.

Chapter 40: Help me Dinky

"One, Two, Three!" I yelled and I pulled up on Dinky with all the strength I had. I almost went over backwards taking Dinky with me, but I managed to hold him upright. I was hurting him, but that could not be helped. I kept in on him.

"Help me, Dinky" I said loudly, "we have to make it to the couch."

Together we shuffled over to the couch. The four feet it took to get there seemed like four miles. I bumped his knees on the edge of the couch and pushed him over gently so he landed on his belly.

I tried to keep him from landing hard, but he did anyway.

Chapter 41: Entry Denied

The scenery changed and Jason and Bart were taking me to the side of our old water bed. The one Baby Girl didn't want but I just had to have. There were many good memories in that old rowboat.

Bart and Jason placed my knees on the side of it and laid me over face down. The cool water and motion of the bed let me know that I had nothing to worry about.

"Dinky, I know you are not comfortable, but I have to clean this wound." Bart whispered as the darkness started enveloping me.

I felt pain in my shoulder and the edges of the darkness seemed to lighten. I could make out someone sitting in an old rocking chair. I heard the voice; there was no doubt in my mind who was addressing me,

"Dinky, you have to go back now."

He slowing rocked the chair back and forth and talked softly.

"We all love you here and we are proud of you. We want you to be with us, but now is not the time. Sarah needs you and so do some other people. Never change the values and ethics that you hold dear."

He sat his coffee cup down and stood up. He slowly slicked his hair back with one hand while placing the ball cap on with the other. He turned around and pointed his finger. Mr. Angus shouted, "Get your ass up, Dinky," and vanished.

The light and the pain stayed.

Chapter 42: Blue Never Barks

I could see fresh blood pooling in the big hole in his shoulder.

"Dinky, I know you are not comfortable, but I have to clean this wound." I said.

I cut the rest of his shirt away and went to work on the big hole with the water and towels. I poured the peroxide into the hole and looked for the fizzing action to help with possible infection. It boiled and bubbled. I kept pouring it on, soaking it into the wound and dabbing it up with the towels.

It was a nasty wound. I kept pouring it in until I had almost used the whole bottle of peroxide and had the hole as clean as I could get it. Dinky winced and groaned when I poured the liquid. He was still feeling something, but he had responded not spoken since the chair.

I got up and went on a search again.

When I got back, Dinky was where I left him. Blue and the cur were sniffing around him and trying to wake him up with their tongues. He would scrunch his face up but didn't reply to them. I could see the cut on his face started to ooze some fresh blood again.

I would have to tend to it later.

I sat on the edge of the couch and went to work. I soaked the needle in the alcohol and just for good measure, soaked the spool of dental floss as well. It was a trick at my age, but I got the floss threaded into the oversized needle.

Now the fun part, I hope I can stand it.

"This is going to hurt but stay with me," I told Dinky, and I pushed the needle through the swollen and jagged skin.

Dinky flinched and groaned as I drew the two pieces of flesh together. There was so much damage caused by the bullet; it was mostly a jagged tear. I know it wasn't, but it seemed like hours to get the wound pulled together.

I put the antibiotic cream on the outside and placed the gauze pads over it. I laid Band-Aid strips to hold the bandage in place.

I sat back and closed my eyes a minute and let the swimming settle down. Blue nuzzled my hand and looked at me with the sympathy eyes.

"I don't know, baby Blue. He has lost a lot of blood. But, if anyone can make, this old fart can," I said and rubbed between his ears.

Dinky moaned and stirred a little. I rushed off the couch and got next to his face and talked softly to him.

"I'm here, Dinky," I whispered.

He opened his old blue eyes, and even though there was a lot of pain in them, there was a lot of love too.

"Thank the old shit-eater for me," he said in almost a whisper.

I laughed and wanted to punch him out at the same time.

He tried to sit up, and I grabbed and helped him.

"Are you okay? I asked.

"I am now that I know you are safe," he said in a croaky voice. I didn't know exactly what he meant by that; I would find out later.

I was crying again, but good tears this time. I kissed him all over the good part of his face.

The old coot just grinned. "Where is that shaky pudding you promised me?"

Blue and the cur came to him like he was Zeus in the flesh and lowered their heads so he could rub them.

"Baby Girl meet Lady. Lady meet Baby Girl," he said to me, as he laid back and closed his eyes while the pain spiked and subsided.

He looked toward the window. "Baby Girl, is it going to rain?"

"Probably. It has been threatening to all day," I said.

He got somber. "Baby Girl, you have got to go and do something for me," he croaked.

He was having a trouble talking; I handed him my water bottle. He took a small sip and let it trickle down his throat.

"You have to go down to the road and cross the bridge. About fifty yards passed the bridge on the left is my backpack and another bag." He let another spike pass and said. "We need both of them."

He looked at Blue and said, "Go with her Blue", and added, "Lady, you stay with me."

I don't know when he learned to speak canine, but Blue got up doing the shaky thing, and Lady stayed lying down where she was. She raised her head and looked around but did not get up.

I pulled the snub nose .38 out of my backpack and put it in my back pocket.

"Let's go, Blue," I said and looked over at Dinky who was sitting back on the couch with his eyes closed.

"Don't worry about me, my love; Mr. Angus won't let me in yet," he said through the pain.

We made it to the end of the driveway and started toward the bridge. The closer I got to the bridge the stronger the smell of carrion got. I wished I would not have, but when I got to the bridge, I looked over the side.

I became fully aware of what had taken place here and why Dinky went into that house.

All the way to where the bags were, I cried tears for the man I loved and the sacrifices that he sometimes made. I would never ask him about it; maybe someday he would tell me. He won't because he knows it would make me upset.

I was about to pick the bags up when Blue took off down the highway at a dead run barking.

He never barks.

A young voice squealed his name and a man's voice try to shush her. She wasn't having anything to do with it because she was still yelled for Blue. I could tell by the sound that they were just around the curve.

"Dinky, are you out there?" a male voice asked.

I didn't know whether to answer or not, evidently Blue trusted these people.

"Dinky is hurt; I am his wife, Sarah," I yelled out. "Who might you be?"

About that time a man and Blue came around the curve. Blue was excited and running all around him. He had a shotgun in his hand and stopped when he could see all around.

"Where is Dinky?" he asked.

"He is in Terry and Juanita's old house up on that hill," I told him and added, "he has been shot."

The man put the shotgun over his shoulder and went back around the curve, Blue right behind him. A woman and a little girl came back around the curve and headed toward me. Blue and the little girl were playing; my jaw dropped because I had never seen Blue act so giddy.

"I am Benjie. This is Belinda and my girl Brittany," the man said and extended his hand. I shook it, relieved that someone was there.

Brittany ran up to me and wrapped her arms around my waist and hugged me.

"Is Mr. Dinky, okay?" she asked.

"He is still alive, baby, but he is hurt really bad," I said. "I am sure he would love to see you, though."

I looked into the beautiful eyes of innocence. She smiled a great big smile at that and run off to play with Blue some more.

I reached and picked up the backpack, and Benjie grabbed the bag.

"We had better get back to him; it is going to start raining any minute," he said.

"There is a fresh body in the house and a bloated one below the bridge on the right," I whispered to Benjie.

He hollered at Brittany to come to him and handed the bag to Belinda who nodded at me and smiled. Benjie grabbed Brittany, put her up on his shoulders, and winked at me. We got across the bridge, and Brittany yelled.

"Pe-uew Wee!" she said, and we all laughed but didn't look over the side. Blue ran around and danced like crazy trying to get to Brittany.

When we got to the house, Benjie asked Belinda to keep Brittany outside for a few minutes. That was not a problem for her nor Blue. Benjie and I went inside.

"What in the wide world of sports do you think you're doing?" Benjie asked, leaning over close to the man on the couch.

Dinky raised one eye lid and focused on the voice. He let out a sigh. "Hey Benjie, good to see you. Please forgive me for not getting up."

Benjie laughed and then got somber. "Sniper?" he asked.

"Yes Sir, he's in the hallway," Dinky replied.

"You need anything?" Benjie asked.

"A kind word and a half-dozen Tylenol," Dinky said.

Benjie laughed and went about removing the body so Brittany would not see it.

When I got to Dinky, the pain in his eyes was evident, but he cracked a smile at me and asked.

"Where did you find Benjie?"

"I didn't," I said. "Blue did."

He nodded. "He sure loves that little princess, doesn't he?"

"Yes, he does," I said.

I changed the tone of my voice a little. "Dinky, I thought I had lost you; don't ever do that to me again."

I was serious when I said it, but he just chuckled. "There is the glow I needed to see. I love you too, Baby Girl."

After about ten minutes, Benjie came back onto the porch and told Belinda they could come inside. Brittany had the attention of Blue and Lady at this point. Lady didn't have the energy that Blue had, but her enthusiasm was right there with him.

Benjie, Belinda, and Brittany came in; Blue and Lady right behind them. Belinda took off like a whirlwind, tidied things up, looked for supplies, and made ready for the night. I went to help her, mostly to have something to do.

Dinky had closed his eyes again, but I could tell he was still awake. Nobody was working at the sawmill right now. After all these years, it was almost hard for me to get some rest unless the old sawmill was working.

Within an hour Belinda and I had the place looking like a livable sanctuary. That was about the time the rain started. By the time we had ate supper and visited, it seemed like we had been friends forever. Little Brittany was the absolute picture of perfectness; I fell in love with her instantly.

Belinda made some warm broth out of some venison she had. I tried to get some of it down Dinky. I didn't get much broth down him, but he did drink a good bit of water.

With a little bit of something in his stomach, I gave him some pain relievers to swallow. I didn't know how much help it would do, but every little bit counted. We made him as comfortable as we could on the couch and within a little while the old sawmill cranked up.

Benjie told the story of how they met, and the little flashlight he had given Brittany. He told me about how much Brittany and Blue enjoyed playing and how much Dinky enjoyed watching them. He told me about how he brought the deer meat to them and showed me the note he had written the morning he left.

If Dinky told him anything of what had happened on his trip, he never let on that he knew. He was just like Dinky and would not have told me, even if I asked him to. He would say that it was for Dinky to tell, not him.

Benjie dragged two mattresses into the living room, and we arranged everyone around Dinky and bedded down for the night. He left the bed on the left alone with its occupant. I sent a prayer to the Lord for her soul. It must have been the hardest thing in the world to do when Juanita left her baby's body and attempted to escape the Pentacle. I wondered how far they made it. I sent up a prayer for Juanita, as well.

Belinda laid out candles and lighters in case we needed to move around in the night. Blue and Lady got by the couch at the foot of it. Blue did his old shaking thing and Lady turned two circles before she lay down. Brittany came over and loved on them both before she went and crawled in between Benjie and Belinda.

With the rain coming down and the sound of it dripping off the roof, it wasn't long until the workforce at the mill had quadrupled.

I listened to Dinky breathe for a few more minutes and thought about how lucky I was to have him. I drifted off and started my labor at the sawmill.

Chapter 43: Day 12, The Journey's End

We spent the next four days held up in Juanita's house. Benjie buried the sniper and the poor man that was in the creek. I do not know how he stood it. Belinda fixed meals and was grateful that Blue and Lady kept Brittney entertained. We continued to nurse Dinky and he improved daily. By the end of that fourth day, even he was getting restless.

The next morning, I woke up to the sound of Belinda stirring around in the kitchen and the wonderful aroma of brewed coffee.

I checked on Dinky, felt his forehead, and watched his breathing. He was a little warm, but I didn't determine he was feverish. His breathing was evident; the lumber was still piling up. I went in the kitchen.

Belinda smiled and handed me a cup; I filled it from an old drip pot. Benjie came in rubbing his eyes and pushing his hair back with his hands, looked at us and smiled. He got his own cup and sat at the kitchen table as if the Pentacle had never happened.

He took a sip and then looked at us.

"How are we going to get Dinky home?" Looking at me, he asked. "How far do we have to go?"

"I can't be more than six miles, seven tops," I told him.

He nodded and stared into his coffee cup. I knew he was thinking about the needs ahead.

"Is the road open?" he asked.

"It's pretty much open all the way," I said.

He stared into the cup and then took a sip.

The day before and tremendous rainstorm moved through for several hours and everything was wet. The good thing about a big spring rain is that it rinses everything clean.

It reminded me of my favorite line in an old Fleetwood Mac song.

We all knew what we had to do, and we got to getting it done.

I went about my chores with Fleetwood Mac playing in the background of my mind. Every once in a while, they would come forward for a second or two and then fade back again.

I cleaned Dinky up and checked the cut across his face. It was going to leave a big scar. It will not set well with his vanity, but he will get used to it.

The wound on his back shoulder looked decent, and I didn't detect any odor coming from it. The hole in the front was draining a little, but it was fairly clear fluid.

The first morning after Benjie arrived, Dinky told me about his foot, and we managed to cut his boot off. The foot was swollen and had turned black around the swelling. He had done a number on this one for sure. I found an ace bandage in the bathroom and wrapped it as tight as I could around the foot and ankle. We took the ace bandage off twice a day to let the blood circulate.

My Dinky almost looked presentable again, and his eyes were not as cloudy; much clearer this morning. He was in and out for most of the morning, occasionally making a pass by the sawmill.

Benjie came in the house about mid-morning with a contraption that looked like a cross between a truck dolly and a wagon. It was just the right size for a Dinky Transport Vehicle, so we named it the "DTV."

Dinky was not impressed, but he didn't fuss when we loaded him up before lunch time and headed out towards home.

Dinky looked over at Lady and directed his sentence at her but loud enough for everyone else to hear.

"Lady, I can't believe they want to load me up in that contraption. Hell, you and I walked this far a few days back, didn't we? They should have been here for that show. Ain't that right!"

He locked eyes with Lady, and she gave him the shut-up-and-get-in-the-buggy look. Dinky smiled at her. Lady was going to fit right in.

Blue and Brittany was outside splashing in the mud holes. Belinda finally just gave up and said she would wash her off later.

Dinky looked at me and softly said, "get Beulah, I can't leave without Beulah."

Benjie came over and laid old Beulah in his lap. He had taken the time to clean her. She was as beat up as Dinky was. Dinky stroked her down her barrel with his good hand until he got to the trigger guard and wrapped his hand around the grip.

"She saved my raggedy ass life, once again," Dinky said lovingly.

Chapter 44: Back Home

Against my better judgement, I got in the cart.

The trip to mine and Baby Girl's house was fairly uneventful; we made it there about an hour before dark. I dozed for most of the trip, except for when a bump in the road would stir up Mr. Pain. Mr. Pain and I would never be bosom buddies, but we found a platform of mutual respect.

It filled my heart with pride to gaze upon the home place; I wasn't sure I would ever see it again. I was damn sure glad to get off the cart Benjie had made.

Benjie helped get me into the bedroom and I sat on a hard-back chair by the edge of the bed. Belinda and Baby Girl didn't even attempt to take my old clothes off. They just cut them away from me. I sat there in my boxers, just like I did that day in Mrs. Sadie's bathroom all those years ago. I was positioned in about the same manner, still trying to hide the manly parts.

Belinda left and came back with a big pan of warm water and some towels. She pulled the door closed and left.

Baby Girl got on her knees between my legs and gently laid her head on my chest and softly started crying. I let her.

I stroked her hair with my good hand and let her get it all out. She never said a word, so I didn't either, but I was as proud at that moment as I was the day I stood before the Good Lord and witnesses and told her that I would love, honor, and cherish her until the day I died.

I couldn't help it; I got a little stirring in the manly parts. "You want to go swimming?" I whispered in her ear.

She went from crying to laughing and looked me straight in the eyes. "You are so bad."

She got up and went to work cleaning me up. I was amazed at how dirty the water had gotten and how much better I felt just being clean. She helped me put on a pair of sleeping pants.

Belinda came back in, and they removed the dressing that Baby Girl had made. Belinda and Baby Girl worked with soft wet cloth to prevent the stuck pad from pulling on my stitches. Once it was removed, they cleaned the wound.

"You did a good job stitching, it pulled together nicely," Belinda commented.

"You're looking at the hardest job I have ever had to do in my life, barring childbirth," Baby Girl said as she coated the wound with anti-infection cream.

"Dinky, we may have to hire Sarah out as a doctor," Belinda said.

"Good Luck with that," I told her, and we all laughed.

"Belinda, I can't thank you and Benjie enough for everything you've done. I don't know how I would have gotten Dinky home without you," Baby Girl said.

"There are only a few men that Benjie has taken a liking to. Dinky is the only man I know that Benjie would consider a true friend since Ezra. When Benjie decides to love someone, he loves them. He made the decision to accept Dinky's offer, not because he needed to, but because he wanted to," Belinda said, holding the pad in place while Baby Girl secured the covering.

"I don't know about Dinky, but I do know about Blue. He is crazy about Brittany. I have never seen that dog act like he does when he is around her," Baby Girl said, and they both laughed.

"The old man has a real bad soft spot for the little princess, too," I said.

When they got through, Belinda left again.

"You need a haircut," Baby Girl said as she brushed my hair back. "Do you want me to see if Benjie would bring you to the living room for a spell?"

"I am pretty well shot for the day. We'll all visit tomorrow," I told her.

"Take these," she said, handing me some pills and holding a glass of water.

Once that was done, she hollered for Benjie. They helped me into the old four-poster bed that I loved so well.

The light outside was fading to dusk; I settled into the mattress and tried not to disturb the shoulder or the foot. Baby Girl raised the window, eased out of the room and closed the door.

I laid there and listened to the crickets, the frogs, and the gentle breeze in the leaves. Jiminy had decided on a harmonious melody tonight and was conducting perfectly.

I closed my eyes, and in the faded shadows, I saw Jason and Mr. Angus just out focus, but enough that I could tell them apart. They were smiling, and Mr. Angus was not wearing the ball cap.

I fell asleep that night like every other night, the most fortunate man in the world.

Epilogue: Fall, 0004 A.P., A Promise to Keep

It was mid-fall. The leaves have commenced their autumn spectacular and have started to fall. There was a slight nip in the early morning air. I was by the lake side with a cup of coffee in my hand. Old Blue walked around the edge of the lake and sniffed everything he could. I looked back and saw Lady. She was on the bottom step of the stone path and looked miserable.

She was going to deliver soon.

"You are going to have to straighten up and fly right. You're going to be a daddy," I told Blue and got the go-to-hell look. He did the hokey pokey and moved up the lake shore. I chuckled to myself.

I hoped the pups would survive, and I could give one to Brittany. That little one has stolen my heart for sure. I hummed the melody from the Gigi movie. The reoccurring thought crossed my mind again; I have a promise to keep.

I had pretty much recovered. My right arm didn't work as well as it did before, but it was functional. I could still beat Benjie fishing on most days. A big lump stayed on the top and side of my foot and was sometimes a little tender, especially when there was a big weather change.

And the scar! Well, the scar reminded me every morning that I was glad to be alive and how much I loved Baby Girl.

She was doing so much better since her medication was steady again. She didn't hide the rash from me anymore. She even wore short pants a month back when the three-Bees came over for supper.

Brittany gets upset because I won't tell her why I call them the three Bees. She will figure it out soon enough.

I picked up a rock from the edge of the lake and threw it out in the water. I took the last sip of coffee and started back toward the house.

"Come on, Blue," I said and whistled.

I got to the house, went in the kitchen, and poured another cup of coffee out of the drip pot. I grabbed a day-old biscuit and took a bite.

Baby Girl stood in the doorway with her arms crossed and the one eyebrow cocked.

"It is time, Baby Girl; I have put it off long enough." I stood my ground.

She pointed her finger at me. "The last time you left, you almost died."

I didn't want to fight with her, but this time my mind was made up.

"There is something that I have to do," I finished before she could butt in. "I don't want to hear any more about it."

Baby Girls eyes misted, and she looked at me with the glow all around her. She came over and put her arms around my neck.

"I love you. Do you know that?" she whispered.

"Yes, ma'am, but I am going anyway," I said, still putting up a front.

She couldn't help it; she smiled. "Okay, let me get my gear," she said.

"No, ma'am, this is only for me and Blue," I said.

She lowered her eyes, reached up and gave me a kiss.

"Please be careful, I love you, even though you're a cantankerous old fart," she said.

That time, I smiled.

I got my backpack out of the hall closet and checked the contents. It was good enough for a day trip. I pulled old Beulah off her place of honor above the mantel and checked the chamber. I retrieved the ammo-box from the top of the closet and got another eight to ten shells. I headed for the back door, went out to the tool shed, and got a shovel.

"Come on, Blue," I hollered.

Blue came running, and Lady came waddling.

"Stay here and take care of Baby Girl. We'll be back tonight," I told Lady and scratched her between her ears. She waddled on up onto the porch, made two circles and lay down.

Blue and I headed out the driveway. I knew Baby Girl was standing on the porch watching me leave, so I did the old Michael Jackson move, without the moon walk this time. I spun around and tipped my old ball cap in her direction. She wanted to be upset, but she laughed anyway.

I blew her a kiss and hollered, "Love you, Baby Girl!"

We made it to the highway; I turned right and headed toward Barkston. We got into a stride, and I found my stamina was not what it was before even though I had walked as much as I could around the home place. We stopped a couple of times, drank some water, let our breath settle, and took off again.

Before I got into Barkston, I took the Ashton Cut-Off road. This went around Barkston and came out on Highway 485.

At the intersection, I took a left and had a mile or so to go. When I got to the big wrought iron gate, I reflected on the knowledge and the events that summoned me there. I hoped that William had found someone to attach himself to in the afterlife.

It was 11:15 according to the new Seiko I had; well, new to me anyway.

I needed to catch a faster gear, if I wanted to make it home before dark.

I found the edge of the fence. It wasn't as easy as I thought it would be with all the new growth. I walked into the woods, followed the fence, and looked for the girl.

About fifty yards in, like William had promised, I found what looked like some rags. It wasn't much left except a skeleton when I looked inside the cloth. I could recognize what the articles of clothing originally were, and it was obvious from where the bones lay in relation to the cloth what had taken place.

A terrible sorrow came over me and tears streaked down my face as I rummaged around the girl's remains. I emptied my backpack and started placing the bones and what few pieces of leathery skin that was left in it. I tried to gather as much of what remained as I could.

When I got to the skull, which had come free of the spine, I saw a gold chain lying across the spine where her neck would have been. I picked the bones up and placed them in the backpack which was starting to fill at this point.

I picked up the chain, on the end of it was a small cross made out of gold. It instantly became aware to me that her grandma had given it to her.

I didn't know how I knew that, but I was convinced beyond a doubt.

I gathered every bone and strip of cloth I could find. I picked her skull up which still had a small amount of leathered skin and some long brown hair. I rolled it up in the old hoodie that I had taken out of the backpack.

Blue sat still about twenty yards away and looked solemn.

I would not bury her in the place where she suffered her indignity and lost her life. I put the necklace over my head and felt the weight of the cross against my neck. Its weight seemed to give me a strength I hadn't had in thirty years.

I threw the backpack over my shoulder. I tied the hoodie into a sack onto my belt. I grabbed Beulah and the shovel and made my way out of the woods and back to the highway.

New-S said 12:55.

With my newfound strength, I started back down 485 with a renewed vigor. When I got to the Ashton Cut-Off, I kept going toward Barkston. Two miles further down 485, I turned into a grown-up driveway and walked on.

I don't know why I did; probably don't want to know.

At the end of the driveway was an old house on piers that looked like it was about ready to throw in the towel. It was probably in pretty bad shape before the Flip.

I never checked up, went up on the porch, and opened the door. The strength that I was enjoying faded away, and I felt all the old man aches and pains of everyday existence.

She had found her way home.

I went inside; Blue stayed on the porch. I looked around the living room of a home that was once full of love and faith. It was small, but it was neat and tidy. Even after this much time, it was obvious that someone had cared for this little home.

I walked over to the fireplace mantel and saw several photographs in frames. One was a young soldier that looked to be from around the Korean War era. This same young man was in a picture with his new bride on their wedding day.

There were some newer ones of two different girls that were dressed sixties style. There were more pictures of these two girls as they were older. There was a picture of one of the girls with a man and a baby girl in her arms. It looked like one of those K-mart Family Photos.

After that, there were pictures of a little girl that grew up before my eyes on the shelf of the old fireplace.

I would never know her name or hear her voice, but I would never forget her face and how beautiful she was.

In the last photograph, I noticed the cross hanging around my neck on a girl in a prom dress standing next to a young man. They looked extremely happy together.

I started crying again. I allowed myself a little time to let it out and reminded myself that I had to Bachman-Turner Overdrive; I had business to take care of. I walked back to the porch, got the shovel from where I had left it, and carried it through the house.

This time Blue came with me.

I looked out into the back yard. She had played in this yard. Before Pentacle, she had probably eased out here to talk to that boy in the picture on her cell phone late at night. She would have watched the stars and made her wishes on them right here in this yard.

This would be a good place; she was home.

I found a spot between a big overgrown azalea bush and a pecan tree and started digging. It didn't take that long because there was not much left to her physical presence anymore. New-S said it was 4:15.

I laid my old backpack in the grave then took the hoodie and placed it above the pack. I took the necklace off of my neck, I kissed the cross and gently placed it on the hoodie.

I bowed my head and prayed.

I prayed to the Good Lord that this girl found peace in heaven.

I thanked him for allowing me to avenge her death and keep other pilgrims safe from the same fate.

I thanked him for letting Baby Girl live through the Flip and assured him that whatever he needed me to do that I was there for him.

I asked him to reconsider the soul of William; he had given his life for Blue and I.

I placed a handful of dirt in the grave.

I covered her remains and took my knife out of my pocket. I carved a cross in the bark of the pecan tree facing her grave. I picked up the shovel and old Beulah. I looked at Blue.

He stood up, did the hokey pokey, and looked back at me signaling he was ready. We headed back down the little driveway and back to the highway.

The walkin' man's heart breathes a sigh of pure relief;
His promise is accomplished and complete.
Blue and I understand the strength of our belief;
That William makes it to the gate to see Saint Pete.

By the time we got through Barkston and on to the house, new-S said it was 8:30. I felt the temperature fall when the sun went down; my jacket was on the ground in the woods.

Baby Girl was waiting on the porch when we arrived and loved on Blue. She couldn't wait to tell him that he was the daddy of five of the prettiest puppies she had ever seen.

He got really excited; I don't know if it was because Baby Girl showered him with attention, or he understood what she said. It didn't make a hill of beans either way.

We went inside and looked at the puppies. I hoped they were immune to the Pentacle Virus, if it is even still around. They truly were a beautiful sight to behold. I stood up and gave Baby Girl a big hug and a kiss.

Benjie will be here at daylight to go fishing," she whispered.

"Okay, some fresh fillets would be good for supper tomorrow night, don't you think?"

We visited a while and heated some water. I took a bath and cleaned up. We went to bed, and Baby Girl cooked me up some *Shaky Pudding*, my favorite.

As we lay there in the afterglow, she whispered, "Did you do what you needed to do?"

"Yes, ma'am, I am right with the Big Man and Mama Nature again," I answered.

"Good," she said, paused a second and then added, "I love you, Dinky."

I kissed the top of her forehead and watched the glow brighten a shade, "I love you too, Baby Girl."

I lay in the dark and listened to her breathe. I reflected about my life before and after the Flip.

Were the basic needs of existence enough to sustain a man?

I have food and water. I have love and faith. I have shelter. I have companionship. I have Beulah, Lady, and Blue. What the hell else do I need?

I thanked the man upstairs again for everything that I have and went to sleep that night like every other night, the world's most fortunate man.

---The End---

The Pentacle Virus drove the human race to the brink of extinction...

Humanity is determined to complete the job.

Doyle Weldon Knight, is a novelist, a short story author and occasional poet that lives in central Louisiana.

He discovered a passion for writing after decades of working in the global oilfield arena.

His short story, *The Matriarch Sin*, was published in the *Halloween Party 2019*, anthology from Devil's Party Press (www.devilspartypress.com) in October 2019.

www.ingramcontent.com/pod-product-compliance
Lightning Source LLC
Chambersburg PA
CBHW031133260626
47153CB00021B/127